The Slash of Savage Swords

Lijena's stomach churned; time did not permit sickness. The clack of boot on rock once more alerted her to a rear attack. She swirled and ducked under a savage sword slash meant for her own neck. Simultaneously, she swung the Sword of Kwerin Bloodhawk hard. The blade sliced into the demon's knees.

"You!" hissed the Faceless Ones' leader. "Fool, you toy with powers beyond your understanding. Zarek Yannis will not be denied!"

Lijena swung around to face the hell-riders...

Ace Fantasy Books by Robert E. Vardeman and Geo. W. Proctor

THE SWORDS OF RAEMLLYN SERIES

TO DEMONS BOUND
A YOKE OF MAGIC
BLOOD FOUNTAIN
DEATH'S ACOLYTE

Ace Fantasy Books by Robert E. Vardeman

THE CENOTAPH ROAD SERIES

CENOTAPH ROAD
THE SORCERER'S SKULL
WORLD OF MAZES
IRON TONGUE
FIRE AND FOG
PILLAR OF NIGHT

Ace Science Fiction Books by Geo. W. Proctor

STARWINGS

DEATH'S ACOLYTE

ROBERT E. VARDEMAN
AND GEO. W. PROCTOR

ACE FANTASY BOOKS
NEW YORK

This book is an Ace Fantasy original edition, and has never been previously published.

DEATH'S ACOLYTE

An Ace Fantasy Book/published by arrangement with the authors

PRINTING HISTORY
Ace Fantasy edition/May 1986

Cover art by Luis Royo.

For information address: The Berkley Publishing Group, 200 Madison Avenue, New York, New York 10016.

ISBN: 0-441-14212-5

Ace Fantasy Books are published by The Berkley Publishing Group, 200 Madison Avenue, New York, New York 10016.
PRINTED IN THE UNITED STATES OF AMERICA

For Melissa Ann Singer, who picked the right nits!

—Geo. W. Proctor

For Frank and AnnaJo Denton

—Robert E. Vardeman

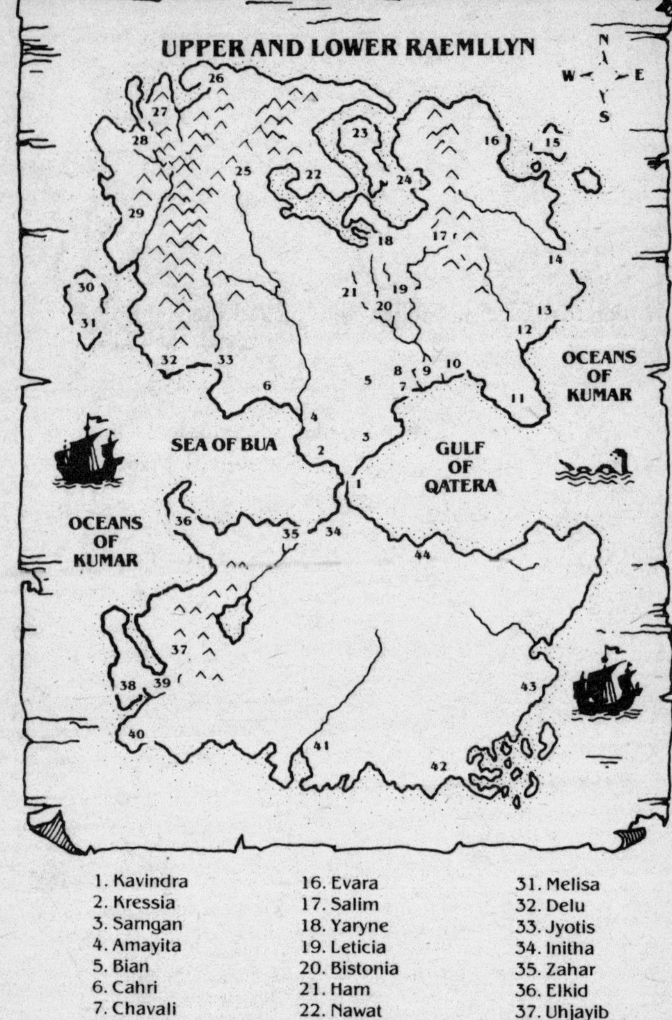

1. Kavindra
2. Kressia
3. Sarngan
4. Amayita
5. Bian
6. Cahri
7. Chavali
8. Degoolah
9. Garoda
10. Jyn
11. Meakham
12. Parrn
13. Qatirn
14. Orji
15. Iluska
16. Evara
17. Salim
18. Yaryne
19. Leticia
20. Bistonia
21. Harn
22. Nawat
23. Vatusia
24. Rakell
25. Solana
26. Faldin
27. Weysh
28. Salnal
29. Yow
30. Litonya
31. Melisa
32. Delu
33. Jyotis
34. Initha
35. Zahar
36. Elkid
37. Uhjayib
38. Fayinah
39. Pahl
40. Rattreh
41. Ohnuhn
42. Gatinah
43. Ahvayuh
44. Nayati

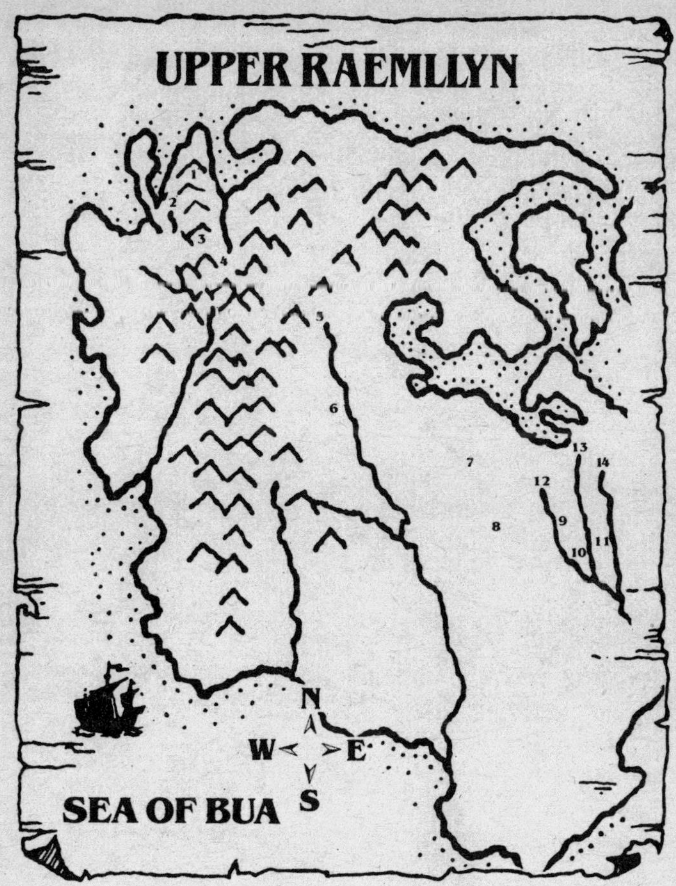

1. Agda
2. Weysh
3. Kou-Garl Mountains
4. Ardevel
5. The River Iet
6. Solana
7. Magic-Sorched Battlefield
8. Hyian
9. Harn
10. Bistonia
11. Leticia
12. The River Kukis
13. The River Stane
14. The River Faor

chapter 1

LIJENA FARLEIGH AWOKE from a restless half-sleep with a start. She leaped to her feet and stood poised in a wide defensive stance. Tempered steel hissed against leather as she freed sword from sheath and leveled it against attack.

Twice her aquamarine eyes blinked to clear the haze of sleep before narrowing to defiant slits. Temples ringing like the blows of a blacksmith's hammer on an anvil, she scanned the periphery of the clearing in which she camped.

Nothing!

Only the predawn purples and grays of the third morning after her escape filtered through the dense foliage of Agda's imposing primordial forest. Amid the shadows of the tangled boughs, the columnlike boles of pine, oak, *morda,* and fir, her imagination gave birth to a horde of demons and elementals escaped from the lowest level of Peyneeha, which men called Hell.

In truth, Black Qar, the God of Death, had not unleashed her, his, its—the Great Destroyer's sex was as varied as the profanities spat into the Death God's face by those whose lives the Dark One claimed—minions on the lone woman. Simple forest trees stood silhouetted against the dim glow of the coming morning.

A nervous sigh of relief quavered over trembling red lips. *A dream . . . the cry of a night bird . . . a forest sound. . . .* Lijena explained away her abrupt awakening. Yet, she scrutinized the camp's perimeter a last time before she eased the broadsword into its scabbard, tossed three new branches atop a low-burning fire, and settled crosslegged before the flickering yellow and blue flames.

Just a dream, she reassured herself while securely hugging a fur cape about her shoulders to fend away the cold breath of winter. It could have been nothing more.

Her three stolen horses stood with hobbled forelegs locked and massive necks drooped in sleep. If a forest predator—or worse—approached, the animals would be aprance, ears perked high, and nostrils flared with the scent of danger.

Only a dream. Memory of that disturbing phantasma evaded conscious scrutiny.

Graceful, long-fingered hand still clasping the sheathed sword that rested in her lap, Lijena Farleigh lowered chin to chest and closed her eyes. She breathed deeply, calming the panicked race of her heart. Tension refused to flow from her taut muscles.

The forest of Agda intruded. The creak of a wind-caressed branch, the screech of a red-hooded owl on wing to roost before the sun rose, the rustling movement of rodents in the winter-dry underbrush, assailed the bubble of surcease she attempted to construct and shattered it.

Her weary eyes slits, Lijena studied the purloined sword balanced atop her thighs—the fabled blade of Kwerin Bloodhawk, Raemllyn's legendary first High King. A silent curse moved over her lips. What hardships this magic-tempered length of steel had brought—still brought—her!

She stiffened stoically when tears threatened to mist her eyes. These last months, the long, lost months, had robbed her of the tears of a lifetime.

She turned her attention to the forest once again. The growing blaze and the approaching dawn did nothing to dissipate the ominous presence of the looming giants of wood that towered around her.

Lijena shivered. For two days, since her escape from the rogues Davin Anane and Goran One-Eye, the sensation that the wood followed her every movement had haunted her. She sensed unseen eyes peering from behind each of the ancient gnarled trunks. When she turned to confront them—there was nothing! Yet the feeling of *wrongness* persisted.

Perhaps, I escaped from Davin and Goran too soon. Doubts niggled free from the recesses of her mind. *No! I would rather throw myself to direwolves than abide those two!*

The bravado rang false. What did she, the daughter of a Bistonian merchant, know of Agda's wilds? Or of swords endowed with magicks cast by a mage at the dawn of Raemllyn's history?

She edged the blade from its sheath, exposing a finger's length of naked, blue steel to the campfire's light. No surge of strength flowed through Lijena's arm. Nor did a tingling of magical energies dance about her body. The sword merely felt cold and heavy.

Faint runes, cuneiform writings worn away by countless generations of use, were barely discernable in the campfire's light. These were the only hint of the sword's power, and their meaning lay veiled in a forgotten past. Had she not seen the sword wielded, seen the burning light that radiated from lifeless steel, she would have mistaken it for an ordinary blade, no different than any sword worn throughout Upper and Lower Raemllyn.

In truth, she admitted to herself, she would not now possess the longsword with which Kwerin Bloodhawk freed these realms from the dark mage Nnamdi had it not been for the Jyotian Davin Anane. She had stolen it and the sheath that gave power to the blade, the three mounts, and her supplies from Davin and his changeling companion Goran in partial retribution for all the suffering they had brought her.

She cared nothing of swords and magicks! She had never hefted a sword until this nightmare journey had begun. Of what use was a sword to a young woman raised to be the gentlest of ladies in Bistonia? What need of honed steel when soft furs, perfumes, gossamer gowns, and the coy batting of an eye were the weapons she had been trained to use?

To be certain, swords and dirks were no longer strangers to Lijena Farleigh. In these long months, she had gained intimate knowledge of fine tempered steel—had killed with both sword and knife! But she was no ebilsis, the female mercenary warriors who matched their skills against male weaponsmen and worshipped Ebil, Goddess of the Frenzy. Even resting on her lap, the Sword of Kwerin Bloodhawk felt awkward and alien.

The sword . . . this forest . . . are not my way. I was never meant for them, she thought for the hundredth time, fully aware that she would now be starving to death were it not for the stolen supplies. Of hunting and trapping, she knew absolutely nothing. The luxury of life as the daughter of wealthy merchant Chesmu Farleigh had ill-prepared her for the long journey that now stretched ahead. Alone she must traverse half of Upper Raemllyn before returning to the protection of her father's house in Bistonia.

Alone. She shivered again at the thought of the unknown lands that awaited her. *Alone*.

The chirping of an awakening songbird drew Lijena from her forlorn reflections. To the east rosy-golden fingers of light announced that a new dawn arrived. Her choice was simple, sit and brood until melancholia beset her and devoured the day, or mount and ride to the southeast, for there awaited Bistonia.

Days . . . weeks . . . months away? She didn't know, nor did she wish to dwell on the long months that it had taken to bring her to Upper Raemllyn's northwestern reaches. All she must focus on—*must*—was that at the end of each day, she would be leagues closer to home and family.

Rising, she hung the Sword of Kwerin Bloodhawk from a wide leather belt encircling the gray doeskin breeches she wore. Satisfied with the balance of the broadsword on her left hip, she kicked out the fire, saddled and bridled the three horses.

She resisted the urge to break fast and gorge herself on the twists of jerked meat contained in one of the leather pouches tied to the saddle's skirt. She had no idea when she might reach a village or hamlet to procure fresh supplies. Rationing herself to two meals a day would stretch what food she had.

Ignoring her stomach's rumbling protests, she swung astride a sorrel mare, gathered the reins of the other two animals in her left hand, and clucked the mare forward. A smile lifted the corners of her mouth as her heels urged the chestnut mount into a canter, then an easy rhythmic gallop. The morning breeze caught her frosty blond tresses, whipping them into disarray behind her.

At least she could ride, she thought. Neither her father nor her Uncle Tadzi, lord of Harn's thieves guild, had neglected that portion of her education. She had been given her own horse at age five and had ridden whenever she had had the opportunity.

For an instant she thought of Orria, her own dappled gray mare. She shoved cherished memories of the beloved animal aside. When she had begun the hellish journey from Harn to Agda's wood, she had ridden Orria.

Now? She knew not what had become of the horse. Lost in the confusion of the escape from the insidious sorcerer Lorennion and his vampiric Blood Fountain, or dead? She could only guess. And speculation did nothing to fill the hollowness the loss left within her.

She rode for an hour, halted long enough to dismount and climb atop the bay gelding, then continued through Agda's forest. Thus it was she travelled; ride for an hour, switch mounts, and ride on. While none of the three horses was ever totally rested, neither were they fully winded.

When the sun climbed to its zenith, Lijena and her mounts stood atop a small rise and stared out over the forest of Agda. Mountains with rugged caps of snow surrounded her. She had no desire to attempt crossing any of those imposing barriers. Better to find a pass, or best to locate a road, whether it be simple cart ruts or a caravan trail.

The young woman's head lifted. A line of slate gray clouds moved eastward, blowing in off the Oceans of Kumar. Snow would fill the air and cover the ground when those moisture-laden forms clashed with the cold mountain air.

Lijena shivered; the reaction stemmed not from any thought of winter blizzards. All seemed quiet, but she could not escape the sense of an undercurrent churning beneath the forest's surface tranquility. Nor could she elude the distinct feeling that spying eyes were focused on the back of her neck.

The sensation mounted, an expanding core of panicked hysteria. The urge to spur her mount forward and blindly flee into the forest swelled, threatening to dominate reason.

Lijena sucked in steadying breaths to retain an outward shell of composure. Panicked flight would serve her naught. Where could she ride, that others could not follow? If there were others; she remained unconvinced that the niggling sensation of being watched was not born in her own insecurity and loneliness.

She had to break through the flotsam clogging her mind and think clearly, examining the possibilities that might lurk ahead. First and most importantly, who could be following her?

Davin Anane and Goran One-Eye? She shook her head. If the two freebooters were that stupid, they trailed leagues and days behind her. After all, she had left them on foot when she had stolen their horses.

Brigands? Lijena doubted it. Like the birds, the roving bands of thieves and cutthroats migrated south during winter to ply their trade in warmer climes.

Another traveller? If so, why hadn't he made his presence known? A woman travelling alone posed no threat. Lijena did not deceive herself on that point. If the traveller were a man, or men, he would hasten to join her, to offer aid and travelling companionship. *In the hope of shared warmth among his sleeping furs during the cold nights, no doubt!*

If the traveller was a woman, she might feel safer with her than if Lijena had been a man alone. Were her watchers were both men and women, the safety of still another in their rank would bring them forward to offer a temporary alliance to the next city.

They weren't casual travellers, of that Lijena felt certain. And if they weren't brigands, that left only the disturbing possibility—

Zarek Yannis!

The bloody usurper had ascended the Velvet Throne of Raemllyn's High King amid a civil war that still raged. Yannis' soldiers might study her, believing her a scout for a band of rebels loyal to Prince Felrad, the rightful heir of the murdered High King Bedrich the Fair.

And a rebel might consider me one of Yannis' spies! Lijena nibbled nervously at her lower lip. Either presented problems.

The cold realization that she had left one possibility unexplored tapped at the base of Lijena's spine like an icy spike when her gaze drifted to a copse of cherry laurels at the foot of the rise. A frigid fear constricted her chest. Her breath came quick and shallow in counterpoint to her pounding heart.

Six eyes, like orbs of burning coal, flared within the shadowy darkness cast by the tangled limbs of the broad-leafed evergreens! Unblinking, they focused on the daughter of Bistonia.

How apparent the oversight was now—*magic!*—be it the usurper's or another's! An ice floe of terror engulfed Lijena, leaving her paralyzed in its wake.

The cherry laurels' boughs opened as though parted by invisible hands. Three massive jet black horses moved into the light. Sparks flew and sulfurous smoke curled each time their hooves—hooves aflame with a hellish fire—touched the ground.

Mounted astride those demonic steeds—three riders with black, woolen cowls drawn over their heads so that the only facial feature revealed within were their fiery eyes. If there were indeed faces hidden by those hoods, no man or woman had ever seen them.

Faceless Ones! Lijena's brain railed against the hell-riders who edged toward her. But her body remained immobile, frozen by unreasoning panic.

Zarek Yannis had resurrected these unholy warriors to hasten his conquest of Upper and Lower Raemllyn. Demons of an era long dead, the Faceless Ones were more than a match for a legion of any human fighters. Not since their defeat at the hands of Kwerin Bloodhawk had they rode within the realms of Man. Now three of them came for her!

"Zarek Yannis summons you." The lead rider spoke in a hollow voice devoid of inflection. The nightmarish creature lifted a skeletal hand and pointed. The tip of the gnarled finger danced with eerie green witch fire. "You shall come with us."

Long, broad tails aglint with silver scales writhed from beneath the Faceless Ones' black robes as the three continued to ascend the slope.

Flee! Lijena's brain screamed, shattering the ice encasing her supple muscles.

Releasing the two horses she led, Lijena jerked her mount's head to the left and dug her heels into the horse's flanks. The sorrel mare snorted and broke into a full run.

"Stop!" the Faceless Ones called to her in unison. Their three separate commands melted to a single voice that grated like steel raked against stone. "There is no escape from the Master."

The command whipped at her brain. Before she fully comprehended the words, sensed the weave of a binding spell, she obeyed, halting the mare and swinging around to face the three demons once again.

"We ride to meet with the Master," the lead hell-rider said, his voice once more a monotonous droning. His hand, a spidery form that poked from a billowed sleeve of the black robe, rose and summoned her.

"I'll see him in Hell—along with you!" She spat the words with all the false courage she could muster.

Although Davin Anane claimed she had conversed with these devil-spawn, she remembered seeing them but once before. Valora, Yannis' mage, and hell-riders had trailed after Davin, Goran, and herself in their escape from the sorcerer Lorennion. Armed with the sword of Kwerin Bloodhawk, Davin had vanquished . . .

"If you will not ride with us," the riders' leader said, "then you shall die."

He flicked a skeletal hand. The burning-orbed demon on his left spurred his mount forward. With a speed that defied the laws of nature, the beast with burning hooves was upon Lijena. The hell-steed's rider raked a longsword forged from crystalline flame from a dark scabbard. Tiny tongues of brilliant fire licked along the blade's length as the Faceless One viciously slashed out, intent on separating Lijena's head from her slender neck.

The lone woman reacted without thought. She ducked, throwing herself low to the mare's neck. The Faceless' sword sizzled harmlessly above her head.

The next instant chaos reigned. Nostrils flared and eyes wide in terror, the chestnut mare reared. Her forelegs pawed the air as her high-pitched whinnies echoed from the rise.

Balance lost, Lijena tumbled from the saddle. Her arms and legs vainly flailed to right her, to find nonexistent support. Breath exploded from her lungs in a cry-groan as she hit the ground, landing solidly on her back. Waves of dizzying pain jolted through bone and joint.

"Kill her!" This time the lead rider's voice hissed, the soul of a serpent held in that command.

Ignoring the aching protests of bruised muscles, Lijena scrambled to her feet. Singular in her purpose now, she focused on the brilliant core of hope that fired within her breast. *Davin Anane defeated the Faceless Ones with the Sword of Kwerin!*

The selfsame blade now dangled from her own belt.

Whipping the entangling folds of her fur cloak from about her legs, she swirled the cape around her left arm. Not only did it free her movements, but it offered some protection for her armorless body.

Simultaneously, her right hand gripped the Sword of Kwerin Bloodhawk and wrenched it from its sheath. No longer cold, warmth radiated from the grip! Gone too was its ponderous weight! The blade felt feather-light in her hand.

Lijena had no time to consider the wondrous transformation. A demon rider charged!

Once again Lijena accepted the only defense open to her. She ducked. The crackling sword of crystalline fire roared but inches above her head as she swung her broadsword with all the strength contained in her slender body.

She aimed not at the demon, but at its beastly mount. Sputtering, hissing, sparks of angry yellow-green fire erupted when the Bloodhawk's steel contacted hell-spawned equine flesh. There was an instant of resistance before the honed blade severed flesh and bone. Together hell-horse and rider toppled.

No bestial scream of agony tore from the horse's throat. The jet steed simply collapsed to a side and lay there, dark, cold eyes staring accusingly at her. Bursts of flame snorted from its distended nostrils with every labored heave of its massive sides.

Of its rider, she saw nothing. The Faceless One had somersaulted down the windward side of the hill.

The crunch of stone beneath booted feet sounded behind the lone woman.

Lijena pivoted. Having seen the effectiveness of her attack against his companion, one of the Faceless abandoned his flaming-hooved mount and ran toward her with hell-fired sword raised high for the kill.

Lijena's left arm flicked, unfurling her cloak in a blinding fan. Flame forged in crystal pierced fur and hide. Its intended target danced to the side, narrowly avoiding the skewering point. The stench of singed hair hung in the air where she had stood a heartbeat before.

Lijena jerked her cloak and yanked the attacking demon off balance as he tried to free blade from entangling folds of the smoking fur. She lunged, her sword flashing in the noon sun.

The Faceless One wheeled back, stumbled, and fell to its knees. There was no escaping the descending blade or the explosion of sparks that showered when spell-forged steel bit through the demon's exposed neck.

The Faceless One's cowled head flew from its torso and went tumbling downhill. A geyser of black ichor sprayed into the air as the headless body thrashed like a marionette with a madman controlling its strings. Preternatural forces powered it. The beheaded demon tossed aside its sword and groped the ground with skeletal hands, lurching away in search of its severed head.

Lijena's stomach churned; time did not permit sickness. The clack of boot on rock once more alerted her to a rear attack. She swirled and ducked under a savage sword slash meant for her own neck. Simultaneously, she swung the Sword of the Bloodhawk hard. The blade sliced into the demon's knees.

This time she did not blink at the blinding shower of sparks. She expected them, as she expected the ease with which the ancient sword parted unholy flesh. The demon toppled to one side, rolling downhill to join its mutilated comrade.

"You!" hissed the Faceless Ones' leader. "Fool, you toy with powers beyond your understanding. Zarek Yannis will not be denied!"

Lijena swung around to face the last of the hell-riders, who had also abandoned his mount. She threw her cloak out to ensnare her remaining foe.

The Faceless One, with the agility of one who anticipated the offense, backstepped and easily avoided the entangling cape. At the same time, the demon's crystalline blade swept out and up, driving toward the woman's belly.

Lijena danced back and lost her footing on the uneven ground. She went down, plopping heavily on her backside.

Instinct alone saved her. Her sword leaped up to meet the demon's downward cut, a blow meant to split her head in twain. Amid the rage of a miniature firestorm, the Faceless One's blade shattered the instant it touched hers.

The demon howled, an ear-piercing ululation that turned Lijena's blood to ice. The Faceless One rose to its full height, sleeves pulled back from skeletal talons. Those savage claws swept downward to gut her, to rob her of her very soul.

Lijena swung the sword awkwardly, its broad blade barely fending off the demon's touch. Even this light caress of steel brought agony to the Faceless One. Shrieking its unholy fury, it lurched upright in horror.

Lijena did not consciously drive the sword in a low arc for the Faceless One's thin body; instinct commanded. The edge of the sword met the Faceless One's robe. Smoke billowed, filling the air with the greasy odor of burning carrion. The blade cut through the dark material and into demonic flesh. This time the hell-rider's shriek built and rose beyond the range of Lijena's ears.

The Faceless One's body separated, then careened down the hill, one body segment going straight downhill and the other off at an angle.

Lijena stood and stared in shock. The hell-warriors were gone! Only black robes remained. From each, dark, writhing smoke curled upward and dissipated in the midday breeze.

Blinking with incomprehension, she staggered about in an uncertain circle. Gone, too, were the hellish horses—even the one whose legs she had severed.

How? Her head moved slowly from side to side. *How?*

She had no answers. Dead or sent back into the universe from which Zarek Yannis had summoned them, she didn't know. Or care. She lived and that was all that mattered.

Wearily, she let the weight of her sword pull her arm downward. The rest of her body followed, and she collapsed to the ground and just sat staring at Agda's distant mountains.

chapter 2

LIJENA FARLEIGH KNELT beside a still forest pool, focusing on the image reflected beyond the veneer of crystal-fine ice that crept outward from the bank. Her hand reached out, fingers hovering above the water's surface.

Who is this? Her head cocked from side to side. The young woman who appeared to float just below the mirror of moisture mimicked her action. *Who are you?*

Bistonia's daughter drew a deep breath and released it in a weary sigh. The reflection's frosty tresses, the aquamarine eyes, the aristocratic mold of eye-pleasing facial features that more than one man had called beautiful, the wide, full-lipped sensual mouth—all were so familiar. Yet so changed.

Where was the high-piled coiffure that once composed those silken tresses? Gone, too, was the hauteur of eyes, mouth, and chin once so carefully cultivated to achieve a lofty regal pose.

And where were the gowns, spun of gossamer silks from the distant Isle of Pthedm, seductively draping willowy curves of blossoming womanhood? The fragile web necklaces of multihued *mardak* stones and firemonds that coolly caressed the alluring invitation of ripe, uptilted breasts?

Replaced by a man's cape, jerkin, and breeches of gray doeskin. Lijena peered at the reflection, denying that this wild woman who stared back at her could indeed be herself.

She shuddered, unable to reject the truth as her gaze drifted to the sword and dirk hung on the mirror-image's broad, brass-buckled belt. Bistonia's fairest flower had sprouted thorns, had killed both man and demon with her own hands!

Tears she thought herself incapable of shedding slid down dirt-smudged cheeks in mourning for the innocent young girl irretrievably lost to the past. Her uncontrollable trembling was for the woman she had become.

How? By Great Yehseen, father of all the gods, how?

A deluge of memories—memories she struggled to keep locked safely in the dark recesses of her mind—unmercifully assailed her. At their beginning stood Davin Anane, and at their end stood the same rogue thief. The young adventurer was the wheel from which the Sitala, Raemllyn's five fates, spun the cruelly knotted thread of Lijena's life.

"Davin." She muttered his name aloud. The evening breeze caught the sound and muted it to a painful sigh.

Davin Anane claimed love. Yet he had kidnapped her from her Uncle Tadzi's palace in Harn and delivered her into the hands of her father's mortal enemy, Emperor Velden, whose kingdom lay in the cavernous sewers beneath Bistonia, whose subjects were that city's thieves. In exchange for her body and soul, the Jyotian had purchased the freedom of his friend the one-eyed, red-maned Goran, a changeling from another realm, locked in human flesh.

The redness of Lijena's lips paled to a tortured white as her mouth grew taut and thin. She had first killed there in the noisome sewers of Bistonia—had killed Velden and escaped.

Lijena's eyes narrowed to slits. *Only to be betrayed by my betrothed Amrik Tohon and sold to the treacherous slaver Nelek Kahl.*

In turn, Kahl put her in the hands of the brutal Letician sorcerer Masur-Kell. The Sitala once more spun Davin Anane and Goran One-Eye into the twisted thread of her existence. The two rescued her, but not before a demon commanded by the great mage Lorennion was bound to her mind and body.

Every muscle in Lijena's body tautened, attempting to twist into tight knots at the remembrance of that hellish possession. The demon had driven her right into the hands of the Jyotian Lord Berenicis, known as The Blackheart. The former ruler of Jyotis chained her like some stray mongrel and used the demon dwelling in her breast to guide him to Agda and Lorennion's castle keep to reunite Kwerin Bloodhawk's sword with the sheath from which the weapon's powers flowed.

Mayhaps there is love. The hard lines melted from Lijena's face. *Davin did follow Berenicis' trail in search of me.*

Here in Agda's wood, the last son of the House of Anane and Goran One-Eye faced and conquered Lorennion's elemental tests to enter the mage's keep. There they freed her from demonic bondage and rescued her and themselves from the vampiric waters of the sorcerer's Blood Fountain.

Love? Lijena's face turned to stone. What did the Jyotian

alley beast know of love? Davin had come to claim the Sword of the Bloodhawk for his own. He was no different than the swine Berenicis who concealed his greedy motives beneath the ruse that he served Prince Felrad in his war against the usurper Zarek Yannis.

Lijena snorted in disgust. She owed Davin Anane nothing! If a debt had ever existed between them, she had more than repaid it when she had allowed the thief to live. In truth, she should have slit his and Goran's throats the morning she had stolen the sword and their horses.

Davin's name remained atop the list of those etched into her brain. He, along with Jun, Velden's captain who had so sorely used her, Amrik Tohon, Nelek Kahl, Masur-Kell, Berenicis, and Lorennion, would one day pay dearly for what they had done to her— pay with their lives!

Lijena sucked in a quavering breath. Did she lie to herself? How could one unable to fend for herself in this wilderness hope to meet and defeat such men? Could she even consider avenging the degradation and humiliation each had heaped upon her shoulders?

She watched the reflection of her left hand climb to the hilt of the sword about her waist. It had been the blade, and not her own skills that had won out over the Faceless Ones this noon. Yet, more than magicks had been at play. She had struck and parried with a surprising agility that no novice possessed.

A humorless smile upturned the corners of her mouth. The demon that dwelled within her for all the long months had left a portion of its existence imprinted on her mind. Unconsciously she had drawn on those dark memories when she had faced the hell-riders.

A spark of an idea glowed alive within her mind. No. It was more than a mere speculation. She could consciously use those memories; she could learn the ways of steel and blades that were the providence of men. She would train herself, fencing the shadows, sparring with mental images of those who she would eventually face.

And her weapon? The same that once filled the hands of Raemllyn's mightiest hero—the Sword of Kwerin Bloodhawk!

The sword! Her possessive hands tightened about the hilt. It did not rightly belong to her, but should rest with Prince Felrad. Only armed with such ancient magicks could the rightful heir to the Velvet Throne hope to stand against the demon-spawned horrors Zarek Yannis unleashed upon the realms of

Raemllyn. *Should I seek Felrad and his army?*

Snowflakes, like miniature feathers, fell from the sky and dropped to the still pool. They rippled the reflected image that had held her attention for so long, bringing her from the depths of her reflections. Beneath the surface of the water a silvery shadow moved.

A fish! Lijena delighted in its movement as it swam toward her.

Drawn by the insect-imitating ripples, its mouth opened and it snapped at a dissolving snowflake.

Lijena's right hand shot out and plunged into the icy water. Her fingers solidly clamped about the scaled body that thrashed wildly to escape the unexpected snare. In the next instant the young woman jerked her arm back and tossed the fish high upon the bank.

A pleased smile slid across her lips as she stared at the flopping form. The fish was food—food she had provided for herself! Elation suffused her, and her laughter rang through the forest of Agda. What need did she have of Davin Anane? Game abounded in this wood. She would learn to hunt and fend for herself!

And the sword? The question pushed back into her mind.

Lijena glanced at the magic-endowed blade. She would not deprive Prince Felrad of its strength. Eventually she would kneel before Felrad and place the Bloodhawk's sword in his hands. But before that time came, she had uses for the tempered steel. Those uses were named Davin Anane, Jun, Amrik Tohon, Nelek Kahl, Masur-Kell, Berenicis, and Lorennion!

"In time each and every one of you will taste my wrath!" she cried into the face of a rising wind.

In time . . . she turned thoughts from revenge to the increasing snow that filled the air. For now she had horses to attend, a shelter to build to protect her from the winter storm, and a fish to cook!

chapter 3

THE SCREAMS ECHOED throughout the great hall until Aerisan wanted to clap his hands over tormented ears to fend off the wailed agonies. Instead, the young man straightened, his formal pose stiffening to a granite rigidity in an attempt to conceal his discomfort.

Caution! The usurper must not sense my distaste for such barbarous displays. I serve the Great One. He tests my faith . . . my ability to endure in His *name.*

Aerisan's green-brown hazel eyes, unable to disguise their disquiet, shifted to Zarek Yannis, who leaned heavily on the balustrade like some winged carrion-eater waiting to swoop down on its prey. A watery blue gaze met the young magician.

Aerisan tried to repress his embarrassed surprise and failed. A hot flush rose up his neck and suffused his cheeks when it became apparent the High King *did* notice his uneasiness at witnessing such torture—and was amused.

The Great One is all-consuming. The Great One awaits all. I willingly walk the path. I rush to the Destroyer's embrace. Aerisan bolstered courage with the litany of his forbidden faith.

"Pain can be so educational." Zarek Yannis' thin lips twisted in a mockery of a smile. "Don't you agree, Aerisan?"

The young mage straightened even more, an action that brought the top of his head but to Yannis' shoulders. The flush left his cheeks as he bridled his emotions. He felt the fulcrum of the time at which he stood. A minor mistake, the slightest slip of the tongue would destroy all he strived to achieve.

When Aerisan spoke no trembling voice betrayed him. "There are other methods for gaining needed information."

Zarek Yannis' smile grew when he looked below once again. He ignored the undercurrent of distaste in the voice of the young man that he had elevated to master of magicks in the month since his arrival in Kavindra, first of Raemllyn's cities. Aerisan was but another moth irresistibly drawn to the flame of the Velvet Throne. And in the end, Yannis would devour him as he had devoured his predecessors.

"Information?" the High King said. He bent forward to rest his chin in a cupped hand. "They can provide me nothing I haven't already learned. I do this to . . . sharpen my skills. Come closer, enjoy the spectacle of death."

And gaze into the burning flame that will eventually consume you and your gnawing hunger for my power, Yannis silently mused.

Aerisan stepped to the railing and peered below. A naked man lay bound to a contraption that confused both Aerisan's eye and magical sense. He tried to discern what forces Zarek Yannis employed to torture the victim and failed.

"What spells are woven, Majesty?" The mage shifted uncomfortably, unable to look away from Duman-nu, the one mage in all Kavindra who had shown kindness to a newcomer in the usurper's court—the very man Aerisan replaced.

"Know you not, Aerisan? I pay you well for your skills. Surely your sovereign does not command more potent magicks than the chief mage of Raemllyn?"

Zarek Yannis toyed with the young sorcerer. Both knew it. Yannis was amused; Aerisan found hatred rising within him. For a moment, the mage considered the poison needle nestled in the sleeve of his black robe. A flick of the wrist, one tiny prick to the usurper's neck and this unbeliever's reign would end.

Only the discipline instilled in him by the Great One held Aerisan's hand. Those of the true faith knew the patience that was inherent in the Great One. In time he would lead Zarek Yannis down the final path of truth. But it would be in the prescribed manner, within the walls of a great temple erected to a forbidden deity.

Zarek Yannis laughed as he leaned back. The movement revealed two Faceless Ones standing on the right side of the balcony. If Aerisan had attempted to harm the king, those demons would have ripped him apart and consigned his soul to the deepest level of Hell.

"I should not taunt you in this way," Yannis said with no hint of remorse or apology. "It is only that my other mages have committed the most heinous crime of all—treason."

"How has Duman-nu betrayed you?" Aerisan knew the error

of his question when he saw the dark clouds of wrath boiling across Yannis' face.

"He conspired with Valora, curse her!" Zarek Yannis stiffened, hands clenched in a white-knuckled grip about the railing. His body shook with rage. "Watch what happens to traitors. Watch and learn, young mage!"

Yannis pointed to the pinioned Duman-nu. The captive sorcerer writhed with the agony of anticipation, the realization that even more diabolical tortures awaited.

"Witness, Aerisan, and see how demons can be summoned from the lowest levels of Peyneeha!"

Aerisan blinked as Yannis began the chants, wove the magical passes with his hands, let his fingers describe the positions of power. The air beside Duman-nu boiled, transformed to a silvery shimmering mist. Within that mist . . .

Aerisan held his emotions in check, stiffling a gasp before it was born in his throat. *The usurper summons a demon! How?*

"For you, Duman-nu, I have summoned Yu-Vatruk." Yannis' voice echoed with the Hall of Screams. "Do you know him, worm?"

"Please, Majesty!" croaked Duman-nu, squirming, but finding no escape from his bonds. "I meant you no harm. I fell under Valora's spells."

"You fell into Valora's bed," snapped Zarek Yannis.

"She held me in total thrall, M–majesty. I did not mean to be rebellious. I meant you no harm. Never! Believe me. *Believe me!*"

Duman-nu shrieked. At the heart of the silvery mist an amorphous mass, dark and sinister, churned. Black, leathery tentacles adrip with an oozing green slime lashed from the shimmering to slash vulnerably exposed flesh. Welts, red and swollen, rose in the wake of each of those living whips. Duman-nu's screams filled the immense hall.

Again the dripping tentacles slashed. Each welt smoked. Flesh charred and burst into crimson flames that refused to die.

Still the demon metamorphosed.

Aerisan found himself unable to look away. The magicks inherent in the demon's changing shape held him as surely as the iron bands held Duman-nu. Yu-Vatruk, Demon of Nightmare reached out a long tentacle and touched Duman-nu with a hard, razor-edged talon. Even as Yu-Vatruk pulled the claw away, it changed into a feathered appendage.

"The feathers are poisonous," Zarek Yannis informed the younger man. "Much worse than simple cutting or burning. Watch. Watch and learn."

Duman-nu learned the full terror of Nightmare when one of nine feathered wings reached out and lightly caressed his face. The mage's anguished howls rent the air as his cheek transformed to a green, putrescent mass awrithe with boils and hatching white maggots hungry for human flesh.

How? The unanswered question railed through Aerisan's brain. Reports categorized Zarek Yannis as an inept, bungling fool who simply toyed with black arts.

Yet, this was no fool, nor did the High King toy with mystical energies. He was a full master who summoned Raemllyn's demons to do his bidding—and there was his guard of Faceless Ones! From where did his power stem? *It's as though he has absorbed the knowledge of all those who have served as his court mage.*

An icy spike embedded itself in the young sorcerer's heart. Was it possible? Icroso, Aglian, M'Rinte, Payat'Morve, Valora, Duman-nu—the names of those who had briefly served at Zarek Yannis' command paraded across Aerisan's mind. Except for Valora and Duman-nu, all had mysteriously died. As for Valora, no one was certain how the witch escaped the High King. And for Duman-nu, it would be only moments before he stood before Black Qar.

Aerisan studied the High King from the corner of an eye. Did this vile unbeliever possess some unknown ability that allowed him to devour the minds of others? Or was he the most powerful mage to walk the world since the legendary Nnamdi, who had first summoned the Faceless Ones and brought Raemllyn to her knees? Both possibilities posed myriad questions that would have to be explored with the utmost caution and delicacy.

"Kill me, please, I beg you, kill me, Aerisan!" Duman-nu's pleas rose to the balcony, drawing Aerisan from his reflections.

The tortured man's gaze fixed on the mage he had befriended upon his arrival in Kavindra. Aerisan watched as dispassionately as he could. To show any sign of weakness before the High King might spell his own death. Zarek Yannis would see it as a passing diversion to have Aerisan join his one-time companion. Aerisan's service to the Great God demanded strength, required he remain at Zarek Yannis' side. He did the only thing he could; he ignored his friend's cries for a quick, clean, merciful death.

This amused Yannis. "You learn, young mage, you learn quickly. That is good. Discard the treacherous and keep only the useful."

Aerisan bowed low, hands thrust deep into the dangling sleeves of his robe. "Would you instruct me, Majesty, on summoning Yu-Vatruk? This appears to be a demon worth cultivating."

Zarek Yannis laughed. "Yes, you are learning. Watch!"

Aerisan watched— and learned. Zarek Yannis chased away Yu-Vatruk, to Duman-nu's relief. But the bound wizard's eyes widened with stark fear as Yannis instructed his new master mage in the art of demonic control. Under his king's tutelage, Aerisan brought back Yu-Vatruk, this time in the form of an odious white slug trailing glowing slime. By the time the Demon of Nightmare reached Duman-nu, the mage had perished from a fear-exploded heart.

"You are a master of spells, Majesty," Aerisan complimented his king. The young mage glanced at the Faceless Ones standing beside Yannis.

"Not yet," the High King cautioned. "Do not think to summon the Faceless Ones on your own. It is a spell that has turned on scores of impatient sorcerers throughout the ages." Zarek Yannis stared at the hell-riders. "They are mine. Any attempt to subvert them and you will end up like him."

Yannis tossed his head in the direction of Duman-nu's body dangling from the chains. With a sneer on his lips, Yannis turned and left, the Faceless Ones a half pace behind and on either side.

Aerisan released an overly held breath. Zarek Yannis would bear careful scrutiny. An unbeliever though he was, the man controlled powers that could be useful when harnessed for the glory of the Great One.

The young mage rocked forward, hands trembling as they rested on the low railing. Once this illustrious hall had been High King Bedrich's audience chamber. Peasants assembled with nobles sat at the foot of the throne to beg their liege's intervention in matters both weighty and minor.

No longer. Zarek Yannis had turned it into a torture chamber. The mute evidence of past bloody successes hung from chains and ropes, the corpses in a spectrum of decay. Some were mere skeletons, picked clean by the insects infesting the hall. Others, such as Duman-nu's lifeless body, retained most of their earthly flesh. Taken together the bodies formed a tapestry of chains and death and misery that extended a full five hundred feet to the arched entryway.

Aerisan smiled, the stench of death around him an exquisite perfume. The Hall of Screams they called this audience chamber now. One day, in a future closer than the High King might imagine, men would give it a new name. For it was here that Aerisan would eventually erect the temple of temples to the Great One. The death Yannis wrought now would look like child's play in comparison to the blood bath Aerisan would unleash.

The young wizard turned and vanished through a small arched doorway. Unless he desired a fate equal to Duman-nu's, he had to consolidate his own power base. One day Zarek Yannis would offend the wrong people—rumors had it that battles with Prince Felrad went against the usurper—and this would provide the opportunity for a ruthless, ambitious man to ascend the Velvet Throne.

A man like Aerisan.

"Tell me of Valora," Aerisan commanded. The mage lounged on a low couch and studied the guard captain.

The soldier's face tightened. A disarray of white scars marched across his weathered face—souvenirs of countless battles and slain foes. Narrowing eyes betrayed a suspicion of the sorcerer's innocently spoken request.

"She was King Yannis' master mage, before you, Lord."

"Fool," snapped Aerisan. "That's not what I meant, and you know it. You and Valora were lovers. Everyone in the palace still buzzes over it. There's not a single gossip in all Kavindra that doesn't whisper of your amorous deeds."

"Then talk to them!" Defiance rumbled in the weaponsman's throaty reply.

Aerisan's wrist did no more than flick; fingers wove intricate patterns. The air before the mage churned, twisting, whirling, taking a form unto itself until a miniature tornado raged.

Beads of sweat glistened on the soldier's forehead, and his eyes grew saucer round. Still no additional answers came from his dry lips.

Aerisan's right forefinger straightened to point at the captain's midriff. The crazily spinning vortex surged, pinning the soldier against a wall. The man's breath hissed through teeth clenched in pain.

"The twisting air can gut you like a swine," Aerisan said. "Or mayhaps I will enlarge it until it swallows your entire body in its churning mouth. Either way, you will die."

The young sorcerer struggled to maintain his outward composure while the fiber of his body and mind threatened to collapse. The skill and energy required to maintain an air elemental taxed him to the limit. Raemllyn's elements were the providence of the gods and not of mere mortals. In another few seconds his strength would fade and his ruse would crumble.

"I'll talk!" The captain's voice rose two octaves.

With a theatrical pass of his hand, Aerisan dismissed the whirling spike of air. He smiled as the captain collapsed to his knees and quaked.

"Tell me of Valora. I care little for the details of your animal couplings." Aerisan hoped that this blatant lie went unchallenged. He lusted to know what his beautiful predecessor and this rugged warrior had done together. "Tell me of the woman. What drove her?"

Aerisan lowered his voice to a soft, caressing sigh like wind through summer's green leaves. "Tell me of her information sources, tell me of her power!"

"You cannot oppose Zarek Yannis." The soldier's eyes lifted, filled with hate and fear.

"Don't instruct me, Captain." Aerisan's voice turned cold. He had hoped the man would not resist interrogation so. "Tell me what I wish to know, and perhaps we can strike an agreement favorable to us both."

"Valora could protect me. You can't. You're little more than a child." Venom seethed in the man's words.

Aerisan's anger flared, tapping the energy needed to send a new whirlwind against the captain's face. The soldier yowled in pain as the spike of air sought his eyes, his nose, his mouth. Aerisan released the spell, not from mercy, but to preserve his own strength. Not since the days of Kwerin Bloodhawk had sorcerers been able to wage extended battles using their magicks.

"She may have protected you, but I can *destroy* you!"

The captain said nothing.

"You live solely because of my mercy," lied Aerisan. "Zarek Yannis knows of your indiscretions with Valora. Only my intervention on your behalf saved your poxy hide."

"He knows nothing!" Still the stubborn soldier resisted.

Aerisan crossed his arms and peered at the man. "I had hoped you valued your life more. But if you insist . . . the High King's ear is mine."

The mage rose and strode toward the door of his chambers without another glance at the weaponsman.

"What do you want to know?"

Aerisan turned. Fear, soul-knotting fear, lined the warrior's face.

"Where did Valora go to get her intelligence reports? Who did she trust most—and least?"

"I provided much. While the Faceless Ones guard Yannis day and night, I am in charge of the palace perimeter and know all that occurs. No one leaves or enters without my approval." The captain's resistance melted.

"She took you to her bed, and you revealed what she needed?" Aerisan frowned. It hardly seemed possible that a man of such courage, of such stature within Zarek Yannis' military corps betrayed his liege so easily.

"She was a beautiful creature. Dark of hair, she was." The captain closed his eyes and a beatific expression crossed his face as he remembered the departed mage's beauty. "That raven's wing black hair floated like a halo, a crown about her pale face. Never have I seen such beauty. I could stare into her jet eyes and vanish into paradise. No god promises more than she did with a simple touch, a caress, a moment's brief embrace."

"And her kisses?" Aerisan said sarcastically.

The captain continued his enraptured remembrance. "Unlike any mortal woman's, Lord. She knew erotic tricks that set my flesh afire. After she'd leave my quarters, I'd continue to burn inside for hours."

"In exchange for this, you betrayed your king?" Aerisan hid his smoldering interior beneath an exterior of feigned interest. The captain was a blasphemer! To compare a mortal to a god was a sin! The soldier spat in the face of the Great One!

"Yes!" The guard captain's eyes shot open, horror etched on his face.

Aerisan smirked. "Fear naught. Your secret is safe with me—for a price. I need similar intelligence. Tell me, Captain, why did Valora depart Kavindra?"

"Mages do not last long in Zarek Yannis' service. She had

blundered. Only by fleeing could Valora save herself from the usurper's wrath."

"What sin did she commit? One of omission or commission?"

The captain's eyes widened, this time in surprise. "Surely, Lord, you know this. She allowed Prince Felrad to obtain the Sword of Kwerin Bloodhawk."

Aerisan hid his surprise. Until this moment he believed the legendary blade to be no more than a myth. With a careless gesture, he dismissed the guard captain then sank back to the low-slung couch to ponder what he had heard, both from the captain and from other sources.

"The Sword of Kwerin!" he mused aloud. Only with this magical weapon could the Faceless Ones be defeated. With the sword in his possession no one could stand before him! Not that pretender to the throne, Prince Felrad. And not Zarek Yannis, even with his amazing ability to summon demons from the depths of Peyneeha.

"High King Aerisan," the mage said in an awed voice. "Yes, it is a fit title for one who devotes his life to the worship of the Great One!"

He clapped his hands. A silent servant glided into the room, bowing low.

"I want a small matter attended to, Miggon. A guard captain. The one Valora used. Remove him. Permanently."

Aerisan turned his attentions elsewhere while his servant-assassin left the room as quietly as he'd entered, already plotting which poison to use on the soldier to keep all suspicion away from his master—and himself.

The palace page slammed hard into the door, unable to slow his breakneck pace in time to avoid the collision. Panting, the boy cried out, "Lord Aerisan, High King Zarek Yannis, Protector of Kavindra and Ruler of Upper and Lower Raemllyn desires your presence immediately, in the Hall of Screams!"

"How long have you searched for me?" asked Aerisan, looking up from a tome of magical spells he had unearthed in a deep palace cellar. The spells written on the crumbling vellum intrigued him, but he needed more time to study their importance before he determined if they might be used against the usurper.

"Less than five minutes. I came directly here, Lord."

Aerisan considered. He might squeeze another few minutes of study in before arriving in the Hall of Screams, blaming his tardiness on the page's inability to find him with any dispatch. Aerisan sighed and shoved himself away from the table.

"I'll be there directly," he said.

The page flashed him a grateful smile of relief and ran off to alert the lord chamberlain that the High King's master mage followed. Aerisan tried to decide how grateful the boy was. He shrugged it off. Not grateful enough to jeopardize his position—and neck—by spying on the chamberlain, Aerisan surmised.

Aerisan smoothed dark blue robes about his slight body and walked in slow, stately strides along the corridor leading to the Hall of Screams. He knew dozens of eyes watched his every move. Nothing in the palace went unnoticed or uncommented upon. It was this grapevine that he sought to make his own.

Aerisan entered the audience chamber of the Hall of Screams from the left side and walked at a steady pace until he came to the foot of reproduction of the Velvet Throne the usurper's artisans had crafted. Such reproductions were in each of the palace's rooms—a constant reminder of Zarek Yannis' power.

The young mage tried to ignore the new additions to the hall's collection of corpses. He couldn't. Yannis had been busy all morning. The man was no more than a butcher, savoring the pleasures of inflicted pain the way others savored the delights of the flesh.

"Majesty, I came as quickly as I could." Aerisan bowed deeply, his brow brushing against the purple velvet runner leading up the steps to the throne.

"You have done well, Aerisan," said the High King. "Your weeks as my master mage have assured me of your loyalty."

Aerisan strained for the slightest hint of sarcasm. Such would mean his death. Could Yannis have learned of his petty intrigues so quickly? They amounted to so little!

"I require someone whom I can trust to perform a mission of the utmost delicacy."

"Majesty, I seek only to serve." Again Aerisan bowed low. Droplets of sweat dampened the velvet runner.

"Yes, yes," Yannis said, waving away the subservient declarations. "I would send a company of my Faceless Ones, but they lack the subtlety required for this mission. You have proven yourself diplomatic—and tactful in your assassinations."

"Majesty!" Aerisan's gaze shot to Yannis' face.

"I know of the guard captain Valora seduced. He was a test—your test. If you had not removed him in the manner you did . . ." Zarek Yannis' words trailed off. The High King leaned back in the mock throne and gestured at the bodies that decorated the immense hall.

Aerisan cursed under his breath. In the future, he'd be more circumspect. And Miggon would have to be the first victim. Of all those in his employ, Aerisan had thought the poisoner-servant the most faithful. It came as a shock to learn he reported to Zarek Yannis, for only Miggon could have betrayed him.

"That is behind us. I need your skills in Bistonia."

"Bistonia, Majesty? Is there something wrong there? It is my belief that Lord Lerel is devoutly faithful to the Velvet Throne. He owes his power solely to you."

"Lerel is my oldest ally," Yannis said. "There is no reason to distrust him."

Aerisan waited. There had to be more. Zarek Yannis did not send his master mage halfway across Raemllyn to pay respects, even to an old and valued ally. Aerisan did not delude himself in thinking his value in Kavindra far outweighed that in Bistonia—unless Lerel had grown unfaithful.

"Yes, I do think that to be the case," Zarek Yannis said, as if reading Aerisan's thoughts. "Rumors, I am sure they are nothing more, come to me that Lerel lives up to his appellation . . .by dealing clandestinely with Prince Felrad."

"His appellation, Majesty?" Aerisan arched an eyebrow.

"He is known as Lerel the Weasel. Go see to my weasel and tame him, Aerisan."

Aerisan backed away from the throne, head bowed. He reached the distant corridor before a wide grin moved across his face. To Bistonia! That prosperous city-state controlled much of the banking and coinage for all Raemllyn. To depose Lerel and claim it for himself would put him in an enviable position of power.

Have I misread the Great One's desires? Only now did the mage recognize the possibility of such a mistake. Was it in Bistonia rather than Kavindra the temple of temples was to be erected? *Surely it must be so. If not, then why would the Great One place such vast wealth before me?*

A prayer of thanksgiving on his lips, Aerisan rushed to prepare for the journey to Bistonia. There were those in his employ who required elimination before he dared leave.

chapter 4

AMRIK TOHON'S RAPIER-SLIM blade sang through the air. The light of brazier and candle glinted off its silver length like myriad flashing stars.

Lijena Farleigh reacted rather than thought. Her own sword leaped from its sheath with a deadly hiss. She ducked and let her former lover's steel whistle harmlessly above her head. Then, with the Sword of Kwerin Bloodhawk glowing warmly in her hand, she lunged.

The broadsword skewered upward in a smooth, fluid motion. Its tip found and plunged into Amrik's vulnerably exposed chest, sinking all the way to his black heart.

Lijena ignored the young man's startled death cry. Wrenching blood-stained steel from his flesh, she kicked out to send his twitching body tumbling to the floor. Without pause to savor the sweet taste of revenge, she spun about, sword raised to fend against a rear attack.

The crimson dripping point of the broadsword was enough to divert Nelek Kahl's poison-tipped dirk. The slaver's arm hesitated for the blink of an eye.

Lijena took full advantage of that uncertain moment. She shuffled to the right in a hasty sidestep, avoiding the plunging fang of steel intended for her back.

Grasping the sword's hilt in a two-handed grip, she struck out with all the strength held in her lithe body. Her frosty tresses of white-gold flew in the air like a wild mane as she guided the honed blade in a tight arc. A path that ended when the sword traced a fine line of scarlet across Kahl's throat.

For an instant total incomprehension filled the slaver's wide eyes. Horror replaced doubt. Kahl's hands jerked up and encircled his throat. Blood, thick and red, sprayed from the second mouth that opened beneath his chin. Neither fingers nor palms could hope to stem the flow fountaining from that life-stealing wound. The slaver's paling lips trembled; only the wet gurgle of blood came from his mouth. Then he collapsed—never to rise again.

For several long moments, Lijena's aquamarine eyes stared at the two men her blade had felled. A humorless smile touched the redness of her lips. How long she had waited to savor this moment of wine-sweet vengeance! How many months . . .

An agitated cheeping like the sound of an angry rodent wedged into that moment of glory.

The room around Lijena Farleigh wavered dissolving to an evaporating mist. The bodies of Amrik Tohon and Nelek Kahl went transparent then vanished, leaving only the brown of winter-dried grass where they had lain.

Lijena's green-blue eyes blinked as she came from the trancelike state that always accompanied her training exercises. Her gaze dipped to the unblooded sword grasped tightly in both hands. Neither Amrik or Kahl had tasted her steel this day, but soon, she thought, resheathing the broadsword.

Since her defeat of the three Faceless Ones in Agda's wood, thus she had practiced her weaponry skills twice daily. Mentally those who had degraded and used her stood before her in twos and threes—and fell before the Sword of Kwerin Bloodhawk.

The high-pitched chirping sounded again.

Lijena glanced around. Three strides away a tiny creature, which she could not identify, poked a head that was more white fuzz than fur out of a burrow. Its tiny pink mouth chittered excitedly as beadlike eyes curiously perused the human intruder.

"Shhhh, little one." Lijena grinned, amused by the creature's obvious alarm. "You've nothing to fear from me."

A louder, spitting and hissing drowned the fuzz-head's cheeping. The creature ducked back into its hole in the ground. A second later a mature, white-capped head thrust from the burrow. A long snout snapped to reveal sharp rows of yellow teeth in warning.

Lijena backed away. She had no desire to challenge either fuzz-head or his mother.

Ten cautious backsteps and Lijena turned to mount a dappled gray gelding. She had traded her three stolen horses for this stout steed and fresh supplies at the village of Ardevel in the Kou-Garl Mountains. The gelding stood nineteen hands at the shoulders and was of little use to mountain people, who preferred smaller pack animals to carry goods over the rugged passes of the Kou-Garls. Morjael, who reminded her so much of her lost Orria, was well-suited to the months of travel that had stretched before her.

Tugging her doeskin cloak about her shoulders, Lijena nudged the dappled-gray southward. Her gaze scanned the broad, rolling plain that opened at the forest's edge. For a moment doubts assailed her. Evening approached, and she had no desire to camp the night in the open. Brigands who preyed on Raemllyn's unwary travellers could sight a flickering campfire from leagues away.

A dark line on the horizon delineating another wood's edge to the south waylaid the lone woman's fears. Morjael, even at a leisurely walk, could traverse the plain ere Horkann, God of Night and Darkness, covered the sky with his inky veils.

A self-amused smile lifted the corners of Lijena's mouth. The months alone in the wilderness of Upper Raemllyn had wrought changes within her. When she escaped from Davin and Goran One-Eye, the differences of wood and plain completely evaded her.

Also, I have this to fend myself against attackers. Her hand touched the hilt of her sword. *And now I can wield it!*

Although, she admitted that she was still untested with Kwerin's blade. Except for the Faceless Ones, neither man nor demon had opposed her journey through Upper Raemllyn's heartlands.

Only in the city of Solana had the need to draw her blade arisen. While supping in a caravansary, a drunken driver approached her with lust and spice-wine firing his veins. Before she could unsheath her sword, another driver gallantly came to her rescue with a wine jug deftly applied to his companion's skull.

The incident would have ended there had not the first driver's brother been present. The brother struck her rescuer. Within seconds the caravansary erupted in a drunken brawl. While fists flew, Lijena quietly crept away and found herself lodging for the night in another of the city-state's inns.

A rancid odor, sharp and bitter, moved on the late afternoon breeze beneath the grassy smell of the plain. Lijena's nose wrinkled when she inhaled deeply. The smell was like carrion left to ripen in the sun.

Reining Morjael toward a high hill on the left, she urged the gelding up the gentle slope with a rhythmic tapping of her heels, then halted the dapple-gray when she reached the crest.

"No." The single word pushed from her throat in rejection of the scene that met her eyes.

For as far as she could see, destruction lay like a burned mantle across the eastward swells of the plain. No natural force had wrought this massive destruction. Only the hands of men and the cruelty they wove could have brought such death.

Bodies of men and horses, grotesquely twisted in an agonizing death, littered the ground. Tiny fires still sputtered amid their charred remains.

Ignoring the stench, Lijena eased her mount toward the battlefield, the horror of what had transpired here repelling and attracting her in the same moment. The sparse winter grass turned to charcoal beneath Morjael's hooves. Blackened lumps sprinkled the ground, vaguely recognizable as human in form. Shields, swords, and great war lances lay scattered about. All indicated more than steel-on-steel had weighed in this battle. Each of the weapons was twisted or melted as though caught in a horrendous inferno.

Mingled with the odors of death and burned flesh was the unmistakable smell of magicks unleashed.

Lijena's right hand closed around the grip of her sword. Her eyebrow arched. Warmth radiated from the weapon as though the ancient steel sensed the spells that had been cast here.

How long since this hell on earth raged? Surely it was recently ended. The blossoms of flame indicated an immediacy to the burnt nightmare. Yet she had heard no battlecries or the din of clashing swords.

Halting Morjael beside one of the fiery flowers, she dismounted and held her palms over a white flame as though to warm them. No heat came from the dancing magical fire.

For an instant Lijena considered thrusting her hand into the flames to determine if they were but an illusion, then discarded the idea. Instead, she lifted the broken haft of a war axe and touched it to the white fire.

The wood ignited and blazed with a consuming hunger. She tossed the fired axe handle away; the wood was ember before it touched the ground.

Whoever cast this magic gave no quarter. She drew a steadying breath and rose. Leading Morjael behind her, she moved deeper into the battlefield in search of a survivor who might reveal what forces had met here today and who claimed victory.

"Prince Felrad's troops? Or Zarek Yannis'?" She could not discern if the dead had worn uniforms, much less which banner they had fought under.

It made no difference to any of those left on the field. All had died.

Felrad's men, she told herself. *The prince's troops foully butchered by Zarek Yannis' magicks.* She could not believe Felrad capable of such wanton carnage.

Lijena poked through the rubble, not knowing what she sought. The death stink no longer caused her throat to constrict, but the sight of so many dead violently churned her stomach.

She pushed on, toward what appeared to have been the center of the battle. A half mile lay behind her when she found fallen banners of unknown royal houses that gave no hint to the troops' identities.

The Sword of Kwerin now glowed warmly on her left hip. Even its sheath could not contain the growing heat.

Around her a dozen flickering magical watchfires burned with their cold light. She used the sword's heat as a guide to find the heart of the magical disturbance. There, if it existed anywhere, she would find the true nature of the combatants—and the victor of this monstrous battle.

The tumbled remains of a command tent that stood before her evoked painful memories of the times she journeyed with her father and mother to the Harnish Spring Fair. King Bedrich's pavilion always sported the finest banners, the most colorful, the most exciting. She would strain to catch sight of the High King or the King's Consort or the ladies in waiting. How she had wanted to be among them, those fine ladies with their luxurious dresses and dazzling jewels and proper manners!

Lijena recalled the last Spring Fair before Zarek Yannis usurped the throne. She had been hardly more than twelve summers then and the pageantry awed her even more than it had in past years. The next year no contingent from Kavindra had appeared. Bedrich the Fair battled for his life.

The year following that, Bedrich lay foully slain and Zarek Yannis had stolen the throne.

The remains of the war pavilion revealed that the usurper had again won a victory. Lijena found it impossible to believe that Prince Felrad had been the victor when his command tent lay so thoroughly destroyed. A bemedalled skeleton, tatters of forest green uniform holding its gold and silver and particolored ribbons, confirmed the defeat of Felrad's forces. Only a field commander loyal to the royal family sported the Defender of Kavindra award. There was no doubt Prince Felrad had lost this gigantic battle— and had lost it badly.

Had the Sword of Kwerin Bloodhawk been with . . . Lijena shoved the half-formed thought from her mind, as she wearily remounted and reined the dappled-gray toward the forest in the south. She could not rid herself of the niggling guilt. The blade she carried might have tilted the scales here today—even in her own hands!

That thought had darkened her spirits as surely as the god Horkann veiled the sky by the time she reached the wood. Intent on finding some small refuge from the horrors she had seen and the night's chill, she moved Morjael beneath the security of overhanging tree limbs. A hot meal and needed rest would divorce her from the tumultuous forces that raged within her breast.

A hundred strides within the wood, she tugged the horse to a halt. A loud crashing sound—combat or a chase?—echoed through the trees ahead. Then came . . . nothing.

The silence distressed Lijena more than the sound. It marked the end of a hunt, the death of the quarry. If she could judge from the outcome of the battle, anyone hunting this night would swear allegiance to Yannis and not to Prince Felrad.

Her hand drifted to her sword's hilt. Nary a hint of warmth came from the blade. A lack of magic—or merely spells the blade could not detect? It did not matter. Steel as well as magicks could kill.

Alert and wary, she moved on, her hand resting on the sword ready to wrench it free at the first indication of approaching danger. Ride deeper into the forest and forget the sounds, she told herself. After all, she was but one woman. What match was she against a troop of Yannis' forces?

The easy route lay in simply riding on, forgetting she had heard the moans of pain and the sudden silence that followed. Zarek Yannis' troops did not even know she was within a month's ride—Yannis did not know her as Chesmu Farleigh's daughter or as anyone of import.

A scream—a human cry of anguish—shattered the wood's unnatural silence. On its heels bellowed cruel, throaty mirth!

Against all common sense, Lijena reined Morjael toward the sounds. She cautioned herself to flee if the usurper's men were too numerous or if the one they had captured already lay dead at their murderous hands.

At the same time, she knew that she would be hard pressed to keep the Sword of Kwerin sheathed. She prayed that Black Qar might celebrate her deeds this day as he entered the names of her victims into the Death Rota. She longed to extract some small vengeance for all the destruction she'd seen. *Aye! I'll well use the blade's magicks!*

Lijena's surging confidence subsided when another blood-curdling scream rent the night. She eased Morjael to an easy walk, suddenly recognizing the folly of riding blindly into a trap. Before she struck—if she struck—she had to determine the size and composition of the opposition.

The yellow-orange flicker of flames filtered through limb and bole ahead of her. Halting the gelding, Lijena slid from the saddle and tethered the animal to a drooping *morda* tree. Eyes homed on the campfire's blaze, she moved in a crouch as a shadow drifting into another shadow. She worked her way to the massive trunk of an ancient oak at the edge of a small clearing. Cautiously, she peered toward the light.

In the center of the camp stood a human soldier—not demon—wearing Zarek Yannis' colors. The man, armed with sword and knife, tossed an armload of dead branches atop the fire. On the opposite side of the clearing were three additional soldiers.

No! Two more of Yannis' lackeys, Lijena corrected herself. The third man was bound to a pine bole with his arms stretched high above his head. His legs were spread wide and tied with rope that snaked about the trunk. *That one is their prey.*

The light of growing flames confirmed her thought. A trickle of crimson ran from a gash above the man's right eye. Another flow of red oozed from the corner of his mouth. Both injuries indicated the use of fists or club rather than steel. The captive wore not a uniform, but a simple blouse and breeches cut from forest green cloth.

Silently Lijena eased the Sword of Kwerin Bloodhawk from its sheath and thoughtfully fingered the blade. To rush forward from her position would be foolish. She could no more than cover half the distance to the captive before being sighted by the soldiers, she thought as she mentally estimated the clearing's width at a full eighty strides.

Even such a potent magical device as the sword required a modicum of common sense in its use. She might be invincible in battle, but this small band had the look of hunters about them. The trio might have longbows nearby, although she could not discern their hiding place. Lijena had no idea if she could defend herself against a well-aimed arrow using the sword.

The thought of dying in a futile rescue held little appeal. Better to use the element of surprise to its fullest. Silently, aware that the slightest misstep of her booted feet, the snap of twig beneath toe or heel, would alert the three soldiers, she inched around the clearing's perimeter.

"The High King chooses ill in his victims," the bound man said in dulcet tones. The voice leaped into the night on lyrical wings.

Lijena paused, her gaze shooting to the captive. Was the man a mage, invoking a spell to ensnare his captors? When he spoke, she felt compelled to listen.

Lijena studied his handsome visage in the blazing light. A thin, straight nose gave his face the aspect of a hatchet blade, yet Lijena found this attractive. Of his eyes she had no clue, but his hair shone like red gold and his skin carried a fair translucence she had often seen in aesthetes.

He tensed against the ropes binding him at the approach of one of the soldiers, but he displayed no indication of fear. For that, Lijena envied him. She remembered all too well her own imprisonment by Velden and the terror that had gnawed inside her.

"We got the right one," growled a soldier. He poked the bound man with a sheathed dagger. "King Yannis has had us looking for you well nigh a month."

"What a wearisome task chasing the likes of me." The captive's chin lifted proudly and the fire's light blazed in his eyes as he grinned.

"Kept us out of the battle," another of the soldiers chuckled.

"Shut up," ordered the first.

While she detected no insignia denoting rank, Lijena sensed authority in the first's voice and posture. Where he led the other two followed, of that she was certain. *He must be eliminated first.*

"Let's get on with this," the third soldier said in a whining voice. "It's cold, and I grow hungry. We've caught the fool. Let's punish him for his verse and get back to a warm barracks."

Lijena paused again, puzzling. *Fool? Verse? Who is this man bound to the tree?*

"A young man from Marduk looked in a mirror, said 'Are

you queer?' " the captive began to recite. "Then let's—aieee!"

The third soldier crossed the clearing and smashed a meaty fist directly into the pit of the green-clad man's stomach. The prisoner retched weakly; his entire body quaked spasmodically.

"You *are* from Marduk, eh?" the man grated out between gasps for air. "I thought as much. The uncultured accent gives away low breeding every time."

"Kill him."

"No!" The leader shook his head emphatically. "We do it as we were commanded. King Zarek ordered him tortured for at least an hour before execution. We obey. Even in these woods our liege may have eyes to spy upon us."

The third soldier spat defiantly, although his eyes surveyed the forest's darkness beyond the glow of the campfire.

Lijena moved closer, readying herself for the sprint across the open space, the three cuts, the three deaths. In the next instant, she hesitated. The soldiers drew their own blades.

Temples pounding, she settled quietly back into a shadow and waited with sword leveled for attack.

There were no battlecries or even a glance in her direction. The three prepared only for the torture ordered by their liege.

However, the three readied weapons required her to rethink her plans for attack—for being here. What was this handsome man to her? Although his clothing was forest green, he did not wear one of Prince Felrad's uniforms. For all she knew he might be nothing more than a rogue who deserved what punishment the three would serve up.

Rogue or not, the prisoner's scream froze her. The leader dragged his sword across the man's left thigh. Scarlet ran from the rent in his green breeches, and the injured leg flopped about as if it had a mind of its own.

"Must we listen to his sniffling?" the second soldier asked. "Isn't it enough we're forced to waste an hour with this loud-mouthed scum?"

The soldier in charge rubbed at his chin for a moment, then nodded. "Come lend a hand. Me thinks I can *cut* some of the noise from his mouth!"

Uncertain what happened, Lijena watched the two soldiers wrestle with their captive's head for several minutes. Then a sword blade flashed in the fire light, rising and falling in the blink of an eye. The soldiers laughed with obvious delight when their leader displayed the captive's tongue between his thumb and forefinger.

No matter what manner of scoundrel this man might be—even if his deeds equalled those of the craven Davin Anane—he deserved better treatment than this! Still Lijena hesitated. The soldiers' bared blades were a harsh reality, while her daily foes had been only imaginary. For all her hours of training, was she ready to face opponents of flesh and blood? Even armed with a sword so magically endowed?

"Bring the brand," the leader ordered. The soldier who'd been mocked went to the fire and returned with a smoldering stick. The soldier stood with the smoking stake until the leader motioned.

Lijena gasped. The burning stick shafted forward, skewering the captive's left eye. His howls of pain were drowned in the soldiers' chorus laughter.

Before the lone woman could recover from witnessing such a brutally inflicted wound, the soldier twisted, withdrew the still smoking stick and jabbed it into the prisoner's right eye.

The man's renewed yowls of agony brought Lijena to life. With a quick downward cut she slashed through the brush and rushed into the clearing. She spun so that the fire warmed her back. *Let these dogs squint into the fire. It will make their deaths all the quicker!*

The three turned, surprise etched on their coarse faces. Past them Lijena saw the ruined visage of the once handsome captive.

"Who're you?" the leader demanded.

"The one who'll send you into Black Qar's embrace!" Lijena gripped the broadsword with both hands, lifted it over her left shoulder and rushed to dispatch three souls into the arms of the God of Death.

Lijena saw the soldier closest to her raise his pathetic blade in a high parry. Her laughter rang out as she brought the Sword of Kwerin crashing down to meet it. The laugh died when steel rang out against steel.

No sparks. No severing of the opponent's blade. Nothing but painful vibrations that jolted all the way down her arms and into her shoulders. Lijena stumbled back, stunned.

The Sword of Kwerin had died! All she wielded was an ordinary steel blade—against three trained, armed soldiers! The weight of that massive weapon tugged heavily at the muscles of her arms and shoulders.

The soldiers spread out, one to the left, one to the right,

the leader in the middle. They advanced. Lijena's fear-rounded eyes focused on three circling points as their swords closed in on her.

chapter 5

THE COACH BOUNCED, jerked, and jostled roughly from side to side before coming to a lopsided halt with one of its forward wheels entrenched at the bottom of a pothole at least three feet deep.

"Why have you stopped?" Aerisan demanded in a highly agitated voice as he picked himself up from the floor of the coach and straightened his disheveled robes. He pulled aside the plush velvet curtains, poked his head out a window, and peered at the driver. "What is it? More brigands?"

"Lord, we have Bistonia in sight. Ye said ye were awanting to enter the city on horseback rather than in the finery of my coach." Shurit made no attempt to disguise his insolence while he locked the carriage's brake and spat a stream of *mylo* weed juice to one side.

Fuming, Aerisan hastily retreated to avoid a faceful of spittle. The coachman Zarek Yannis assigned for the journey had taken every opportunity during the trip to show his contempt for his sole passenger. Shurit grew dangerously close to overstepping the limits of the mage's tolerance.

A small spell might teach a needed lesson, Aerisan considered. Preferable would be to give the overweight ass into the hands of the two Faceless Ones Yannis had commanded to accompany the sorcerer. *Mayhaps they would find the boorish oaf amusing. That is, if hell-riders derive any enjoyment from a human's death.*

"Where is the escort? Summon them and get me a mount. I will enter the city at sunset as planned." Aerisan called from the safety of the carriage.

The sound of another well-aimed mouthful of spittle striking the ground just outside the door reached Aerisan's ears before Shurit leisurely answered, "Of course, my *Lord.*" The driver's inflection twisted the honorific into profanity.

Aerisan had wavered in punishing the coachman overlong, believing the *mylo*-addicted man to be yet another of the usurper's tests. No longer! Shurit had served his purpose; Gajo, the man's apprentice, would take the journeyman's place at the reins.

Waiting for the Faceless Ones to ride beside the coach with his mount, Aerisan swung the door open and stepped to the road. He pointed to a set of saddlebags resting beside the driver. Shurit passed them down with the contemptuous speed of a slug.

The young wizard glanced to one of the Faceless as he swung astride a sleek bay mare. "You may have him. Now."

Aerisan mentally intoned a prayer to the Great One, offering Shurit's body and soul as a sacrifice to secure the deity's blessing on this holy venture the magician undertook for the glory of his god. He felt the Great One's presence. Like a cloak it covered him. Threads of power wove outward from the mage's divine aura to touch the coach's driver.

But it was not the Great One's pleasure that coursed through the mage as he bathed in the terror that awoke on the driver's face. That moment—the realization of true fear—was well worth the base insults Aerisan had suffered throughout the journey from Kavindra.

"Lord, no!" the driver shrieked.

The cry died in a bloody gurgle when a Faceless One shot out an arm and with a flick of a wrist drew a ragged skeletal talon across the man's throat of double chins.

Steam rose from the severed arteries as they pumped lifeblood into the cold afternoon air. The coachman slumped forward, then fell in a tumble to the road and lay there, his body atwitch with the last spasms of life.

Aerisan's gaze lifted to a trembling youth of no more than fifteen years who cowered on the driver's board. "Learn from your former master's impudence, Gajo. Life is a fragile thing. Only in strict obedience to the one you serve may you preserve it."

He paused allowing his words to penetrate the youth's terrified mind. "I am your master now, Gajo. You will deliver the coach to Bistonia, stable it there, and await further instructions from me. Is that understood?"

The boy nodded, and Aerisan pointed to Bistonia. "Then go!"

Without a word the youth kicked the brake free, snatched up the reins, and popped them against the teams' backs. The coach bounced forward toward the spires of the distant city-state.

"You have done well," Aerisan said when he turned to the two demon riders who remained at his side. "King Zarek demands your presence along the River Stane. Ride there and conceal yourselves near the great ducts that empty Bistonia's sewage into the river's waters. Your wait will be long, but I will eventually bring orders from the High King."

The Faceless Ones departed silently. Aerisan released a soft sigh of relief while he watched them disappear in the distance. That had been easier than he expected. He had feared Zarek Yannis had given the two orders to return to his palace in Kavindra after reaching Bistonia. While the Faceless Ones were not necessary to his plans, they would be a most useful tool.

Perhaps one day they will truly be mine to command. Aerisan remembered the Sword of Kwerin Bloodhawk. Were he to gain that legendary blade, he would possess the key with which to rule the fiery-orbed demons.

Aerisan glanced at Shurit's body and nudged the bay forward to avoid the flies that already gathered on it. At least three hours remained before the sun set. He needed time to think before riding into Bistonia and could ill-afford even a minor distraction such as the buzz of hungry insects.

Aerisan rode slowly, sharp eyes soaking in detail. The farmlands surrounding the walls of Bistonia had yielded well. Even this late in winter evidence of excellent harvests showed in warehouses brimming with grain and the fruits of a bountiful summer. Nowhere was there evidence of starvation, as he had seen in some parts of Raemllyn between Bistonia and Kavindra.

He nodded and smiled. Dealing with Lerel would be easier than anticipated; such overflowing granaries suggested moral complacency among Bistonia's citizens. A land of plenty produced soft men, unprepared to face unsuspected dangers.

The weak, wintry sun had fled the sky when Aerisan halted his mount in front of a guardhouse beside the south gate to the city. The helmeted man within gave him a lazy glance and waved an arm toward the open gate as though he cared not who entered or left Bistonia.

"You, there," called the mage. "I seek shelter for the night. Can you recommend an inn to a weary traveller?"

The guard blinked up at Aerisan, eyes bloodshot. The smell of heavy liquor wafted to the sorcerer's nostrils. When Lerel was disposed of and Aerisan had a firm grip on the city guard, such slovenliness would cease.

"Can't say I know much 'bout places to sleep—all night," the guard replied, words slurring over his tongue. "But ye might try the Inn of the Winged Ram. They got this serving wench who's known for—"

"Swine!" Aerisan spurred the bay past the guard and through the gate. When he took Bistonia's reins, things *would* change.

Skirting the market areas and keeping to torch and brazier illuminated side streets, the mage wended toward Bistonia's heart. While there were people to contact within the city walls, they could wait for a day or so. He wanted to get a feel for the spirit of the people—a soul that was easily discernible in the countless merchant shops that lined each avenue.

Money lenders, gem traders, silk merchants, purveyors of gold and silver—these were the veins through which flowed Bistonia's lifeblood. For a people such as these there was but one maxim by which to rule—profit! They would follow a man who assured that their profit was protected.

Aerisan's lips twisted in an amused smile, recalling the long hours he had spent poring over the volumes of Bistonia's history during the journey from Kavindra. How these merchants would pale and tremble if they realized the methods he intended to employ to guard the profits they cherished so!

Three hours of wandering, watching, and absorbing brought him to a wrought iron fence worked with a confusing panoply of characters.

"Good evening, sir," came a soft feminine voice from beyond the gate. "You admire our iron work?"

"The artistry is unique. I've never seen such fine work," Aerisan admitted while squinting into the shadows. His gaze found the voice's owner. A sullen-eyed blond wench, an earthen jug of wine clutched to her abundant bosom, stood in the veiling darkness.

"It depicts the hero Kaga stealing the winged rams of the God Brykheedah." The woman coyly batted long, silky eyelashes.

"Winged rams?" Aerisan's eyes widened in half-remembrance.

"Aye, this is the Inn of the Winged Ram." The woman shifted her stance to give the stranger a better view of womanly flaring hips. "And I am called Belatha."

Aerisan chuckled.

"You find this funny? Or, mayhaps, I am the one who amuses you so!" Indignity colored Belatha's tone.

"Not at all. This is the very spot recommended to me. I had . . . despaired of finding it. I am newly arrived in Bistonia," Aerisan replied.

"Pray, good sir, dismount and let the stable boy groom your horse. And allow me to show you to our taproom."

Belatha stepped into the cone of light cast by a nearby brazier. Aerisan felt a stirring in his loins. From atop the bay, he surveyed the broad expanse of the woman's ample breasts. All but their very tips lay wantonly exposed by the revealing plunge of the neckline of her pleasant blouse. A shower of blond hair fell in soft ripples around her face, and sparkling emerald eyes lingered in a unmistakable invitation.

"Please, good sir. Join me in the public room of the inn?"

Aerisan tried not to show unseemly haste as he dismounted, but a hot flush rose into his cheeks when he heard her musical laughter. He was making a public spectacle of himself and hated it—and at the same time, he didn't care.

"The stable boy will carry the saddlebags," Belatha said, then called a youth to take the mage's horse.

"They stay with me," Aerisan replied, his voice harsher than he'd intended.

Belatha's eyes widened in surprise at the tone, but she said nothing. Holding the iron gate open for the stranger, she stepped aside to admit him.

"The hospitality of the Inn of the Winged Ram is known throughout all Bistonia," she said. "We will do everything to make your stay a pleasant one."

Her gem-green eyes locked on Aerisan's, leaving no doubt as to her meaning. The mage felt heat suffuse him once again when the woman pressed close, shoulder and hip brushing his side. Her closeness was strangely flustering.

He covered his nervousness by dropping the saddlebags atop a table inside the inn. The loud clattering focused the attention of those in the room on his entrance, but that was better than becoming tongue-tied in front of the lovely blond wench.

"Ale," Aerisan ordered. "And a meat pie. I've ridden long leagues this day and must satisfy a growling stomach and a parched throat."

While Belatha scurried away to fill his order, the young

mage found a chair near the fireplace and warmed himself against the gathering chill. His keen ears heard the muted conversation of the others in the room discussing him.

Aerisan glanced at the coat and breeches he wore in disguise, his robes tucked within his saddlebags, and cursed an oversight in his arrival. Two wine-sotted patrons noted that he wasn't the least road-dirty, and another commented on his seeming lack of fatigue. Aerisan hadn't wanted attention; his mission depended on secrecy.

But, he thought, perhaps this would work to his benefit. He swallowed hard while he watched Belatha's sway while she returned to his table with the tankard of ale. She put it down, letting the foam billow over the battered rim and onto the table. Aerisan didn't notice the sloppy service; his gaze was on the serving wench.

"Do you come from far away?" she asked. "Your clothing has the cut of Kavindra about it."

Aerisan cursed his inattention to detail anew. He knew so little about such things. His life had been a sequestered one, his every waking hour focused on learning the skills required to achieve the abilities of a mage. His mentor, Roan-Jafar, had been a harsh taskmaster and tolerated no frivolity, and the demands of serving the Great One left little time for the ways of common men.

It had never occurred to Aerisan before Belatha mentioned it that anyone, even a serving wench in a quaint tavern, might be able to glance at him and know that he travelled from Kavindra.

"These?" he said, looking down at his clothing, as if for the first time. "I bought these in Leticia. Are they of Kavindran cut? Did you mistake me for one of the Royal Court?" He allowed a hint of eagerness to slip into his voice.

When Belatha laughed, Aerisan thought silver bells rang out in the night. "Hardly that, but you look prosperous enough, even in a fine city like Bistonia."

"One day I might be." Aerisan smiled as the wench's eyebrows arched.

"A scion of a royal family?" she asked, impressed.

Aerisan was grateful for his earlier carelessness. It added weight to his hints.

"I can say little of it. There are unfriendly ears listening everywhere," he said, glancing around the room. No one met his gaze.

"You are a relation to Prince Felrad!" Belatha cried, then put a hand to her mouth. She smiled. "Your secret is safe. Curse Lerel, the weasel!"

"You oppose the Weasel?" Aerisan asked. His heart beat faster. He had so quickly unearthed a source of information in the lowest classes of Bistonia—that class where rebellion sparked and could be easily fanned to flame.

"Who doesn't?" Belatha said. "Even if he . . ."

"Yes?" Aerisan urged. "Even if Lerel does what?"

She seated herself beside him, a well-fleshed thigh pressing warmly against his. The woman leaned to his ear. Her breath carried an aroma of mint. "Your secret is safe with me. I swear it on my honor. I'd never do anything to betray Prince Felrad!"

"And what," Aerisan asked, "is my secret?"

"You have come to deal with Lerel!"

Aerisan went cold inside. How had she learned? His hand slipped under his cloak and rested on the brass wire-wound hilt of a dagger. One quick movement would silence the wench's inviting lips forever.

"Oh, I won't tell. Don't look so shocked. It is widely rumored—aye, known—that Lerel deals with Prince Felrad. You are Prince Felrad's emissary come to parlay with the Weasel." Belatha laid a soft, warm hand on Aerisan's. "Lerel is treacherous, playing both sides against each other, but any aid he gives Prince Felrad is welcome."

"What sort of aid is rumored?"

"A full one part in ten of the crops travelling up and down the River Stane by barge never arrive at their destination." Belatha winked at Aerisan. "But you know this."

Aerisan smiled. *So Lerel feeds Prince Felrad's host, eh? While the Weasel publically claims to be Yannis' most ardent supporter. The man comes by his name honestly.* Here the Bistonian ruler's probity ended. Aerisan would enjoy removing him and succeeding him as despot of Raemllyn's richest city.

"Will you take a room for the night?" Belatha asked. "There is a special one just at the top of the stairs."

"And what's special about it?" Aerisan asked.

"It is the quietest room in the inn and has the best furnishings and—I come with it."

"Show me the room." Aerisan waved an arm for Belatha to lead the way.

He followed without stumbling over his own feet in his

eagerness. Behind the locked door his awkwardness no longer mattered. Nor did his inexperience in the worldly ways of men. Belatha was a most experienced teacher.

chapter 6

A CACOPHONY OF steel clashing on steel rang through the night forest as the soldier's sword slammed into Lijena's awkwardly poised blade. The bone-jarring impact jarred through muscle and sinew ill-prepared for the force of that blow.

A piteous cry of desperation twisted from Lijena's lips. Her left foot lost purchase on the forest floor. She stumbled and fell to one knee. Her wrist turned; the soldier's blade careened down her length of steel, deflected to the ground.

Time for even one quick easy breath was denied the lone woman. Her assailant's weapon leaped up in a tight, circular arc, its tip meant to slash across her wrist.

Lijena threw her sword out in a clumsy block rather than a graceful parry and scurried backward, rolling to a side. The campfire formed a flaming shield between her and the three soldiers.

For an instant, her eyes dipped in disbelief to the inert Sword of Kwerin in her hand. No sparks danced from the blade, no arcane magicks flowed to slice through common steel as though it lacked substance. What had gone wrong? Was the wondrous blade drained of power?

Thoughts of failed spells fled her mind as Zarek Yannis' three henchmen raised their swords and stalked forward. The firelight reflected in their eyes like glowing flowers of blood.

"Whoever you are, we welcome you." This from the leader while he edged around the blaze. "'Tis been long since we've shared the company and pleasures of a woman."

Lijena backstepped. Her gaze focused on the foremost of the three, but she was aware that the remaining two eased to each side of her once again.

"Lay aside the blade. We've no want to kill you." The leader's tone left no doubt as to what he *did* desire.

Lijena sucked in a steadying breath. Magic or not, the sword in her hand was still honed steel and deadly. The soldiers numbered but three; she faced that many daily in her training sessions! She refused to consider the fact that those who matched skills with her during those sessions were only the stuff of her imagination rather than flesh and blood.

"Let her keep it, Kele!" The soldier to Lijena's left called out, his leer never leaving the frosty-tressed blonde. "Daoh and me like'em with spirit!"

"Quiet, Rorke! We've no want to force the lady—unless she pushes us." Kele paused his steady advance, his gaze shooting to his companion.

The lead soldier's momentary diversion was a ruse to lull the woman he faced. Before his eyes darted back to Lijena, he lunged. His sword swept out like a club with the obvious intent of knocking the woman's blade from her grasp.

Lust rather than swordsmanship was his mistake!

Lijena's blade dropped, letting his sword sail through empty air. Her wrist flicked upward, and she answered with her own lunge. The tip of the Sword of Kwerin Bloodhawk sank home, driving into Kele's exposed throat.

Neck skewered on naked steel, the soldier stood, blinking as though unable to comprehend what had occurred. He lurched back, weapon falling from his trembling fingers. The embedded sword jerked free in a spray of crimson that his clasping hands could not stem. Kele turned and swayed, his gaze on Daoh as though seeking aid from his companion in arms. Then he toppled forward like a felled tree to lay face down in the dirt.

The shock of seeing their leader easily bested by one so delicate froze both Daoh and Rorke. Not so Lijena. Kele had looked to Daoh, and it was to him she leaped. Her sword swept back, then lashed out.

The hard slash raked along the soldier's thigh cutting to the bone. Daoh's yowl of pain—and life—ended as Lijena deftly lunged once again. Her blade's tip skidded off a rib and forced inward to pierce the craven's black heart.

Blood dripping from the Sword of Kwerin, she spun about. Her eyes narrowed to slits, and her mouth tautened to a thin white line. She moved toward the last of her opponents in the step-glide, step-glide of an experienced fighter.

"Come to me, my beauty. Come feel the caress Rorke of Initha's blade . . . come embrace death." Bravado filled the soldier's defiant hiss, but caution and a hint of fear colored his alert eyes.

Lijena halted, sword leveled to fend attack, sensing that her own movement was exactly what Zarek Yannis' lackey wanted. Why she did not fathom, but she had no intention of providing Rorke of Initha the opening he sought.

The soldier's eyes widened when she stopped. He spat and scowled. "So be it, bitch! If ye'll not come to me, then I come to ye."

From chest and throat, he roared a howling battlecry. At the same instant Rorke leaped forward, his sword slashing in a broad cut aimed at Lijena's left side.

Only a briefest glint of firelight on steel saved the daughter of Bistonia from dancing to the right and directly onto a treacherous dirk Rorke brandished in his left hand!

Instead Lijena backstepped, clutched her sword's hilt in both hands, and with all the strength in her supple body swung the blade high over her head. It descended with the accuracy of an executioner's axe. Steel sliced into the side of Rorke's neck, leaving his head half severed from torso when he fell to the ground, body twitching while life fled it pulsing sprays of blood.

Breast aheave with labored breaths, Lijena surveyed the gory remains of the three who had faced her this night. Skill, not spells had claimed their lives!

Lijena stared at the crimson streaking the ancient blade of Raemllyn's first High King still grasped in both her hands. She knelt and cleaned the steel on Rorke's tunic before easing the weapon back into its sheath. Even without the spells the long-dead mage Edan had forged into the sword, it had served her well.

The sword draws its power from the sheath in which it rests, she remembered Davin Anane saying after their escape from Lorennion's keep. She shook her head; the Jyotian rogue apparently had been wrong. There was no magic in the blade now.

A groan from behind spun Lijena around. The Sword of Kwerin Bloodhawk was two-thirds clear of the scabbard before the blonde realized the sound came from the prisoner still tied to the *morda* bole.

"Everything's all right now. The soldiers who did this are dead." She stepped to the man's side, freeing her dirk to slice the rope binding his hands and arms.

A wave of compassion swept over the lone daughter of Bistonia when the red-haired man lifted his head. The blinded pits that had once been eyes seemed to search the face of his savior.

"Yehseen, sire of all Raemllyn's gods, delivers Chal son of Chalt into your able hands, fair lady."

The poet's voice swept through Lijena like the caress of a soft, warm spring breeze—a voice that was the heart of gentleness itself. In the next instant, blood gurgled over the young man's lips and dripped from his mouth like spittle. His chin dropped to his chest, and he collapsed into Lijena's arms.

Easing the burden of his weight to the ground, Lijena quickly cut the ropes holding his ankles and dragged him beside the campfire. Returning to the night-darkened wood, she found Morjael and led the horse to the clearing. In her own sleeping furs she wrapped the ill-abused poet, then washed his wounds and bandaged them with cloth she tore from the dead soldiers' uniforms.

Would that I might somehow treat his severed tongue, she thought while she bathed his drying lips with drops of water squeezed from a cloth. *In the morning, I will seek* calokin *buds in the forest to ease his pain and stonewood leaves to aid the healing. If he lives through this night.* In truth, she doubted this Chal son of Chalt would survive. He appeared too frail to endure . . .

Lijena's thoughts faltered. Her eyes widened to stare at the golden red haired man she nursed. It couldn't be! She had seen Kele and Rorke slice the poet's tongue from his mouth. Yet, she had *heard him speak!*

Uncertain, she edged away from Chal. With arms hugging knees, she sat staring at the unconscious man. She gave voice to her thoughts as her head moved from side to side. "By Yehseen, what breed of man speaks when his tongue has been cut from his mouth?"

chapter 7

AERISAN LEANED AGAINST the wall of the inn, hands discreetly concealed beneath the folds of his cape. He disliked the odorous thief standing in front of him, but for the time being such ruffians were his lot in life. Nor was he likely to consort with others of higher station for some time to come.

Except for the lovely Belatha. Aerisan mused in spite of the danger the man before him presented. The buxom blonde seemed totally captivated by his charms—and the mistaken idea he carried the lineage of Prince Felrad's royal house in his veins. The delightful woman could stretch a single night into a lifetime of ecstasy. For the past two weeks they had spent eons of pleasure in each other's arms.

Each bedding brought new and more wondrous revelations of the flesh, erotic activity Aerisan previously had known only in his imagination. When he assumed control of Bistonia, Aerisan considered elevating Belatha to the position of consort.

He chuckled at the unintentional pun.

"Somethin' I said amuse you, Lord?" the thief demanded.

"Keep a civil tongue or I'll have the pleasure of ripping it from your mouth!" Aerisan snapped, distraught by the daydream's interruption. As enticing as the sweet Belatha was, she also served as his emissary to Bistonia's less savory elements—those which the young mage might mold into a force to serve the Great One. Belatha was responsible for bringing this thief to his room.

"You want to meet with the Emperor or not? Your choice."

"No," Aerisan said, his voice turning oily and menacing. "It is your so-called Emperor Jun's choice whether he wants to live. I hold it within my power to dispatch him." Aerisan snapped his fingers to indicate the ease with which the task could be completed.

The thief yawned, obviously unimpressed by the threat. "You want, you can see Jun now. You don't want, then Nyuria take you. Makes no difference."

Aerisan considered using his dagger on this impudent man. Or creating a small but deadly whirlwind in his mouth. A slow smile crossed his face. Aerisan stood straight. "Very well. Now."

Surprise washed over the thief's scarred features. Obviously he'd not considered the possibility that this haughty noble would accept. "We got to go into the sewers."

"No," Aerisan replied firmly. "We'll meet by the River Stane, where the sewers discharge. That ought to provide safety enough for both Jun and myself. He can retreat into the sewers if he feels cowardly."

"And you can go drown yourself," the thief chuckled.

"Then, Jun can simply stay in his noxious sewers and forfeit the opportunity of regaining control of Bistonia's public thoroughfares." Aerisan refused to abandon his original plan. The sewage ducts that emptied into the Stane were his territory, although Jun, Bistonia's Emperor of Thieves, would never suspect that.

"The streets? We haven't been free above-ground in the streets since Farleigh banded the merchants together." Awe filled the ruffian's voice.

"All things change." Aerisan smiled. "Chesmu Farleigh's chapter in the history of Bistonia is written in quicksilver." He saw the thief didn't understand his allusion. "We can change what has been," the sorcerer said simply.

"The Emperor'll see you at the mouth of the sewer. Now," the thief replied, then cautiously added, "No tricks."

"Lead the way." Aerisan waved an arm to the man.

The unlikely pair hurried through Bistonia's streets. City guards glanced occasionally in their direction, but the speed of their passage gave no hint of lingering to pick pockets or commit petty crimes. For their part, the guard heaved a sigh of relief to see them continue on. Night turned the riverfront cold by the time the thief pointed to a large sewer pipe opening into the Stane.

"There. Wait. Jun'll be here."

Aerisan made his way down the sludge-covered embankment and brushed off a rock. He sat and stared out across the gently rippling river. Massive flatbed barges moved lazily on the water, transporting the bulk of Bistonia's wealth to Raemllyn's other realms. The sands of an hourglass were fully spent before the magician heard a sloshing behind him.

"You wait well," came a cold voice. "What else have you been trained to do—spy?"

Aerisan didn't turn to face his accuser. "The river is lovely, except for the refuse you dump into it."

"Add his body to the shit floating there," Jun commanded.

Aerisan heard boots sucking in the mud. He tensed, even though he knew the approaching men presented no danger.

"Jun, reconsider," Aerisan said. Strong hands seized and jerked him to his feet. "I'm no mere spy. Zarek Yannis sent me with an offer."

"Cut his throat before you throw him in," Jun amended his command.

Aerisan closed his eyes and muttered a small chant. The hands holding him vanished, and Jun gasped.

"Don't try to run. They will kill you. Even in the sanctuary of your precious sewers, they can find you." Aerisan's eyes opened, and he turned to face the ruler of Bistonia's thieves.

"Nyuria take you!" Jun, a tall, slender man, stood draped in purple robes, their hems dripping with scum. Silver sword and dirk, hilts encrusted with a wealth of gems, hung from his waist, but his clenched fists made no move for either.

The reason—on each side of the emperor of Bistonia's thieves stood a hooded demon, mounted on steeds with burning hooves and nostrils that snorted flame. Scaly tails writhed from beneath the dark robes the hell-riders wore, and red eyes burned with hellish fury out of the depths of cowls as black as bottomless pits. The two thieves who'd seized Aerisan lay with their throats ripped out, expressions of intense horror now permanently etched on their faces. Such was the speed of the Faceless Ones.

"Zarek Yannis' trusted emissaries. Will we talk now, or should I . . ." Aerisan's voice trailed off. The smile on the mage's face indicated what the alternative to talk—and full agreement—would be.

"Call them off," Jun said with ill-disguised fear.

Aerisan waved an arm in a broad theatrical gesture. The fire-orbed demons slumped in their saddles, but remained ready should danger threaten. Jun's gaze shifted between the two, beads of sweat glistening on his brow. Aerisan smiled with amusement. His hiding the two Faceless here on his arrival to Bistonia had been sheer genius.

"So the High King takes note of the lowly thieves?" Jun eventually found the courage to question. "What is it you're wanting? Does the son of a whore want some petty pilfering done?"

"His thievery is done on vaster scale," Aerisan said, resting leisurely on the rock. "We require information, for which we are willing to pay handsomely."

Jun nodded slowly, noting how Aerisan used the royal "we." Whether he and Yannis were comrades in arms meant nothing to the emperor of Bistonia's thieves. Command over the Faceless Ones brought a quicker response to his lips than the mutterings of a mad tyrant in far off Kavindra.

"Rumors have it that Lerel is less than the loyal servant of the Velvet Throne he might be," Aerisan began.

"I know nothing of the Weasel's dealings."

Jun spoke too quickly; Aerisan seized on this. "You know how Lerel diverts as much as ten percent of all foodstuffs leaving Bistonia to Prince Felrad's army."

Jun shrugged. "Not hard to do. Just a little rerouting of the barges. The thieving of the arms and tax revenues is something I don't understand."

Aerisan said nothing. He had suspected Lerel of giving more than food to Prince Felrad, but Jun confirmed it.

"These thefts amount to a considerable sum over the course of a year," Aerisan continued. "A smart man—a knowledgeable thief—might do well if that went to himself and his friends rather than a rebel prince."

"You're sayin' that King Zarek is going to depose Lerel?" Jun's eyes nervously darted to the Faceless Ones.

"Let's say that Yannis is unhappy with the idea of a traitor in his rank."

"And you'd replace Lerel?"

"I?" Aerisan laughed. "Hardly. My position is somewhat more important in Zarek Yannis' court." Aerisan hoped the lie rang as the truth in Jun's ears. If the thief were greedy enough, he might pounce on the opportunity Aerisan offered.

Jun struck for the obvious. "You're lookin' to put someone else in power? Bistonia might see a face other'n Lerel's ugly one at the parades?"

"Who might you suggest as Lerel's successor? I have heard

favorable reports on this merchant Chesmu Farleigh. He has command of the streets." The young wizard noted the anger rising in the Emperor of Thieves. Aerisan held his delight. Jun was as easy as a child to maneuver.

"Farleigh!" bellowed Jun. "He knows nothing of Lerel's doings. If he did, he'd approve of Lerel supporting Prince Felrad. Pah!"

"Perhaps I was hasty in my judgment. Perhaps someone, shall we say, closer to the people, able to come and go with no one noticing. Perhaps such a person might be better suited to assuming total control of all Bistonia," Aerisan suggested.

Aerisan waited for what he proposed to penetrate. Jun smiled slowly.

"No longer *just* Emperor of Thieves. You, friend Jun, ought to aspire to more. With my aid, with the aid of Zarek Yannis and the Faceless Ones."

Aerisan had calculated well. The promise of total dominance over Bistonia coupled with the threat of the Faceless Ones had its effect.

"I will serve King Zarek well."

"There is more," Aerisan said.

"Name it. Your lordship's slightest whim will be fulfilled even if a thousand of my followers labor a year and a day."

Aerisan ignored Jun's attempt at what the thief thought to be courtly speech. "I require information. All the information you can find about Lerel's dealings with Prince Felrad."

"Consider it done."

"Further," Aerisan interrupted, "we require a tribute to proclaim your sincerity and devotion to the Velvet Throne."

Jun waited expectantly.

Aerisan said slowly, "We desire a temple constructed."

"It will be the finest in all Bistonia!" cried Jun. "It shall rise above all the holy houses on the Avenue of Temples!"

"On the morrow send a messenger to my quarters, and I shall provide him with the temple's design," Aerisan said. "Land must be purchased, and the construction started immediately."

"There are those who will serve as our agents for such matters," Jun nodded. "By sunset tomorrow, a site for this temple will be secure. What else do you command?"

"For tonight, that is enough." Aerisan motioned to the two hell-riders, who galloped off and disappeared along the banks of the river. "I grow cold and weary. Tomorrow will be soon enough for talks of greater matters."

Without so much as a glance toward Jun, the young mage worked his way up the sloping bank and back onto Bistonia's streets—streets that would soon be his!

chapter 8

"THEY ROB ME of sight, and the *only* penalty you extracted from them is death? Never again will I see the subtle colors of sunset, the soft curves of a lover's face, the dark clouds filled with storm and thunder."

"Be glad you're alive. It's more than you would have been, if I hadn't come along." Lijena waved away the man who sat before. Her gaze avoided the fire-scorched sockets that once held a poet's eyes.

"Aiiiieeee!" A scream shattered the warm summer night. "Father! Mother! By Yehseen, you can not be dead! Gentle souls killed by the hand of Man!"

The forest tumbled, spinning on its head as though the anguished cry wove threads of awesome magicks that shook the very foundations of the world. Lijena's own cry rose as the earth opened beneath her . . .

Lijena jerked upright, breaking through the mists of restless sleep, and stared around her. The forest clearing and the campfire lay undisturbed. A soft sigh escaped her lips as she clutched arms about her to fight away the night's chill. *Only a dream. Not warm summer, but cold winter remains.*

She closed her eyes and attempted to repress a shiver that writhed up her spine like the squirming of an ice worm. For five nights phantasmas had haunted her sleep—and even intruded into the hours of light. *Is this place accursed? Do the spirits of the three soldiers I slew and buried haunt this wood?*

A wave of unbridled terror washed over the woman. Her eyes flew wide to stare at the groaning form of a man who thrashed from side to side in a bundle of sleeping furs. Although the poet Chal's lips did not move, she heard:

"Run, Calana. Hide before their spears find you!"

Love broke over Lijena like a flowing river, and then came the words, "Maili, I bathe in the luxury of you."

Then there were only gurgled groans, and fevered moans that shuddered from the lips of the man with the golden red hair.

Lijena pushed from the ground and moved to Chal's side. She lifted a bowl of murky water containing a thin mixture of *calokin* and *dragonroote*. The first for the narcotic it held to ease his suffering; the latter for the time dilation it produced, with the hope the drug's effect would hasten the poet's recovery.

"Pray forgive me, dear lady." Lijena once more heard words that came from no lips. With those unuttered sounds a sensation of flowers and rich perfumes swept through her senses. "I am something of a poet and inclined to a poet's excesses."

A beat of her heart later sadness as deep as a bottomless well swallowed her, and Chal said, but did not speak, "Unto the Great Destroyer Qar, God of Death, I deliver the souls of my father and mother. May Yehseen, from whom all life flows intercede on their behalf so that they might dwell . . ."

Again silence reigned through the night-shrouded wood.

Chesmu Farleigh's sole child tried to tell herself it was impossible, but she could not escape the evidence that had pressed on her for five days and nights. Even without a tongue, Chal spoke to her. She shared the fever dreams that wracked his brain.

The man beside her twisted and groaned. He worked an arm from beneath the furs and clawed at the cloth tied across his eyes.

Lijena reached out and tucked arm and hand beneath the furs once again. "I don't understand how or why, but the gods have somehow bound us together—your mind touches mine. Your thoughts become mine."

As she untied the cloth bandaging eyes that were no longer, she realized that thoughts and words floating between Chal's mind and her own did not describe what had repeatedly transpired these past five days and nights. What she sensed was a swell of emotion that washed over and through her—sensations she was certain originated from the blinded poet. In this the words were born, as though they were her own brain's feeble attempt to translate the overwhelming feelings that enveloped it.

"Why would the gods unite me to one such as you—a poet without eyes or tongue?" She lifted the rag and gently removed the layer of crushed leaves she had placed there to heal his brutal wounds. "You are a weight without purpose. My shoulders balance burden enough."

As she drew a handful of fresh tonewood leaves from a pouch on her belt to lay across his seared eyes, Chal's eyelids flew open!

"No!" A gasp of terror tore from Lijena's lips. She pushed from the ground and ran to the edge of the clearing before turning back to stare at her ward.

An orb of the clearest blue, transparent like the warm waters of the Gulf of Qatera, like some rare sapphire filled the socket of Chal's left eye. His right remained charred and empty.

"By the gods, how can such be?" Lijena's frosty blond tresses trembled as her head moved from side to side in denial of what her eyes perceived.

Chal pushed to quivering elbows. That orb of bluest blue focused on Lijena. A flooding deluge of warmth, gratitude, and peaceful surcease filled the woman's heart and soul. From these dominating sensations formed the words, "Fear not, fair one. In time this too shall pass."

Before Lijena could react, the young poet's eyes closed and he collapsed, once more held in the arms of Ansisian, God of Sleep.

"Yehseen, protect me." Lijena whispered her quavering prayer aloud. "From this man—or demon—you have set before me!!

Lijena wearily dropped the hare beside the low-burning flames of the fire. The morning hunt had been winding and long, and she had but one small rabbit to show for hours of effort. And still the creature had to be dressed, cleaned, spitted, and roasted before she could sate her and Chal's hunger.

She glanced at the fur bundled poet asleep by the embers' glow. The last week had only brought greater puzzlement. No demon, this one, of that she was certain—almost certain. But whether Chal was truly a man was another matter.

Could he be another such as the giant Goran? A changeling from another realm of existence trapped in these lands? Or mayhaps he is a mage in bard's disguise. She shook her head, certain of only one thing—more that her medicines of leaves and herbs worked within Chal's slender body.

Gone was the deep wound Kele had slashed across the red-haired man's thigh. No scar remained to even hint that Chal's fair flesh had ever been injured. Gone, too, was the orb of transparent blue that filled his left socket, although such an orb had inhabited his right socket last night. Chal now sported a fully formed left eye with red-veined white and an iris that challenged the sky in its blueness.

Not fully formed, Lijena admitted, squatting beside the hare and drawing her dirk to begin the messy task of skinning the animal. Chal's iris was without pupil! However, the man's miraculously returned sight did not seem hindered in the least by the lack.

"But you've yet to get your tongue back, have you . . ."

Lijena swallowed her words when she looked back at the poet. She rubbed her eyes to make certain some veil had not dropped over them. The vision remained. Her mouth tried to form the simple protest "no" and failed. It had gone as dry as the Great Desert of Nayati.

Chal's head, poked from beneath the furs, wavered, flickered, and faded to a ghostly image.

"Why is this visited upon me?" Lijena forced words over the dryness as she backed away. Her right hand clasped the Sword of Kwerin and slid it from its sheath. The blade's hilt was warm and alive as the day in Agda when she faced the three Faceless Ones.

"Magic!" Lijena's mind saw and wove the threads together. *The sword comes alive only in the presence of magicks!*

The wisdom of the ancient sorcerer Edan was not lost on her. The mage, now dead for centuries, had forged a blade whose power could not be turned against mere mortals, but used only in the fight against sorcery-born dangers!

Was Chal such a threat?

There was but one way to discover the truth. With sword extended before her, Lijena crept forward and used the tip to ease back Chal's sleeping furs.

In the blink of an eye, Chal solidified then turned a transparent phantom. She saw *through* him to the insides of his clothing, to the blanket beneath him—*through* him! The Sword of Kwerin Bloodhawk grew warmer in her hand.

"Magicks! Chal is ensorcelled." Of this she was certain. But were the magicks his own, or did another hold him in his power as Lorennion's cruel spell had trapped her?

Lifting the blade, she rested it atop Chal's transparent chest. No shower of fiery, actinic sparks exploded. The sword simply lay there, still warming her hand. She eased the enchanted steel away.

Chal's flickering form gave momentary glimpses of the man's body that wavered before becoming meaty solid. Torso, legs, arms, neck, and head all returned and remained. The poet's eyes blinked open. A hand, almost effeminate in its graceful slenderness, reached up to brush across dried lips. He moaned softly as his head rolled toward Lijena. His gaze focused on the unsheathed blade.

The instant the corners of Chal's lips lifted, Lijena felt a swell of unfearing mirth break over her, giving birth to words in his remembered voice. "After nursing me back from Black Qar's embrace, do you now intend to send my soul to Pey-neeha?"

"To Hell's lowest levels—if I had any sense about me!" She answered, in spite of the gentleness that flowed around her, calming the fears within her mind. "What manner of man—of creature—are you?"

"A thirsty and hungry one!" The sensations of both doubled within Lijena.

"If you thirst so, then why not rise and walk twenty strides to the stream?" Lijena's eyes narrowed, and she kept her sword bared. "Your legs are fully healed and sight is returned."

Lijena sensed a dark doubt radiate from the young poet, then a bright light of reassurance in which formed the words, "Yes! By the strength of Father Yehseen, you are right! The healing seems complete enough. And I do believe I feel capable of the task!"

As though he were a man awakening from a long restful sleep, Chal rose, nearly jumping to his feet, and hastened to the stream to cup a palm and lift the clear water to dry lips. For an instant his body went transparent, then solidified. His head jerked to the sky, then twisted around to Lijena.

Lijena stood with mouth agap. She had watched the young poet's unnatural recovery during the past two weeks—yet she still could not believe her eyes.

"You saw me fade," his emotion-formed words came as a statement rather than a question.

"How?" Lijena sputtered. "You recover from wounds that would be mortal to most men. You wink in and out like some ghost. How?"

"The clouds have fluttered across the face of the sun most

this morning," Chal's flowing emotions took the shape of words. "My people draw their strength from Yehseen's fiery light."

Lijena blinked, her doubt mounting. "Yehseen's light? For centuries we have known that it is Yehseen's son Punmacih who truly rules the sun. Are you some member of a forgotten cult?"

Chal shrugged and walked to the campfire. He squatted by the fire, withdrew a knife from inside the high top of his right boot and began to skin the hare. "It is enough to say that my people gather strength from the sun."

"Enough?" Lijena's fuming anger replaced fearful doubts. "I killed three of Zarek Yannis' soldiers to save your worthless hide. I've nursed you for two weeks! And you deny me any explanation of what powers you weave to heal your wounds! Or a telling of the means by which you speak in my mind!"

"It is not enough that we may share our words?" Chal spitted the rabbit and hung it over the fire. "Can you not accept the gifts the gods bestow without questioning?"

The lilting lyrics of a soft, haunting melody began at the center of Lijena's head, and streamed out to cloak in her the gentlest of sounds. The voice that sang those tender refrains was Chal's, but there was more. It was as though a lute accompanied him and a reed flute, both played by accomplished court musicians!

"'Lorra's Lost Love,'" Lijena mused, lulled by the tune's intricacies. "It's one of my favorites. My mother sang it to me when I was but a . . ."

She stopped and spat. Her sword lifted menacingly. "I won't be so easily disposed, Chal! I demand answers to my questions. Tell me of yourself . . . of these people who drink strength from the sun."

"Or else?" Chal added the threat she had not spoken. He glanced at her while he turned the spitted hare. "Or else nothing, Lijena Farleigh. You are not one who heals a man only to run him through with your sword."

"But I am one who will not be denied." Lijena's tone was firm.

"Come sit with me and enjoy our repast. For you I will sing the songs and recite the verses that so angered the usurper Zarek Yannis that he placed a price of five hundred gold bists on my head and set ten companies of his weaponsmen on my heels." Chal grinned, obviously pleased at having gained such an infamous reputation. "It's a good and true story. You will enjoy the hearing. I promise . . ."

"Tell it to the wind!" Lijena reached down and snatched the skewered hare away from the fire. "And find your own 'repast'! I've wasted more than enough time on you. Even a street mongrel displays more gratitude for simple kindness than you!"

She pivoted angrily and pointed to four horses tied to limbs just beyond the edge of the clearing. "There, pick one of your would-be murderers' horses. Ride directly south and you will eventually come to Hyian. You may select weapons from those piled near the horses."

"That's the nearest city?"

"It is." Lijena nodded.

"You do not travel there?"

"I'm already late in arriving in Bistonia," she said.

"You would not abandon me thusly. Allow me to ride with you." Sadness flowed from the poet. "I can entertain, can give insights into matters befuddling to you, can . . ."

"I ride alone." Lijena spoke in clipped, flat tones.

"Would I be such a burden? See me to Bistonia. That is a prosperous city worthy of my talents."

"Hyian is closest," Lijena said, her voice colder than any winter wind. "I'll not travel with one who'll not provide simple answers to simple questions."

"So be it." Chal shrugged and without further protest rose, walked to the horses, saddled a roan, mounted without selecting a sword or longbow, and rode southward. The strands of a bawdy tune describing the erotic positions preferred by the women of Kavindra resounded in Lijena's head for minutes after the poet had disappeared into the forest.

In disgust, Lijena spat again. Were all men the same? She wanted nothing to do with any of them—especially one who was spell-ridden. The Sword of Kwerin Bloodhawk held all the magicks she had need of.

Sheathing the blade, she lowered herself cross-legged to the ground and began eating the half-cooked rabbit. She wasted enough time here. Now she must once again return to the task that glided her toward Bistonia and revenge.

Harn first, Lijena decided her course as she reined Morjael along what appeared to be a deer path. She'd stop in the city-state of Harn and there visit with her Uncle Tadzi, who ruled

Harn's thieves. She smiled without humor, realizing Tadzi's fury would be unleashed when she told him of all that had happened since Davin Anane kidnapped her from his care.

She frowned. Or should she tell him of the abuses that had been heaped upon her shoulders? If Tadzi knew she rode to Bistonia seeking vengeance, would he not insist on handling the matter himself? Or tell all to his brother, her father?

Chesmu Farleigh, for all his merchant's ways, carried the same streak of obstinance and savagery that made his brother such an outstanding leader of the Harnish Thieves' Guild. Her father had driven Velden off the streets of Bistonia and into the sewers. He would never rest until Jun and the others perished by his hand.

Lijena wanted her tormentors' blood dripping from *her* blade. She would not be cheated of that—not even by her uncle or father!

The strands of "Lorra's Lost Love" floated lyrically in the air around Lijena.

Jerking on Morjael's reins, she halted the horse and stood in the stirrups. She turned slowly to locate the source of the music.

Chal son of Chalt stood twenty strides to her left atop an oak stump. His hands rested on his hips. He sang, although his lips did not move.

"You!" she cried.

"Good day, fair one," Chal's emotions swelled in impish delight to wash over her. "I had hoped you would hear and come."

"How did you get here ahead of me? And where is your roan?"

"This is not unknown terrain, Lijena. With or without mount I travel easily. Although I much prefer a companion of the road." He tipped a non-existent hat toward her.

"And I would travel with *pletha* snakes first!" Lijena nudged Morjael forward, tugging the dead soldiers' two mounts after her.

"Stay your haste for but a moment." Chal now sat on a drooping pine branch that overhung the forest path. "At least give the courtesy of hearing me out."

Lijena jerked upright. *How?* In one instant the poet stood on the stump, in the next he perched atop a limb ten feet in the air. What power could transport a man thusly, and in the blink of eye!

"Courtesy? You haven't an inkling of the word's meaning." Lijena reined to the left to about the man in green. And yanked Morjael to an abrupt halt for a second time.

Chal leaned against a *morda* trunk directly before her!

"I am alone . . . as are you, Lijena Farleigh. I sense, as do you, something binds us as kindred souls. I speak in the manner of my people—and you hear," Chal said. "I sing and my song touches your heart. No other man or woman I have met in the realms of Upper and Lower Raemllyn have ever heard the songs I do not speak. Does that not tell you Great Yehseen has joined us together for some purpose?"

A song, a tune Lijena had never heard before, engulfed her. She soared like some bird on wing with each note that flowed through her.

"No!" She shook her head violently, breaking the spell of his unspoken voice. "My business in Bistonia is personal. I do not wish to involve anyone else. Especially one who surrounds himself with the mysteries of magicks!"

"Then don't. But nothing says we cannot travel and enjoy one another's companionship. What blazes more brilliantly than friendship along a dark and rocky road?"

"You appear pale," Lijena said.

"The sun danced behind clouds most of the day," Chal said. "As I said earlier, I need the sun."

Lijena urged Morjael closer to stare directly at a handsome face that held no trace of the fiery brands that had gouged out his eyes fourteen days earlier. The skin had a strange, fired ceramic appearance which unsettled her. This wasn't the flesh of a feverish man, or a sick one—nor was it normal.

"Who are you?" asked Lijena, not certain she really wanted to hear the answer. "Answer me that straight forward without rhyme or riddle."

"Then shall I ride at your side?" Chal's pupilless blue eyes lifted. His gaze locked to hers.

"At least to Harn," Lijena answered, admitting to herself that she had grown accustomed to the poet-minstrel's company during the weeks she had tended his wounds. "And then only if it is understood we travel merely as *friends*."

"Both conditions accepted, fair Lijena." Chal laughed without hint of humor in the sensations that radiated from him. "'Who am I?' That is not the proper question to pose to one such as I. You ought to ask '*What* am I?'"

chapter 9

"BUT EMPEROR, HOW can you trust a *mage*?" cried Jun's captain of the guard, a tall, scrawny man called Scrounge. The chief bodyguard to Bistonia's Emperor of Thieves worried fingers through long strands of slicked back hair that hugged his skull like a shiny cap. Whether Scrounge's hair was black or merely a dark brown lay concealed beneath a pomade of thick grease. "And this'un's carried about in Zarek Yannis' hip pocket. Not natural, I say. Can't trust the whoreson."

Jun lounged back in his elegant throne and peered across the empty audience chamber. The fingertips of his right hand idly stroked a thin white scar that ran a finger's joint across the tautness of his right cheek. The small souvenir was a reminder of Jun's last meeting with a Jyotian thief named Davin Anane. However, the man who had so marred his visage did not now occupy the muscular Emperor of Thieves' mind.

Jun's gaze swept across the chamber hidden away in the bowels of Bistonia's sewers. Through the haze of frankincense burned to cover the constant presence of sewer fumes Jun studied a room that had been expertly hewn from bedrock. Years of toil had gone into its careful fashioning. The intricate carved figures adorning the rock, the false pillars etched into granite were the work of generations of skilled artisans, craftsmen who had long faded from the memories of those who inhabited the city above—or the one below.

A perpetual light radiated from mosses that dangled from a lofted ceiling, casting its soft glow on an amazing treasure trove of wealth; a vast fortune relieved from those who lived overhead. The finest of carpets covered the stone floor, thick and plush. Hangings woven by the most skilled tapissaires in all Raemllyn adorned the walls. Jewels, knobs and posts worth more than the citizens of Bistonia paid a year in taxes to Lerel lay strewn in disregard about the chamber. All this had fallen to Jun when Lijena Farleigh killed his predecessor Velden.

Yet there was a shabbiness defacing all, an undeniable sense of decay. Like a blossom kept too long from the sunlight, this kingdom beneath the earth rotted. The stench lay heavy in Jun's nostrils, and he hungered for the purity of the open air.

"Tell anyone coming into my presence to clean his boots. The sight of muck on the carpeting annoys me." Jun pointed to the stains left by boots soaked in the detritus of Bistonia's sewers.

"That I will, Emperor, but shouldn't you be thinkin' on this mage's claims?" Scrounge urged.

"I am, damn your eyes!" Jun shot to his feet and paced before a replica of the High King's Velvet Throne. "I've thought long on the matter. How would you suggest flaunting the power of the Faceless Ones?"

Even mouthing the name brought a frigid chill to Jun's innards. He saw no way of escaping Aerisan's demands, yet he knew the mage played him for the fool. What did the man want? It made no sense to remove Lerel, install Jun and then remove Jun. With the power of the Faceless Ones at his command, what need did the mage have of Jun—or anyone in Bistonia?

"How goes the temple's construction?" Jun's thin eyebrows lifted when he glanced at Scrounge.

"Well, my liege," his captain replied. "The tower already rises to the height of ten tall men. The priests along the Avenue of Temples eye it from sunrise to sunset. They openly wonder which of our deities will be worshipped within its windowless walls."

As do I! However, the damnable sorcerer deftly sidestepped uttering the name of the god to whom the tower was erected whenever the matter was broached. Jun's doubts surfaced to gnaw at him as they had for countless hours since Aerisan's arrival in Bistonia. *The temple is a keystone.*

The Emperor of Thieves' mouth tightened grimly. That had to be the reason! Aerisan wanted the temple, but not the onus of building it himself.

"But why?" he muttered aloud. "What does Yannis gain from this? Aerisan is his pawn. Why does the High King concern himself with the construction of a temple? And why is it veiled in secrecy?"

"May be Zarek Yannis don't know about the temple," Scrounge suggested.

Jun stared at his captain of the guards. Doubt washed from the Emperor of Thieves' face. "I wondered why I kept a scurvy pile of bones like you around. Now I know! Today you've earned the thousands of gold bists you've stolen from me!"

Jun dropped back to his throne. A smile moved over his thin lips as he steepled fingers over his chest.

Scrounge waited expectantly, began to fidget and finally left the audience chamber when it became apparent Jun had no intent of revealing his thoughts.

"There can be no quarter given," Aerisan told the Emperor of Thieves. "I will give the signal; you will attack. Any hesitation and it will be our heads."

Jun snorted derisively. "You are in no danger. Not with the Faceless Ones as your guard." He tilted his head toward the two shadowy demons standing behind the young mage.

Aerisan caught himself before he swallowed nervously. The hell-riders were a double-edged sword. Their mere presence bolstered his aura of power whether it be with the likes of Jun and his army of thieves or Bistonia's respectable citizenry. The sorcerer could not have asked for a more powerful tool to be placed in his hands.

Yet, the Faceless Ones were not his. In truth he was surprised they still remained at his side and had not returned to Kavindra. Although they responded to his every command, he realized their true master was the usurper who sat upon the Velvet Throne. If they stood with him, it was only because Zarek Yannis had so ordered. The question was—did the demons guard him, or guard against him?

"Our High King has no desire to overtly overthrow Lerel. He prefers for the situation to appear as though the people rose in revolt against the Weasel's rule," Aerisan answered. "How many cityguards will you face?"

"Enough," grated Jun.

"We are in agreement on the plan then?" Aerisan asked.

Jun stared at the mage and wondered how one so young became so devious. "There must be another way."

"Are you afraid to do the deed yourself?" Aerisan arched one eyebrow as if he'd heard the most incredible tall tale in all Raemllyn.

"I will slay the Weasel, with pleasure," snapped Jun.

"As I said, it is decided. Be prepared for the ceremony. It begins soon." Aerisan whirled and left the tiny anteroom off

Lerel's audience hall. The Faceless Ones glided on silent feet after their master.

Not for the first time Jun wished he could summon the nerve to take one of the creatures aside. What bribe would a demon consider sufficient to change allegiance?

Disguised in the finery of a court leech who lived on the grace of Lerel's generosity, Jun paced nervously, occasionally peering out through a partially opened door into the hall that led to Lerel's throne. He had no choice but to follow Aerisan's orders.

Or was there an alternative?

Desperation drove the thief into the cramped corridor to hurry along the way until he reached the chamber where Lerel prepared himself. Guards stood just inside the door, waiting for the ruler of Bistonia to don the robes of state for the ceremonial greeting of High King Yannis' emissary.

The certainty he had felt two days ago had long since fled him. Just when he was sure he grasped the scheme Aerisan wove for the usurper king, the threads he held unraveled leaving him drowning in doubt. Would it not be better to call out, to beg a private audience with Lerel? He loathed the man and his policies, but Jun's subterranean empire was real and not just the promises of an unproven sorcerer. It was his duty to his followers—to himself—to protect that kingdom.

Jun's mouth opened. His shout of warning died in his throat when a hand gripped his shoulder.

He flinched, looked back, and stared into twin pits of glowing red. Where a face should have been, he saw only inchoate whirls of black.

The talonlike fingers tightened and edged Jun away from the open door and back to the anteroom. The Faceless One left without uttering a sound. Jun crouched down and held himself like a small child. He shivered while rivulets of sweat poured from his forehead.

"I have to do it," he told himself. "I have to."

That the Faceless awaited should he fail did not make the assassination any easier.

"All pay obeisance to Lord Lerel!" the chamberlain's bass voice rang through the great hall, echoing back upon itself.

A shifting of heavy robes of state whispered throughout the chamber like wind in tall trees. Lerel strutted into the room, adjusted his robes, and sat on the gold-flaked throne. Only when he deemed the proper level of anticipation and uneasiness had built did Lerel, known as the Weasel, call out, "My people, attend me on this great day!"

Aching joints relieved by the command to stand, those in the audience looked up at Lerel. He smirked. Whispers passed among those gathered. It was well known that Zarek Yannis' emissary and Bistonia's lord had met in secrecy for the past two weeks. What had been achieved in those veiled talks? Surely something that favored Lerel to warrant the self-pleased expression on his royal face.

"Loyal followers, nobles and citizens of Bistonia, harken. High King Zarek has sent an emissary to us. Rejoice! I declare a week's celebration."

More murmurs rippled through those assembled. Whenever Lerel proclaimed celebrations, the merchants paid for it. Any who protested too loudly found themselves taxed into oblivion—or worse. Many were later discovered face down in the River Stane, victims of nebulous "brigands."

"Lord Aerisan is in Bistonia to adjudge our preparation against the pretender to the Velvet Throne. He . . ." Lerel's words trailed off; a frown furrowed his brow. He half rose and peered over the heads of those before him.

At the rear of the chamber a horde of dirty, disheveled thieves swarmed into the great hall.

"Guards! Stop those ruffians!" Lerel's cry of alarm came too late.

The chamber's vaulted doors slammed closed. Great beams of stonewood fell into niches, barring the massive portal.

Jun stood a dozen paces away, poised for this moment. While all attention focused on the rear of the chamber as the guards within the hall hastened to dispatch the invaders, the Emperor of Thieves slipped a silver-bladed dirk from beneath the flowing cloak he wore. He leaped toward the weasel in human form who sat upon Bistonia's throne.

The twelve paces shortened to three.

Lerel turned, eyes widening in shock. Two paces. Lerel's red-rouged lips worked like a beached fish. One. Lerel began a scream.

Jun's knife swung upward in a sweeping arc, then fell. The tip of the blade drove through Lerel's robes of state, penetrating rib cage and lung to skewer the heart.

Lerel's mouth gaped, blood trickling from the corners of his mouth. The Weasel grasped the handle of the knife in a vain attempt to wrench it free. He twisted and fell across his gold encrusted throne, dead.

"Death to the tyrant! Death to the tyrant!" The cry resounded from Jun's own thieves. Others in the assembly took up the booming chant. City guards froze, eyes darting between the crowd and the thieves uncertain whether they should strike.

Jun stood speechless. His own gaze shifted from the dead ruler and Bistonia's citizens. Could it be they truly rallied to him? Jun had accomplished what so many had tried and failed—and he felt no sense of triumph.

Aerisan stood directly before the throne, smiling with obvious amusement. The mage's expression told Jun that, in the moment of victory, he had lost.

But how?

"That's Jun!" A shocked gasp transformed to an angry roar. "Kill the thief!"

Jun stood and stared at the assembly of nobles. He expected no less. They might harbor no love for the dead ruler, but they cherished the Emperor of Thieves far less. He had stolen with impunity from most of them, and taunted his victims at every turn.

The crowd surged forward, ready to deal with Lerel's assassin and put one of their own on the throne.

Like a man standing distant from the scene, Jun saw it all falling into place perfectly. He killed Lerel for Aerisan, who would let the crowd kill him. Then Aerisan placed whoever he wanted on the throne.

"Wait!" Jun's heart almost stopped when the mage lifted both hands and shouted. "He has done us all a favor! Stop!"

The crowd stumbled to an awkward halt, although the desire for blood did not drain from their scowling faces. *A spell artfully woven*, Jun realized, for no mere words had the power to stop the tide of nobles and merchants.

"Here stands a hero. Honor him. He has done what all you, deep in your hearts, wanted to do. Place Jun on the throne!"

Aerisan spoke with conviction—or magic. Jun cared little which it was. That he still lived mattered most.

And this startled him. He had thought Aerisan would play him for the fool, use him and discard him once Lerel had perished under his blade. Yet, the mage honored their agreement. *Why?* What did Aerisan gain by placing a thief on Bistonia's throne?

"We would meet with your leaders," Aerisan cried.

The hush that fell over the assembly closed about Jun's chest like an icy band of steel. He wanted to cry out, to run, to leave the sorcerer and his schemes far behind. When he had taken Velden's place as Emperor of Thieves, he had achieved his life's ambitions—and more. Why had he hungered to rule above the ground as well as below?

Five men pushed from the gathered mass to stand before Aerisan. The mage signalled for the doors to be swung wide, then motioned to the assembly. "Return to your homes and rest assured that what will be done here today will be for the good of all."

When neither noble nor merchant moved, two demonic forms hovering at the sides of the great hall stepped forward. Their skeletal talons wrenched flaming swords of crystal from metal sheaths.

"The Faceless Ones!" a terrified gasp rose, and man, woman, and child hastened to obey the young sorcerer's command.

"Now we may discuss the future of Bistonia," Aerisan said, his gaze shifting to the five still standing before him.

Jun's mind raced. This was the pivotal point; he sensed it. Here the course of events might be diverted one way or another. But how to wrest control from the mage? An answer evaded him. With his command of magicks and the Faceless Ones, Aerisan rolled dice that came up with Emperor's eyes every time.

No way to beat him at his own game—whatever it might be! Jun perceived a glimmer of hope. If he could not name the game, perhaps he might turn it to his favor, subtly change the rules. While he still placed little faith in the young sorcerer—how could he—no man walked into Bistonia and offered rule over the city-state without some devious scheme of his own—Aerisan *had* honored his words with deeds. *The course to take might be in simply waiting.*

"Nobles, these are perilous times," started Aerisan. The young mage looked from man to man. He ignored Jun. "Prince Felrad threatens the sanctity of Bistonia."

"Better Prince Felrad than Zarek Yannis," grumbled a merchant, a man so fat that three chins bobbed when he spoke.

"You do not swear fealty to High King Zarek?"

The tone Aerisan used froze the man. Frightened pigeyes, twinged with fear and doubt, peered at the mage.

"Lord Aerisan." A tall, stately man with white-blond hair stepped forward. "What is your interest in the internal affairs of Bistonia? This . . . this thief is not master of Bistonia. He is scum—offal come floating up from the sewers. Such as he is not fit to rule an ant hill, let alone a city!"

"Chesmu Farleigh," Jun whispered over Aerisan's shoulder, his hate-narrowed eyes never leaving the man responsible for driving the thieves underground.

"Did you deem Lerel a man fit to rule?" Aerisan asked calmly.

Jun sneered not in memory of the now dead ruler, but at his long time adversary. Farleigh looked much like his daughter. Lijena and Chesmu shared the same hair and striking aquamarine eyes. The similarities went beyond this. The determined set of the jaw, the sense of invulnerability, the haughtiness; all were shared. But Jun had used the daughter as another man might use a common street slut before she had escaped from the sewers. He only hoped Aerisan would arrange some suitable degradation for the father, before taking his life.

"You would replace one tyrant with another!" Farleigh challenged without hesitation.

"Kind sirs . . ." Aerisan began his answer.

Farleigh's voice drowned his words. The influential merchant turned and stared at the four others summoned to this meeting. "No! My friends, they are not the ones to rule Bistonia. Don't let Zarek Yannis gain even more of a hold than he had with Lerel."

"Lerel supported Prince Felrad," said Aerisan.

"There! See? Do you understand now? Yannis employed Jun as nothing more than a hired assassination to rid himself of Lerel and his wavering aid for Prince Felrad. *We* are the ones to seize the reins of control over Bistonia. We are, we who care."

"A pretty speech, Farleigh," said Aerisan with a faint sneer. "But it means nothing. You are not the one to decide. Jun is the new ruler of Bistonia. He will decide all that transpires within the city walls."

Chesmu Farleigh would not be denied. "Friends, we must take a stand straight and true or have our knees and backs forever bent beneath Zarek Yannis' damnable yoke!"

"You would accept rule?" Aerisan asked.

Jun's head twisted toward the young sorcerer. Was this the mage's plan? To raise Farleigh to the throne?

"I have no desire to rule, but better me than you or Yannis or this . . . trash!"

"Lord Aerisan, I detect rebellion. What is the punishment for such a high crime?" Jun moved on instinct alone, fighting to save his own life. To remain mute would have been the same as suicide.

"Death." Aerisan answered without hesitation.

"For you and your sewer-spawned lackey!" Farleigh's right hand dropped toward a ceremonial dagger dangling at his side as he swung around to face mage and thief.

His fingers never reached the hilt. The two Faceless Ones leaped forward and grasped his arms. Aerisan flicked a hand and the cowled demons lifted their captive from the floor as though he were a mere child, and carried him from the hall. Aerisan allowed Farleigh's echoing curses to die before he looked back at the remaining four leaders.

"Are there others who share Farleigh's views? Aerisan eyed those standing before him.

The four shifted nervously from foot to foot; their gazes lowered to the marbled floor. It was the fat one with bobbling chins who finally spoke, "J–jun might p–prove popular."

"It is so good to hear how Bistonia's leading citizens have united behind their new ruler. Tell your fellow citizens that Jun's justice is quick and unswerving." Aerisan dismissed the men with a wave of his arm. An amused smile moved across his lips as he watched Bistonia's finests42scurry from the hall.

"And Chesmu Farleigh?" Jun's voice drew the mage's attention to the thief elevated to ruler of a Raemllyn city state. "Shall I personally oversee his torture in the dungeons below?"

"Farleigh is mine," Aerisan answered. "Even now the Faceless Ones carry him to the temple you built for me. Tonight all of Bistonia will know a god has come to dwell in the city—a god not even Zarek Yannis may summon!"

"A god?" Jun frowned uncertain what the sorcerer meant.

"Lord Jun, Farleigh shall be our first sacrifice to the Great One—to the god men give the name Black Qar!"

"Death." The whisper trembled over Jun's lips. Only now did he realize just how Aerisan had manipulated him—the horror he had unleashed on Bistonia.

chapter 10

Tears welled in Lijena Farleigh's eyes. Stoically she contained them, keeping the moisture from leaking out and trickling down her soft cheeks. She rode onward, the grassy plain ahead a blur of browns and tentative greens that signalled Jalya, Goddess of Seasons, slackened her winter rage and allowed spring to creep closer.

The cause of those tear-misted eyes and the soul-rending emotions that wrenched within her breast—Chal, son of Chalt.

The golden red haired, pupilless blue-eyed poet-minstrel sat astride a bay mare with one knee hooked about the saddle's horn. In lap and arm he cradled a simple lacquered lute. The instrument had been purchased in the hamlet of Ionar and was common to such farming villages. Neither paint nor carvings adorned its stonewood neck or cherrywood bowl. Its strings were cured gut rather than the spun silver and gold employed by court musicians.

But in Chal's hands, cajoled by his nimble fingers, the instrument sounded as though it were some lost treasure of the gods themselves. With eyes closed and a soft hum coming from his lips, he sat and played. The long graceful fingers of his left hand seemed to contort into impossibly tangled knots while thumb and fingers of his right hands hovered above the lute's sound hole plucking the strings with an expert deftness.

The Tears of the Elyshah—how Lijena had come to know the lament during the weeks Chal had ridden with her. Each time the melody grew more intricate, more revealing—for it was through his song that Chal told her of himself and his people.

That first evening they travelled together he simply sang the emotion-words, letting the rhythm of their mounts establish the tempo of his song. It was then Chal fulfilled his promise and revealed his identity. No man this fair poet—but Elyshah!

Lijena's mind had spun dizzily with that revelation. The Elyshah were beings spoken of only in children's tales—a race said once to have walked Raemllyn beside humankind in those ancient days when magicks ruled the realms. The gentlest of people, they drew life itself from the sun, nor would they harm any creature whose strength came in part from Yehseen's warming, heavenly fire.

Which are all creatures, Lijena thought. Even when the blackest wizard of all, Nnamdi, first unleashed the Faceless Ones on the face of the world, the Elyshah had not fought, but fled before the tide of dark power. Children's tales said the race had been slaughtered, totally eradicated by the Faceless because the Elyshah were the complete opposite of the demon riders.

There had been death. *The Tears of the Elyshah* told of great suffering, of Chal's parents' murder, the death of his sister. It also spoke of flight, of refuge found . . . where Lijena did not know, nor would Chal reveal that secret. His emotion-words ceased to flow whenever she questioned him about his people's new homeland.

Chal's humming, the sound of the lute, and the pictures he wove within her head faded to silence. Lijena glanced at her companion, the loneliness that always signalled the end of Chal's emotion-words growing.

"You play beautifully." She groped for words that seemed so inadequate to describe the poignancy of the Elyshah's melody.

"It's the lute," Chal answered, his words the flow of emotion and a slur of sound produced by his slow-healing tongue. "It was a rare find. Although, I do not flaunt false modesty. I am considered an excellent minstrel among the Elyshah. Today I chose a minor key to elicit even greater feelings. Mere words often fail to convey the proper messages. Songs help bridge the chasm between thought and emotion. I am a master of such blendings."

The poet-minstrel's words came not as a boast, but a simple statement of fact. Lijena smiled. In Chal's presence she sensed a great, aged wisdom, yet underlying that was a childlike naivete. The latter evoked a passion to protect this open, vulnerable creature of the light. He was like spring's first opening blossom, to be sheltered from cruel winds rather than picked.

"I have remembered another song," he said. "One I haven't played in many years."

"Please play it," Lijena urged him. "Your songs make the leagues pass quickly."

Chal began. He had sung only a few bars of the song when Lijena rode closer and reached out to mute the strings of the lute with flat of a hand.

"Do not mock me!" Her aquamarine eyes flared with an angry fire.

"Mock you? How did I mock you, fairest Lijena?" A sense of hurt swept out from the Elyshah. "This is a song of revenge and the afflictions to the soul such deeds attract."

Lijena's anger rose. "You know I go to Bistonia to seek the blood of my . . ." Her voice trailed off in sputters. Just thinking of those who had used her reduced her to incoherency. "Chal, revenge . . . killing is unknown to your people. When you sing of such, it comes out as a mockery of human feelings. It's no wonder that Zarek Yannis set his men after you. How your songs must have twisted his desire for power."

"There might be other remedies for your grievance rather than silencing my song," Chal suggested softly. "Blood spilled only tempers the links of a chain leading to more blood."

"You can't know."

The laugh Chal emitted was the voice of a child, free and innocent. "I, Lijena, do not know? How can you say that?"

Lijena fell silent. Of those who ought to feel the fire of vengeance burning the brightest, Chal was the one. Zarek Yannis' soldiers would have killed him that night.

Lijena studied her companion from the corner of an eye. Chal wasn't human. The fineness of his features came from no human mother, his lilting voice wasn't inherited from a human father. Chal was a child of the sun; he would fade into oblivion without exposure to bright light.

Lijena didn't want to consider the tortures that could be meted out to one so fragile. She had been Velden's prisoner in the sewers—Chal would have faded into transparency after only a few days of imprisonment in the dark cells of the underground emperor.

"We are too different for you to fully understand, my friend," Lijena said with a helpless sigh.

"And that is our greatest difference!" Chal shook his head. "The Elyshah sees the sameness in all creatures. You humans look for differences. Even among yourselves you see nothing but the things that separate. Two humans stand together, and you carefully ascertain whether they be male or female. You look to see if they are tall or short, fat or slender. If the shade of the skin is a different hue, that, too, is given great weight. You fear differences, yet you seek them like a leech seeks blood. You build great walls from those differences—isolating yourselves behind such minor things as the way a man's pronunciation of a word differs from your own."

"I have no need of your lectures," Lijena snapped. "Were it not for our differences, *you*, friend Chal, would now be *dead!*"

"And were it not for our shared sameness, you might not have rescued me from Zarek Yannis' soldiers." Chal's childlike laughter rang out once again. "Would you have bared your sword to save a giant slug, no matter how piteous its cries?"

"You press too close, Chal." Lijena's eyes narrowed menacingly. Her right hand slipped to the hilt of her sword.

"Nay," Chal's head moved from side to side. "I merely present a clear view of the differences you so desire."

Lijena gritted her teeth and glared at a dark green line of trees in the distance. Though she had told Chal all that had befallen her since Davin Anane kidnapped her, he still didn't understand the spurs of vengeance that drove her. *Nor will he ever! He has no desire to understand!*

"Yon wood lies between the cities of Hyian and Harn," Chal said as his fingers once more danced over the lute, strumming random chords.

"Aye! And I'll finally be rid of you!" Lijena spoke without looking at the Elyshah. Yet, from the corner of an eye she saw an amused smile on Chal's face as he began an unknown song recounting the happiness and woes of two star-crossed lovers, separated by an ancient feud between their families.

The barrier rose twelve feet tall ahead of the two riders. Lijena's heart doubled its pace, racing with unashamed excitement. "Chal, look! The boundary of my uncle's estate!"

The Elyshah glanced up, his eyes of unbroken blue perusing the massive obstacle at the end of the forest path with disinterest. "It's but a wall."

"A wall?" Lijena glanced at the minstrel-poet in disbelief. "That *wall* is built of Norggstone! It is said fifteen hundred men lost their lives mining and transporting the stone from distant Norgg Province. A wall? It encompasses a full eight hundred acres of the richest land in Harn!"

The frosty-haired young woman turned back to the looming

barrier. She nudged Morjael's flanks with her heels to urge him into a canter. Even at a distance of a quarter of a league and cloaked by early evening dimness the opalescent sheen of Norggstone was unmistakable. She could almost feel the interior warmth of the stone radiating outward.

Chal, lute secure in the crook of his left arm, clucked his bay mare after Bistonia's daughter. "It is said fifteen hundred *slaves* died securing the stone from that land of perpetual hoarfrost. And it still remains a wall. Behind it dwells a lord of thieves. The citizens of Harn should be grateful to your uncle; Tadzi has constructed his own prison."

Lijena frowned, remembering similar thoughts when last she visited Tadzi's palace. She shook away the memories. Then she had been infatuated with Amrik Tohon and longed to be in his arms. Her father had placed her in his brother's care while he journeyed south to Kavindra on business.

He sought to prevent my marriage to Amrik, Lijena's teeth gritted as a seething rage rose within her breast. Hindsight revealed her father's wisdom. Her treacherous lover had sold her to the slaver Nelek Kahl after her escape from the sewer kingdom of thieves beneath Bistonia's streets.

"No wall, Chal, but family!" Lijena refused to allow the intruding dark thoughts dampen her high spirits. This was the reason she had travelled months from Agda. "Next to my own home in Bistonia, my friend, there is no other place in all of Raemllyn I would rather be!"

"If you live to actually see this wondrous place once again." Chal pointed to a gate opening in the Norggstone wall. "You'd best inform the guard of your identity, else we will find a dozen arrows sprouting from our limbs. I, for one, have little desire to emulate a tree with its leafy branches."

Lijena drew her mount to a halt as a shadowy figure stepped from the gate. A guard, with bow pulled taut and broadhead arrow menacingly aimed at Chal, challenged them. "Lest ye've a desire to be wearing quills this night, I'd turn them horses around and ride back into the forest. Lord Tadzi has no wish to receive uninvited visitors."

"Hold your hand!" Lijena's voice rose an octave. In her excitement she had forgotten about the small army who guarded her uncle, as well as an assortment of spells to waylay would be assassins. Drawing a calming breath, she announced slowly and distinctly, "I am Lijena Farleigh, Lord Tadzi's niece."

"Lord Tadzi's niece has been kidnapped," the guard answered with a snort. His bow remained homed on Chal. "And who be this? The rogue who kidnapped you?"

"*I am* Tadzi's niece, fool!" Lijena repeated, trying to disguise her frustration. She hadn't traversed half of Raemllyn to be shuffled aside by an overly cautious guard. "I demand that you take us to my uncle immediately."

"If you're Lijena Farleigh, then I'm the demon Nyuria and you can kiss my scorched arse." The guard snorted again. "Be off with ye before my arm grows weary and I give this scrawny lad a feather to wear in his chest."

"Then your name be Nyuria, though neither I nor my lovely companion have any intention of . . ." Chal began.

"What's the trouble, Mahr?" Another guard, wearing a sergeant's insignia on his chest, approached holding a torch above his head. He opened the gate and stepped beside the man with raised bow.

"Rabble from the city I'd say," the first guard mused. "The wench takes me for a fool. Claims to be Lord Tadzi's lost niece, she does."

"Lijena?" The sergeant of the guards strode forward, lifted the torch high, and squinted at Lijena. An instant later, his eyes went saucer wide, and his jaw sagged. "My lady? Can it truly be you?"

"Aye, and it gladdens my heart to see an old friend, good Bassonio." Lijena grinned. "Would you see that my uncle is informed that I'm waiting?"

"Tell the lord you are here? Nay! I'll take you to him myself!" Pausing only the time needed to give Mahr a reprimanding cuff of the hand, Bassonio swung the great iron gate wide and waved Lijena and Chal inside.

chapter 11

"THIS PLACE HAS the feel of a house under siege." A sense of weighted oppression wove through Chal's emotion-words while his gaze travelled over the vaulted hall in which they waited. "I count a dozen guards in our sight. How many henchmen has Tadzi in his employ?"

"Hundreds, but I know only a few." Lijena's attention focused on a massive mahogany door at the end of the hallway through which Bassonio had disappeared seconds ago. "The sergeant is an old and dear friend. I played with him when I was but a child."

"A most unusual upbringing for a gentle flower of Bistonia," Chal commented, his face twisting in a sour expression. "Thieves and cutthroats for playmates! What pets were you given? Cobras from the Great Desert of Nayati?"

"Unusual now, I suppose," Lijena smiled with amusement. "But then it seemed like a world filled with wonderment. I could not image a palace more grand than my uncle's, not even the High King's in Kavindra."

"*Lijena!*" A joyous cry boomed down the hall as the mahogany door flew open.

A tall, heavyset man draped in robes of royal purple stood at the threshold with arms thrown wide. Lijena's own arms opened and closed around the man. Tadzi's embrace enfolded, crushing his niece to him.

"You're alive! By all the gods, I never thought I would live to see this day!" Tears streamed down Tadzi's cheeks into a beard as frosty as Lijena's tresses. "Your father and I thought you dead."

"And I thought myself the same on more than one occasion." Lijena lovingly kissed her uncle's cheek.

"How I have prayed for this day—yet never truly dared to believe it would come to pass. My men scoured the forest in search of you for weeks. I offered rewards all over Harn for any information concerning your abduction. No one admitted even knowing your kidnapper." Tadzi gave her another tight squeeze.

"Even after you interrogated them?" This from Chal whose words came over his still healing tongue as a burst of unintelligible sputterings.

"Who's this?" Tadzi's right hand dropped to a sheathed sword slung from a broad leather belt about his waist. "Is this the man who . . .?"

"No, Uncle." Lijena reached out and stayed his hand. "This is Chal, son of Chalt, a companion of the road. He offers his gratitude to Lord Tadzi for welcoming him into this magnificent palace."

Her liberal alteration of the poet's emotion-words drew an arched eyebrow from the Elyshah and a reply, "Would that I could speak for myself! Neither your uncle, nor any of his gorillas seems capable of truly hearing me!"

"Uh?" Tadzi eyed his niece. "You understood those grunts?"

"Zarek Yannis' soldiers robbed Chal of his tongue, and he is attempting to . . . " Lijena started and shook her head. Giving Tadzi another warm hug, she maneuvered him into the room. "It is a long story that will take some time in the telling, Uncle. Please let's go inside. Chal and I have ridden hard and far for long weeks. Food and drink would make the telling easier."

"Of course! At once! Chlorisa, Susonna, fetch food. Make it a feast." Tadzi called to two serving wenches who stood within the immense hearth room. "Bassonio, Maite, drag that table and those chairs before the fire so we may warm ourselves!"

While servants and soldiers scurried to comply. Lijena moved with her uncle to the blazing hearth. How familiar and secure this was. The dozens of statues representing Raemllyn's pantheon of gods the sweet aroma of blue *limna* roses in jade vases, the tapestries depicting battles of men and mythical creatures—she could almost believe that she had just awakened from a long nightmare, that the past months had been nothing but a frightening dream. Almost!

"Ah, food and mulled wine. Fill yourselves, and if you need more, simply nod. Either Chlorisa or Susonna will fetch it." Tadzi waved niece and the Elyshah to the table set before the hearth. He took the third chair, poured himself a goblet of the hot spiced wine, and sat gazing at his niece, disbelief still in his eyes.

Lijena's attention centered on a meaty joint of roast pork. She noted with a rootless sense of distress the way Susonna and her sultry dark eyes kept track of every move Chal made. As for the Elyshah, Chal's pleased waves of satisfaction while he busied himself with orange-glazed pheasant mingled with Lijena's own contented warmth. Only after devouring half of the portion of meat did she begin her story.

"Cens was the only survivor of the guards with you," Tadzi said, after she recounted how Davin Anane had single-handedly overcome her bodyguards in the woods beyond Tadzi's high walls. "He insisted on going off to find you."

"I never saw him." Lijena sipped from her goblet. "Portrevnio died?"

"He did," said Tadzi. "This Davin Anane has been a thorn in my side since he and his partner Goran One-Eye robbed the Spring Festival here last year. Now I shall issue his death warrant. Ten thousand gold bists reward on his head should get results! And another five thousand will assure the same fate for the one-eyed rogue with him!"

"Uncle, it's not necessary. I'm safe now." Lijena attempted to conceal her anxiety. She had no desire for her uncle to rob her of the revenge she sought. "What matters now is letting Father know I've returned."

"Chesmu . . . your father . . . yes . . . yes." Tadzi's tongue stumbled over the words, although his face was an expressionless mask.

"Surely he has returned from Kavindra?" Lijena tensed, sensing something was terribly askew.

"A month after your abduction, he returned," Tadzi nodded slowly. "And he was successful in his meeting with Prince Felrad's agents."

"Felrad's agents?" Lijena wasn't certain she heard correctly. Her father had always maintained he had no interest in who sat upon the Velvet Throne—Yannis or Felrad.

Tadzi nodded. "Chesmu and I have always been loyal to Bedrich's rightful heir. My brother was instrumental in swaying Lerel's support away from the usurper. He silently rallied Bistonia's merchants and nobles to . . ."

Again Tadzi stumbled over his words. Tears welled in the man's eyes. "Last month . . . Lijena . . . your father . . ."

"Uncle, what is it?" A fist of ice squeezed around Lijena's heart. "What has happened to Father?"

"Your father, my only brother, is dead." Lord Tadzi shuddered and tears poured from his eyes as he spoke. "I am sorry, Lijena." He wiped ineffectually at his eyes. "I thought I'd gotten over it. But one never truly . . ."

Lijena didn't listen. Her father was dead! It could not be—could not! She was the one who had been driven to Agda by Lorennion's demon. She had faced and defeated the Faceless Ones. What dangers were there in Bistonia that could have claimed her father's life? "Lerel did it?"

"The Weasel?" Tadzi shook his head. "That is the only good news to come from Bistonia of late. Your father's killer also murdered Lerel while he sat on his throne."

"A political assassination, then?" Lijena supressed the grief that tore at her soul. Later there would be time to mourn—later after she bathed the sword she wore in the blood of her father's murderer.

"That and more. Jun, who succeeded Velden when that sewer-crawler mysteriously died, is responsible for killing Chesmu. Or perhaps it was the mage Zarek Yannis sent from Kavindra. I am not certain; the details are sketchy. The only thing of which I am sure is that your father opposed Jun's ascendancy to rule Bistonia."

"Jun!" Lijena fought a surge of dizziness that sent her thoughts into a crazy spin. The very man whose life she sought was responsible for her father's death. "No! By Yehseen, no!"

Chal reached across the table taking her hand in his. The almost effeminate grace of those fingers belied their power. Lijena drew strength from him. Her spine stiffened, and she sat straight, staring into her uncle's eyes.

"Jun is cunning and cruel, but he isn't the power in Bistonia," Tadzi continued. "Zarek Yannis' wizard, a master mage by all description, a mere boy named Aerisan, appears to have masterminded Lerel's overthrow. For all his youth, he has learned quickly and well. He holds the city in a state of constant fear."

"Have you recovered my father's body?" Emotion drained from her heart, leaving one burning purpose—to return to Bistonia and slay this mage Aerisan!

And Jun! Oh, how the thief would suffer before the last breath of life passed from his body! The tortures he had inflicted on her would pale beside those she would devise for him. He would live a full year, knowing intense suffering each of those days before she allowed him the escape of death!

"With Zarek Yannis' forces so strong in Bistonia, I have tripled my own defenses. Spies have carried word of the ethium stored in the vaults below," Tadzi said.

"Ethium?" Chal's emotions tautened at the mention of that rare luminous metal. "Yes, I sense it now . . . a vast, priceless horde of ethium directly below me."

Lijena shoved the Elyshah's random thought-feelings away. "Then you've not recovered Father's body nor provided proper burial rites?"

Tadzi's head lowered and moved from side to side in shame. "No, it lies beyond my power."

"Beyond the power of the great Lord Tadzi?" A cruel edge crept into Lijena's voice.

"I've had to employ mages to secure my own land and castle. Even now they renew ward spells about the wall for the night. Simple patrols no longer suffice to give adequate safety. Even with the mages' spells, I wonder. This Aerisan is a demon in his own right. It is said that like Yannis, the Faceless Ones answer to his command."

Tadzi swallowed, licked his lips, then reached for a goblet of wine. He downed the contents and signalled for more before continuing. "There are darker rumors. Aerisan is a worshipper of Black Qar. In return for Bistonia's throne, Jun permits a return to the old ways, the dark ways."

"They sacrifice to Black Qar? In Bistonia?" Pieces to the horrible picture tumbled into place. "You said this Aerisan might have killed my father?"

"Aye." Tadzi's broad shoulders sagged as though they carried the weight of a world upon them. "The Great Destroyer demands human sacrifices. And Aerisan needs the blood for the twisted magicks he invokes."

"Once Nnamdi named Qar his god and released the Faceless Ones." Chal's voiceless words floated in Lijena's head. "How similar these times are to those. Only there are fewer Elyshah."

"Chesmu fought to make the streets of Bistonia safe for all citizens. Now no one dares walk after sundown. Jun's city guard will kidnap and take the unsuspecting and unwary to Black Qar's temple where Aerisan performs his demonic rites."

"To what end?" Lijena still reeled under the revelation that her father was dead—in all likelihood his life spilled as a sacrifice to the God of Death!

"Not a whisper of that has reached me," Tadzi replied. "We

in Harn feel safe enough for the moment, but all fear that Aerisan will seek to expand his power."

"You speak of him as something other than Zarek Yannis' pawn."

"That one has his own schemes." Tadzi finished his wine, but motioned away the serving girl before she could refill the goblet. He then rose to clasp Lijena's shoulder. "This is no fit homecoming for my niece. Even in these black times, your return brightens these rooms. You are all the family I have left, Lijena."

"What of the family holdings in Bistonia? Of my father's house?" Thoughts of material objects were far from her mind—Lijena probed for more information about Jun and the sorcerer.

"Who cares? There's enough in Harn for us. You'll have no want for the rest of your life." Tadzi's hand tightened on her shoulder.

Who cares? Those words would have been alien to the Lord Tadzi Lijena had known all her life. The way he brushed the matter away said much. Tadzi's own network of spies were unable to glean what was happening inside Bistonia.

She was certain of that, just as she recognized that the clench of her uncle's hand indicated he would never let her leave the estate if she revealed her plan of returning to Bistonia. She intended to give him little opportunity to impede her plans.

"Uncle, I need time to be alone."

"I haven't heard of your escape from this Davin Anane. Where have you been? Tell me all!"

Lijena heard the hurt in Tadzi's voice; it didn't matter. Perhaps one day, she could be the family he needed, but not now. "Uncle, I arrived at your gate weary from months of endless wandering. Now your words have burdened my soul. I must have time to rest and be alone with my memories."

Tadzi sighed and nodded. "I apologize. I thought only of myself. To have lost you and then regained you once again is overwhelming." He looked at Lijena as though searching for a hint as to what to say next.

She smiled and lightly kissed his hand. "Tomorrow we will talk at length. Now, those two rooms at the far end of the west wing would serve us well. You know the two?"

"You always did like that section of the house, Yehseen knows why." But Tadzi had received the information he desired.

Lijena smiled again. She had specifically asked for two rooms, not one. Her uncle appeared relieved. For years he had tried to match her with one after another of Harn's society scions. Lijena had rejected each of the suitors. She saw nothing wrong in letting Tadzi assume—rightly—that there was no intimate bond between her and Chal.

"Susonna, take my niece and her friend to their rooms." Tadzi called to the young serving girl.

At the girl's heels Lijena and Chal moved down a series of wide corridors until they reached the west wing. Two doors from the end of the final hallway, Susonna halted and opened a door. She motioned for Lijena to enter, then stepped inside to light a candle.

As she left, Lijena noted the serving girl slipped her hand into Chal's, leading the Elyshah to the next room. Lijena frowned. For the second time that evening she felt disquiet over Susonna's obvious interest in Chal. Why?

Closing the door, Lijena waited until she heard Susonna's footsteps retreat down the hallway. She then slipped from her room and darted into Chal's.

The Elyshah sat on the side of his bed, surprise on his fair face. He ran a hand over the sleeping silks. "Such fine bedding, but they have not drawn you to my room."

"Surely Susonna voiced such interest?" Did she detect a hint of regret in his emotion-words? That possibly she had only served it increased Lijena's disquiet. "This room holds a secret I discovered when I was seven years old."

"Ah, a secret! What would draw the attention of such a young girl?" Chal's pupilless eyes made a slow circuit of the room, before alighting on an ornately carved wood armoire. He rose and walked to the standing closet and let his nimble fingers run over the top and sides.

"Do you have some magical power I'm unaware of?" Lijena asked, amazed by how quickly the poet homed in on her secret.

"This is not what it appears," the Elyshah said simply.

"Let me show you." Lijena found the release and pressed her thumb hard into it. The armoire rolled silently outward to reveal a narrow, dark passage. "It leads directly to the stables. One of the many escape routes hidden in this old palace."

"You would leave your uncle without saying goodbye?" Chal stared at her.

"We must—or I must. If you wish, you can stay. I hadn't planned on this course, but that was before I learned of my father's murder." Lijena searched herself, but found no sorrow, no mourning, only the desire to send the souls of her father's killers into the embrace of the dark god they worshipped.

"Despair often doubles strength," Chal said. "You can conquer any adversity because of it."

"You'll come with me?"

"Yes."

"Then we waste time. You heard my uncle say mages cast protective spells around the house. We must be outside the walls before those spells are woven. Otherwise we'll be trapped for the night." Lijena ducked into the hidden passage.

"And if you stayed another day, Tadzi would trap you forever," said Chal as he followed after her.

Ten minutes later they rode from Tadzi's stables astride fresh horses. Another ten minutes passed, and they successfully evaded the legion of guards Tadzi posted around the estate. An hour after that Chal began a song of leavetaking that tore at Lijena's heart.

She finally found the strength to cry for her uncle, her father—and herself.

chapter 12

"I'LL HAVE YOUR head on a spike if anyone saw you." Jun, Ruler of Bistonia and Emperor of Thieves, twisted his mouth in a bestial snarl when Scrounge stepped onto an upper level balcony of the palace's eastern tower.

The tall, scraggly thief picked at discolored teeth with the tip of a slender steel spike. Scrounge spat and shrugged his shoulders.

"Did anyone notice you enter the tower?" demanded Jun.

"Doubt it, Emperor. You know the ol' Scrounge. When I want to vanish, nobody sees me. Not even my own shadow." Jun's old captain of the guards smiled.

Jun cringed. Did a thought ever spark behind that smile? Or was Scrounge the imbecile he appeared? "What did you find?"

Scrounge's smile widened with obvious self-satisfaction. Dipping a hand inside a soiled jerkin, he pulled forth a tattered handkerchief, untied its knotted corners, and proudly held out the contents for Jun's inspection. Myriad jewels glittered in the afternoon light.

"You fool!" shrieked Jun. He slammed his fist into the side of Scrounge's head, sending the skeletal man sprawling.

Jewels showered the balcony's polished marble floor, clattering like a spring hailstorm on a tiled roof. Scrounge stared up, confused. His expression was that of a man unsure whether to object or scramble after the spilled riches that careened dangerously close to the balcony's edge.

"Fool! I'll *give* you all the jewels you want. The cellars of this damned palace are filled with them. I want *information*. That's more precious than your weight in gold bists!" Jun turned in disgust from his fellow thief.

His gaze searched over the city. A frigid chill shivered through his core when his eyes alighted on the tower that rose high above the Avenue of Temples. Aerisan's accursed tower, reaching a full thousand feet toward the sky, dominated all of Bistonia. Even Jun's own palace was reduced to a dwarf in the shadow of the massive structure.

It grows darker with each passing night. Another shiver of horror worked through the former thief. Every man, woman, and child in the city well knew what unholy rites turned pure, white virgin marble to jet.

"But, Emperor." Scrounge's whining protest drew Jun's gaze from Aerisan's obscene house of Death.

In a fury that stemmed from fear too long confined, Jun lashed out with his right boot. The impact of foot to exposed rump set the medals on Jun's fine jacket dancing in disarray. Bistonia's lord sucked in a calming breath, then straightened the neat rows of unearned medals he prized so highly before looking down at his henchman. "Get up from there, you oaf!"

"Didn't mean nothing by it," Scrounge mumbled as he pushed from the floor. His head hesitantly bobbed about to scan the scattered treasure. "Good jewels."

"Pick them up. They're all yours." Jun held the urge to send Scrounge tumbling back to floor. Was the man's head so dense he could comprehend but one thing—thievery?

Scrounge jerked around and stared at his emperor more befuddled than before.

"I'll only take thirty percent," Jun amended, recognizing his slip.

This Scrounge understood. Matters took their usual course, even if Jun was overly generous. Ordinarily the Emperor of Thieves demanded—and took—a full half of any booty purloined by his subjects. But Jun couldn't tell Scrounge why he'd lightened his cut.

How he yearned for a compassionate ear! The desire to turn and run, never stopping until he reached the sea often swelled within him. Once he had panicked only when being chased by the city guard. Now, with that the same guard was under his control, fear gnawed at his entrails every waking instant. The nights were worse—he'd been unable to sleep in the fine bed Lerel once occupied.

The name of that fear was—assassination. It stalked him. There had been four attempts in the past two weeks, all awkward bunglings of amateurs, but all disconcerting. He had lived by his wits in the sewers; none had been better at petty thieving along Bistonia's prosperous streets. But this existence went far beyond anything Jun had ever imagined, even in his worse nightmares.

Lerel the Weasel had always appeared an unapproachable man, secure behind the high walls of his palace and with legions of well-armed city guards to protect him. Now Jun wondered how Lerel had lived as long as he had.

Wealth was his for the taking. He hadn't lied to Scrounge. Women? All he had to do was ask and one—or two or a dozen—were sent to his chambers. He had stopped asking after the last one. A comely wench barely sixteen summers had smiled and lavished her wet kisses on him and then tried to drive a knife into his back.

The last attempt stemmed from his own fancy-dressed guards. Of that he was certain. It had come only this morning when Jun passed a young private who stood at attention outside the audience chamber. A movement, a vagrant current, a shadow out of place—Jun wasn't sure, but his street-honed instincts sent him diving forward. The private's hard-thrust halberd raked empty air above his head.

The other guards posted along the corridor had rushed to slay the would-be assassin.

To save my life, or merely silence a loose tongue? Jun believed the latter.

Every guard posed a threat now. Every woman might want him in Black Qar's arms before her own. And now Scrounge persisted in petty thievery when Jun wanted *information*.

"What did you learn of Aerisan?" Jun began again.

Scrounge, down on hands and knees recovering his spoils, bobbed his head up and down. "Much, my liege. He's been seen in some odd places out and about the city. Doin' peculiar deals with the bargemasters on the Stane. There's one in particular he's been beggin' to see."

"Who?"

"This one's a puzzle, Emperor. It really is."

"Get on with it!" Jun dropped to his knees and seized Scrounge by his collar, shaking the man violently.

Scrounge sputtered when Jun loosened his grip. "Kahl! He's been lookin' for Nelek Kahl!"

"What does a mage want from a slaver?" Jun's brow furrowed.

"Can't say for sure, but the rumors have it your mage wants slaves that won't be missed around here."

Jun swallowed hard. Weren't the men, women, and children

who disappeared daily from Bistonia's streets enough for the young wizard? Apparently not. His gaze darted to the Black Qar's dark tower. He knew for what purpose Aerisan needed slaves.

"The other thing. What about that?" Jun pressed.

"Strange request, Emperor. Why'd you want to go and leave Bistonia when you're sitting pretty up on that gold encrusted throne and havin' people bowin' and beggin' you for the smallest crust of bread?" Scrounge stared at Jun, his expression devoid of even a hint of understanding.

Of the palace staff, Jun trusted none. The chamberlain spied on him. The major-domo sold off pieces of the palace treasure. Advisors were potential assassins. Scrounge alone could be trusted, the sole captain from the days of ruling over the sewers who had remained loyal. Yet, Jun feared to tell him the truth, feared the thief would view his constant worry as a weakness.

"Affairs of state. You wouldn't understand," Jun lied. "I want to, uh, pay my regards to the ruler of Leticia."

"What's Rynatvis going to tell the likes of you? He's one of them high and mighty rulers who don't consort with lesser folks." Scrounge scratched his head. "Even newly crowned rulers of Bistonia, if they don't come from the right class."

"I want to work this out with Lord Rynatvis. He and I might be able to trade. Leticia and Bistonia. Trade. Yes." Jun stopped himself before he babbled out of control. His fear rose and cloaked him like fog, blurring his senses and obscuring logic.

He needed information on Aerisan's activities—and possible safe routes out of the city. Before, the Bistonian sewers had provided ample protection. No one sought a thief for long in the dangerous underground empire. But with the Faceless Ones, with Aerisan's magicks, with Jun's feeling of being an expendable pawn in the mage's unfathomable game, he required an alternate escape route; one that was ever ready. When the time of flight came, it would be without any warning.

"There's this bargemaster that's willin' to book passage 'tween here'n Pretty's Wharf," Scrounge said.

Jun's desperation rose. "Just to the wharf? That's not ten miles down the river!"

"Bargemaster's got commitments, he says." Scrounge shrugged. "Can't stand around with his thumb up his arse waitin' for somebody who might never show."

"I'll buy the damned barge!" Even as he shouted this, Jun realized the futility of such an act. Aerisan's spies were legion.

Buying off a bargemaster and having him do nothing but sit on the docks would attract unwanted attention.

Jun never considered having horses ready to flee. The nightmare image of the Faceless Ones galloping after him, snuffling at his spoor, baying as they closed in for the kill churned his stomach.

"Find me a way out of the city. Buy a barge. Yes, that's it. Buy one almost completed, one that won't be launched for a week. But no more." Sweat beaded Jun's forehead as he considered enduring another week of Aerisan's unctuous presence in a place filled with people who hated him. "Have it ready in one week. Buy it with this."

Jun tossed Scrounge a bag filled with bists. The scrawny thief's eyes widened, gleaming with greed.

"There'll be that much more, just for you, when you arrange it." He gripped Scrounge's shoulder and squeezed in what he hoped was a comradely gesture. "You're my best friend, Scrounge. Don't fail me in this."

"You'll give me twice this amount when I get the barge?" Scrounge blinked as a hungry grin split his face from ear to ear.

Jun almost throttled the thief. Instead, he held his anger in check and said, "Twice that. From Bistonia's coffers."

"You'll let me sneak in and steal it myself?"

"Of course."

Jun watched Scrounge slip behind a curtain inside the tower—a shadow melting into other shadows. Jun swallowed his apprehension and went inside. Aerisan had asked for his presence at a state dinner.

Jun would attend. A request from the mage was an order not to be disobeyed.

The dinner had been a death match with raw fear for Jun. The chamberlain had quietly informed Aerisan—but in a voice loud enough for Jun to overhear—that the official food taster had died in convulsions. Jun had been unable to hear the chamberlain's further explanation concerning which dish had been the assassin's vehicle. As a result, he merely pushed his food about with gold utensils. His stomach complained noisily over lack of food, but his head told him starvation was slow, poison quick.

If that had been all, Jun might have gotten through the affair with some semblance of humor. As it was, his dinner companions, all of Bistonian society, took the opportunity to make slighting remarks about him. Oh, they were clever, those lords and ladies. They carefully hid their insults with flowery phrases, thinking Jun too ignorant to understand.

But he knew.

Somehow, he would get even with them. Each and every one who heaped such scorn on his head. And Aerisan. He wouldn't forget the mage and the way he goaded on those assembled. How he would retaliate against the wizard he didn't know, but he'd find a way.

Peyneeha recall the Faceless Ones! He silently prayed for the removal of the main obstacles between him and the wizard. Were the demon riders gone, he might be able to slip a blade in Aerisan's back.

Jun had left the table without announcing his departure. This produced another round of titters and mocking comments. He didn't care. Instead he hastened in long strides toward his sleeping chambers, wearied to the bone from the day's strain. Pushing through the heavy door to his rooms, he crossed to his bed intent on falling headlong into the silks, and sleep as he was, fully dressed for a state function.

The alert senses which had kept him alive in the sewers again saved him.

He examined the bed carefully and found a tiny tripwire just under a gold-weave comforter. Jun traced it to the foot of the bed and up one massive post to the canopy above. He blanched when he saw the mechanism hidden there.

His weight on the tripwire would have triggered an arm mounted with hundreds of stout needles. From the bed's canopy it would have descended to strike him full face. The sticky, dull tips of those needles told him all he wanted to know. They were poisoned.

Leaving the death trap untouched, afraid to tamper with the delicate device, he walked on quivering legs to a chair in front of a writing desk and flopped into it. Too tired to care, he slumped forward, head on crossed arms. Within minutes, he slept.

Jun came instantly alert when he heard soft footsteps in the corridor outside his quarters. His hand dropped to the ornately wrought gold chased handle of his dagger. The blade whispered softly from its scabbard when the heavy wooden door to the chambers opened.

He had barred the door after entering. Someone had betrayed him!

"Jun," Aerisan's voice slid softly across the room. "You are well?"

"Why do you ask?" Jun could not conceal his suspicion.

"There are rumors." Aerisan replied while he approached Bistonia's ruler. "My . . . sources claim another attempt is to be made on your life this night."

"You came to warn me of this?" Contempt seeped in Jun's tone.

"And to protect you, if necessary. I am a mage, and my powers are at your disposal, my lord."

Jun laughed harshly. Halting before he mentioned the trip-wire and needles. Doubt furrowed his forehead. Could Aerisan be telling the truth? If so, he should show him the trap. If not, he wanted to keep Aerisan in the dark as to how he avoided the poisoned death.

Jun decided. "I fell asleep at my desk working on . . . on papers," he finished lamely. Only blank sheets lay scattered across the desk. Jun was unable to read or write beyond simple phrases necessary for his trade of thievery.

"Walk with me in the garden." When Aerisan spoke, it came as a command.

Jun rose, pondering the man's true intentions.

"These assassination attempts grow bolder each day. We must seek their source and cut it out like a rotted core of a fruit." Aerisan walked with hands tucked in the folds of his robes as they entered the garden.

Jun studied the mage. For an instant he sensed a shifting veil about the sorcerer as though a smoky mist cloaked his form. In the next instant, the mist was gone—or was it merely imagined?

A trick of light and shadows, Jun decided. Although he did discern changes in Aerisan. The wizard appeared more mature, had a firmer command of himself and others. If Jun had seen Aerisan for the first time this night he'd not have thought him a callow youth. With Aerisan's newfound maturity came a sense of power.

Jun shuddered involuntarily. It wasn't confidence Aerisan reeked, but power. Stark evil power!

"There are fewer ears to overhear along garden paths," the wizard said.

The constellations had wheeled through their nighttime path. The War Dog vanished over the horizon, the Lesser Rat already gone. Within an hour the first streaks of sunlight would force their way into the sky.

Jun felt renewed, in spite of the lack of food and interrupted sleep. This was his portion of the night, the time he worked best and felt most alive. Let the Bistonian citizens sleep heavily; a talented thief could make a fortune in a few hours on a night like this.

"My inquiries have proven fruitless, but I will endeavor to find the source of your peril," Aerisan continued.

"Why do they want me dead? Who would profit?"

"Everyone. No one." Aerisan shook his head. "There are those who consider any ruler's death an opportunity. For looting, for seizing the reins of power themselves, for myriad other reasons. The 'why' is unimportant. Unmasking who is behind these attempts is vital."

Jun remained unsure whether Aerisan lied or not. Did the mage play some deeper game that required lying to his puppet ruler? Jun had no illusions about his status in Bistonia. Aerisan attended to the day-to-day details. The only time Jun made a pronouncement came after Aerisan provided him the proper words to say from the throne.

"Your thieves might prove worthwhile in gathering such information. I believe the people behind the attempts to be members of Bistonian nobility. They had no love for Lerel, but the idea of a lowborn on the throne is abhorrent to them."

"Contact with my men is fading."

"Reestablish it," Aerisan said.

The command startled Jun. With his legion of thieves again firmly under his control, he might challenge the mage for all Bistonia.

Or had Aerisan progressed beyond such petty concerns?

They came to the far end of the garden where the trees rose to rival the height of the wall. Even above this Jun could see the black tower challenging the night's sky.

The tower he had ordered built—a temple to the God of Death. Jun closed his eyes. Did he hear faint shrieks of pain emanating from the structure? Or was it only the whistling of morning wind through barren winter trees? He had no desire to find out.

"We can . . ."

Aerisan's voice trailed off. The mage cocked his head to

one side, then whirled about, his dark blue robes flowing outward like ink spreading through the murky night.

Jun turned more slowly. His eyes widened when he saw the flash of a naked sword. Another assassin!

The swordsman lifted his blade, bellowing, "Death to the tyrant!"

Jun had no chance to defend himself. Nor did he need to. Aerisan's hands moved in quick, intricate patterns.

A dark tornado cloud formed about the would-be killer. The man screamed as the air was ripped from his lungs. The whirlwind caught up dirt and hid the tormented face from Jun's sight.

As abruptly as it had formed, the tornado died. The swordsman, released from its magical power, slumped to the ground. His eyes had exploded and blood trickled from ears, nose and mouth.

Jun stared up at Aerisan, who stood with arms crossed and a frown on his face. Above him and to one side rose the black tower of Qar. Bistonia's puppet ruler trembled. The power he had sensed earlier was oh, too real. And now Jun realized the source of that power—and feared the man even more.

chapter 13

Lijena Farleigh drew her mount to a halt atop the crest of a bluff. From the vantage point, she saw the River Stane on her left, its muddy waters running a third of a league to the east. However, the young woman's gaze traced southward following the Stane's flow.

"Bistonia." The city state's name came in the strange emotion-words and garble of sounds from Chal's healing tongue that Lijena had grown accustomed to during her travels with the Elyshah poet-minstrel.

"Bistonia." She brushed a stray strand of blond hair away from her eyes.

The sound of that single word and the sight of the distant walls rising out of the rolling grassland brought a catch to her throat. It had been so long. After all the months, the seemingly endless leagues, home lay so close—yet felt so far from her grasp.

Home, it repeated in her mind. She refused to acknowledge the hollowness in its sound. Bistonia had been her goal—now it would be hers again! No one would deny her that.

She turned and stared along the course of the River Stane. A few barges sluggishly moved with the river's current. She remembered days when traffic so crowded the river that it was hard to glimpse the water that carried the vessels.

Jun's rule? Or merely a seasonal lull in shipping? Lijena bit at her lower lip. Surely it was the latter. Trade and banking were the city state's life blood.

"The sun will set within two hours," Chal's voice intruded into Lijena's thoughts.

The young woman watched the Elyshah's head tilt to the sky and the fiery orb that slowly settled toward the western horizon. With the late afternoon light playing over his fine features, she once again saw her companion as some rare, delicate spring flower to be carefully protected from nature's cruelties.

Chal's pupilless blue eyes locked to hers, holding them in a gentle caress. A rootless, disquieting sensation suffused Lijena—the same distressing feeling she had experienced when Susonna's covetous gaze had hungered for the Elyshah. She jerked her head away and stared at distant Bistonia once more.

"It's only an hour's ride from the walls." Lijena's tone held a nervous edge for which she could find no cause. "The north gate lies directly ahead. Beyond that is a small market district. To the left, along the Stane, are the wharves and warehouse district. Just south of the market begins a residential area. The heart of the city is Porsno Square, a great plaza surrounded by the oldest businesses and banks in Bistonia. Halfway between market and square stands my father's house."

"There is longing in your voice . . . the need to be with friends . . . with your own," Chal said. "Is it here our paths part?"

Lijena turned to the Elyshah again. The same stolidness that so unsettled her remained on his face. Why couldn't she read him? Why did this man who was not a man effect her so strangely, especially now when both her thoughts and feelings were knotted in a thousand confusing crochets?

"Part? But you . . . we . . . ride to Bistonia." Lijena's words faltered.

"There is need of me, fair one?" No smile or arching eyebrow broke Chal's expressionless mask.

"Yes," Lijena answered, suddenly aware that she had no desire to be alone when she rode into Bistonia. That in spite of myriad times she had told herself that she had need of no others in this world, she needed Chal at her side. "Yes, Chal, there is need of you."

A smile lifted the corners of the Elyshah's lips, which did not move as he spoke. "Yes, I know . . . have known for weeks."

"For weeks?" Lijena stared in exasperation. "Then why did you speak of parting paths?"

"I wanted *you* to know as well," he answered simply.

She snorted as she reined her horse toward Bistonia. "Be not so smug, Chal son of Chalt. Raemllyn's cities have little use for a minstrel lacking his tongue!"

Chal's impish grin widened. "I am more than capable of fending on my own, dear Lijena. I am an Elyshah—no delicate flower."

Lijena did a double take when his words settled in her mind. "You read my thoughts!"

Chal's only answer was rolling laughter that echoed off the hills about them.

Lijena shifted in the saddle to peer between the limbs of a stand of oaks. She studied the city's walls from the copse's concealment. A thousand repressed doubts broke free from the back of her mind. She shook her head. "Bistonia must be greatly changed. I can't imagine a city where the nobles and merchants would let the ruler—any ruler—openly murder my father."

"Your mother was murdered and her killer escaped," Chal replied, his voice a gentle breeze in her mind.

"Her death triggered a protest that drove the thieves from Bistonian streets and into their underground empire of sewers," Lijena answered defensively. Velden, Emperor of Bistonia's thieves had killed her mother, and, in turn, Lijena had killed the swine. Now his successor was responsible for her father's death. Blood did indeed seem to beget blood.

"Do we ride openly into Bistonia?"

Chal's question returned her attention to the wall.

The stone barrier around the city was a reminder of a more violent time, a past when the brigands roamed freely over the surrounding lands. The walls were maintained as old fears were hard to forget, but normally the gates were manned only by a token sentry, if they were guarded at all. Now a full ten soldiers, armed with lance and sword, stood at the north gate.

"There are posterns that will serve us better than the main avenues into Bistonia," Lijena said as she nudged her mount toward the west. Ten minutes later she halted and pointed to the wall and a forgotten gate half hidden by ivy vines. "Dismount; we'll have to lead the horses through. My blade will clear the path."

Dropping from the saddle, Lijena freed the Sword of Kwerin Bloodhawk and hastened from the wood about the city. Two quick cuts eliminated the vines, but it took both her and Chal's shoulders to loosen rusted iron hinges and swing the stubborn gate inward. Sword leveled to meet an unexpected attack, Lijena led her horse into the city.

No attack came, nor did a single eye lift to question their entrance. There were no people on Bistonia's streets!

"Things have changed," she said while she climbed back into the saddle.

"Changed?" Chal shook his head, his eyes scanning the empty streets. "I'd say Bistonia is deserted. It's as though the citizens have fled before some great plague."

Lijena ignored the shiver that worked coldly down her spine with the echo of their horses' hooves on the cobblestone pavement. Nothing Tadzi had mentioned prepared her for this. They rode eight blocks before sighting a man stepping from the doorway of a home. The instant they hailed him, he fled back into the house, slamming the door behind him.

They covered another five blocks before entering peopled streets, if these avenues could truly be described as peopled. It was as if some master thief had come in the night and replaced the Bistonia she had lived in all her life with this pallid imitation. There was no hum of the throng, no angry shouts, nor joyous laughter. A few tight knots of citizens stood and watched her and Chal pass. Their gazes had metamorphosed from a challenge to haunted fear.

Filth littered both gutter and street, the accumulation of months of neglect. Children, the few to be seen, huddled in doorways, eyes large and woeful. Even the scattered city guards who marched along the streets displayed no sense of duty—only fear.

Everywhere Lijena turned she saw the scars of fear. In the months she had been gone Bistonia had died and been reborn as this distracted, uneasy beast lurking in shadows.

"I hear no music. Is Bistonia always so glum? Mayhaps I should lighten the hearts of these sad souls." Chal tilted his head toward the lute tied behind his saddle.

"Better not," warned Lijena, and Chal answered with a nod that said he had little heart for music at this moment.

Memories long hidden within Lijena's mind awoke when her gaze returned to the dreariness around her—memories of Bistonia in times gone by. How often her mother and she had ridden along these streets in their family's carriage. There, to the right, stood the house of Waymare Ega whose son was the first to steal a kiss from Lijena Farleigh—a quick peck on the cheek at Lijena's seventh nameday celebration. How heavy the air had smelled then, heavy with the aroma of sweetcakes and sizzling sausages peddled by street vendors who pushed tiny carts. And there were flowers! Even when the snows of winter blanketed Bistonia there seemed to be some enterprising soul who . . .

"Five rings."

Chal's words shattered the parade of memories, to bring Lijena back to the harsh reality of the moment at hand. She drew her mount to a halt beside a weathered post from which five brass rings hung, marking the beginning of the Street of Five Rings, which opened to their right.

She reached out and touched the largest of the rings. Fingertips found a tiny nick near the center that neither time nor polish had worn away. How long had the nick been there before she had first felt it at age ten? How long would it remain? The marred metal had out-lived both her mother and father.

"My father's house stands at the end of the street," she said, turning her horse in the direction she nodded.

"There is an uneasy quiet to this street." Chal's words echoed Lijena's own feelings. "I hear nothing, I see no one. And the only smell in the air is that of the river. Night approaches. The aromas of roasting lamb and stewing vegetables should taunt our nostrils!"

Lijena's mount stopped before a chained and locked gate that enclosed the front of the Farleigh home. A yellowed parchment clung to the gate, officially proclaiming that the house and its contents were forfeit to the state. The decree was signed "Jun, Lord of Bistonia and all surrounding lands."

"Jun!" Lijena spat as her right arm snaked out and snatched the notice from the gate. She tore the parchment in twain, then ripped the halves again before tossing them to the ground. "He will pay dearly for this!"

"You do not wear your thoughts of vengeance well," Chal said. "Best we should leave this place and find lodgings for the night. A city's citizenry does not abandon their streets at the approach of night without good cause."

"We spend the night *here*! No low-born thief will deprive me of my own home!" Lijena made no attempt to conceal her fury. "There is a way to enter at the back of the house."

Not giving the Elyshah the opportunity to comment, Lijena reined her horse to a side street, and rode a block to a service way that led behind the houses on the Street of Five Rings. She reached an abandoned stable that had once housed her father's carriage and team. Both were gone now, but the empty stalls provided shelter for their horses.

Dismounting, she unsaddled and unbridled her horse while Chal did the same with his mount. Making a mental note to find grain and hay for the animals on the morrow, she closed the stall door and strode to the back entrance of her family's home.

A similar notice, complete with Jun's signature was nailed to the entry. It received the same treatment as the first. She then tried the door and found it locked.

"We can break a window," Chal suggested. "I dare say no one would hear us."

Lijena shook her head and pointed left to a chute that led to the door of a supply cellar. Walking to the chute, Lijena slid down it. The door here was also locked, but her fumbling fingers found a brass key neatly tucked into a niche in the stone wall above the door. In seconds she and Chal stood in the cellar.

"A pleasant place," the Elyshah said, inhaling deeply. "Your family stored many fine things here. I especially approve of the *phorra* brandy."

As though led by his nose, he strode to a dusty corner and with uncanny accuracy selected a slender-necked bottle from a shelf. He popped the cork and inhaled the aroma rising from the bottle before lifting the mouth to his lips for a small sample. He sighed with pleasure while he recorked the brandy and replaced it on the shelf. "Truly a fine vintage."

"Take all you like," Lijena offered. "It's mine now, and I am not especially fond of brandy."

"I've had enough. Your presence is all the euphoric I require."

Lijena blinked and stared at the poet-minstrel. Had another said such she would have laughed scornfully. But she felt, truly *felt*, Chal's sincerity. That rootless disquiet Chal had awakened in her earlier returned. Still the source of her nervousness evaded her. Lijena tried to edge the unrest away as she surveyed her surroundings.

The bottle of fine brandy was one of the few survivors within the cellar. Looters, she realized as she stared at ripped crates and items of no consequence thrown off shelves to lay in untidy piles on the floor.

Lijena waded through the debris, to climb a narrow, winding flight of stairs to the kitchens. Looters had done their work well here, too. The room had been stripped. The pantries loomed bare and dusty, indicating the thievery had occurred many months ago.

"This might have been done immediately after I left Bistonia to stay with my uncle. But why didn't Father clean it up?"

The mention of her dead father brought a catch to her voice. Lijena ignored it and went into the dining room where the Farleighs had given parties for a hundred years. Her great-great grandfather had built this mansion and been the first to entertain nobility in this very room. Only the splintered remains of a single chair lay within the dusty chamber.

"Once, High King Dumarrik stayed here," Lijena said. "That was over seventy years ago. Prince Felrad was to have visited us. That was before the usurper Zarek Yannis rose to power."

"The furnishings were well wrought," Chal said, his sensitive fingers running over what remained of the chair's back.

Lijena didn't answer, but walked to a broad marble staircase that ascended to the living quarters on the third floor. The tapestries, the fine oil paintings by Bistonia's and Raemllyn's most noted artists, the furniture—all gone. The looting had been thorough. What hadn't been stolen lay smashed. Lijena didn't even slow when she came to the second floor where her father's library and business offices had been.

The third floor landing looked untouched. Lijena hardly dared hope that the rest of the rooms shared this serenity. These were the rooms of her youth, of her entire life. She had been born in the fourth room to the right down the hall, as had her father and his father. Her room opened to the left and gave a fine view of the street outside.

Lijena gingerly opened the door. Sacking had occurred but most of the furniture had escaped unscathed. Who took a bed or a simple straightbacked chair when there were gold fixtures to rip out of the wall elsewhere?

She pushed aside the debris and walked to the window and peered out onto the Street of Five Rings.

"The view is nice," Chal said softly behind her.

"It was intriguing to a small child," she said, remembering, feeling the full weight of what once had been. "To see the people come and go, the activity, the *fun*."

The hours she had played here with her dolls; how she and her best friend Fria had confided the secrets of their adolescence; the first time Amrik Tohon had climbed the vine-covered wall from the street and stole into her bed—all this and more had occurred here. Now it was gone, and only the discards of thieves remained.

No, Lijena tried to steel herself against the tears that welled in her eyes. The sorrow, the burden of all that had been lost, her father's death, were too much to bear. She shuddered, and the tears flowed in gasping sobs.

"Fairest one," Chal whispered. His hands turned her then tenderly drew her quaking form into the warm comfort of his arms. With her head buried in the hollow of a shoulder, he held her, his palms gently soothing over the silken strands of her frosty hair.

There were no soft assurances that time would make all right again, no false promises that all her wounds would eventually heal. There were only the calming hands and the love that flowed from the Elyshah to enfold and cradle her.

When the tears at last dried from her eyes and the final shuddery quake passed from her body, Chal lifted her chin with a finger. For a long, silent moment, his blue eyes searched her face, then his head lowered, his lips slightly brushing hers.

And Lijena found the root of her disquiet. Hesitant, stumbling over memories of other men and how they had used and degraded her, she realized that the love enveloping her came from two sources—one being her own heart. Her arms encircled the Elyshah, her own mouth returning the kiss.

"Chal," she started to question when they parted.

"Yes, I know." he whispered. "Since the day I first sang for you, I knew my love was returned. I am Elyshah and sensing such is my nature."

Emotions, both quiet and intense reflecting a passion that had been bridled within the Elyshah for months, swelled outward and waited there for the taking or the sharing. It was the latter Lijena chose when their mouths met once again and they sank to the bed in each other's arms.

Lijena quietly slid from beside Chal's warmth and stood. *More than a flower* . . . his words echoed in her mind while her gaze traced over his moonlight-bathed nakedness. A loving smile touched her lips. Sleep only increased the aura of innocence surrounding the Elyshah.

Amrik, Velden, Jun, Berenicis, Davin—she shuddered coldly, remembering the names and the faces, many whose names she had never learned, of all those who had used her body since that day she had been kidnapped from her uncle's care. Yet, Chal who was not a man gave her what no man had ever given—love.

Her smile grew as she walked to an open window and gazed out over the city. Raemllyn's two moons seemed to wash clean the streets. How fresh Bistonía appeared—how new! If she could only hold tight to this moment forever!

"You can," Chal said. "There is no need for us to remain in Bistonia. There are wonders in this world just meant for our eyes, my love."

Lijena turned and watched Chal rise and walk to her. She nestled snuggly into his warmth when he opened an arm to her. "You *do* read my thoughts!"

"Easy enough when one shares them," he answered without answering.

"You know why I must remain here," she said without her eyes lifting to his, afraid those orbs of pupilless blue might sway her from her avowed task.

"Yes, I know, but do not understand." His arm tightened about her slender, bare waist. "But understanding is not necessary. I will stay or I will go with you."

Lijena looked up and kissed his lips. She felt desire stir and rise in him. His reaction awoke a new wave of desire that until this evening she was certain had died in her. While her fingertips explored the warm smoothness of him, she idly wondered if a child could come from their lovemaking. She would have to ask Chal, but not now, not with the bed so close.

The clack of hooves and the crunch of wheels turning on cobblestone echoed outside.

"A carriage below." Chal tilted his head toward the window.

Lijena frowned when she saw a carriage coming down the street from the east. Who dared travel the Street of Five Rings when everyone else in Bistonia avoided it?

The carriage was finely appointed, and the driver wore a livery both costly and unusual. Lijena smiled wanly, remembering other carriages carrying nobility.

Her smile vanished.

Edging from Chal's arms, she pressed closer to the window to be certain she had not been tricked by the lack of light in the street and the carriage's moving shadow. Lijena went cold. She *had* seen it!

A black cloud—a cloud born of no natural phenomenon—swirled above the carriage, a miniature thunderstorm replete with tiny bolts of vivid lightning.

The driver looked over his shoulder, saw the danger and raised his whip to urge more speed from the team of four matched grays.

He acted too late. The cloud descended and engulfed the carriage.

Lijena heard a man scream. Then, as swiftly as it had dropped, the black cloud lifted and dissipated.

Driver, horses, carriage, any passenger within—all vanished as if they'd never existed.

"By the gods!" Lijena's arms sought and found Chal. "What was that!"

"Not the gods, my love," the Elyshah said, and Lijena felt a cold shiver shudder through him. "Only one god moves thusly—Black Qar. The Great Destroyer now rules Bistonia!"

chapter 14

LIJENA STUDIED THE massive black tower that loomed skyward from the center of Bistonia. Its sleek, windowless surface emphasized the ugliness of the structure. What was it? And how had such a towering edifice been constructed in the months—less than a single year—she had been gone?

She shook her head, once again overwhelmed by the multitude of transformations that had swept through the city during her absence. *Soon*, her hand dropped to the hilt of the broadsword strapped to her waist, *the man behind these changes will be no more*.

Turning from the window, her gaze alighted on the empty bed in which she and Chal had slept the night in each other's arms—the reason she had originally moved to the window. When she had awakened an hour ago, she found herself alone. Chal and his lute had disappeared.

Where? Her gaze moved back to the Street of Five Rings. She repressed a shudder that attempted to quake through her slender body. The Elyshah, whether he admitted it or not, was so vulnerable. She cursed the differences that separated his race from the humans who dwelled in this city. Even if his own life were at stake, Chal would take no action that would harm another living creature. Only for sustenance did an Elyshah take life, and then with a deep sense of sorrow.

In spite of the strength she had felt hidden within Chal's core last night during their lovemaking, she could not rid herself of the image of that first blossom of spring. And she was the one who chose to protect that flower.

The fool! Where has he gone . . .

Lijena's mental ranting faltered. Her head jerked around, and her eyes searched. She frowned; nothing!

From the corner of an eye, she was certain that she had

seen a blur of shadowy motion across the street, moving toward the abandoned house of Magister Reslo Pusdorn. Stare as she might, there was nothing now. Not even the rustle of a breeze through the untidy hedges that fronted the house.

My eyes play tricks on me. It comes from a lack of sleep. She smiled; she had no regrets about how the hours last night had been spent. Night was a time for either sleeping or love-making. Chal and she had chosen the latter.

"Lijena." Her name formed in her mind amid an expanding globe of love.

A wide grin spreading on her face, she turned to the room's door. Chal's footsteps rose from the staircase. *Here, my love, where you left me cold . . . and alone in our bed,* she thought rather than spoke.

"It was unavoidable," Chal replied when he appeared in the doorway, lute strung hung over his back and a bundle tied in red cloth in his right hand. "I was hungry."

He stopped and eyed the supple young woman who stood slyly grinning at him. The Elyshah arched an eyebrow in question. "There is more than happiness at my return in that expression."

You can *read my thoughts!* Lijena mentally answered.

Chal made no reply, but stared expectantly at her. "Well, do you intend to share the reason for that bright grin?"

She bit her tongue. For whatever Elyshah reason, Chal refused to admit his ability to read her thoughts. If he wanted to play games, so be it. Eventually he would trip himself and have to reveal his talent—and the reason for his secrecy!

"No reason, other than I am glad you've returned," Lijena lied.

"You thought me but a thief who came in the night and stole your virtue," Chal chuckled.

The thought that Chal had abandoned her had never entered her mind. She had *felt* the Elyshah's love last night. Unlike human lovers, Chal could not disguise his true motivations with whispered meaningless promises and empty eyes trained to imitate the gaze of love in the classrooms of countless feminine conquests.

"I thought you injured or worse. The streets of Bistonia are dangerous, especially for . . . ," Lijena's words trailed to an awkward silence.

"Especially for a minstrel without a voice," Chal finished

her sentence."Which is exactly why I took to Bistonia's streets alone."

He tossed the red bundle to Lijena. "Your breakfast, fair one, compliments of Chal son of Chalt. Freshly cooked sausages, dried apples, bread fresh from the oven, and a fine young white cheese. And this!" He untied an earthen jug from his hip where another man might wear a dirk or dagger. "A sweet wine!"

"How?" Lijena knelt and unknotted the cloth on the floor beside the window. A feast spread before her. "Where did you get this?"

"While my tongue is lacking," Chal answered when he settled cross legged at her side, "these fingers can speak a language of their own. By the gods, there *are* still people in this dismal city who appreciate a fine tune!"

Lijena popped one of the small roasted sausages in her mouth. "Mmmmmm, it's still warm from the fire!"

"Of course! Would an Elyshah bring his lady love cold, greasy sausages?" Chal passed Lijena the jug to wash down the meat, then recounted how he had found his way to a market. "I simply stood on a corner and played. While no crowd gathered, I saw the stolen glances in my direction. And when the men and women left with baskets under arm, they passed by me dropping coins at my feet."

Chal paused long enough to use Lijena's dirk to slice a piece of cheese. His face was radiant in the morning light as he stared out the window. "There's still life here, Lijena. I felt it. Desperation to be certain, but beneath that an urge to grasp life and hold it close. Do you realize that one woman dropped a silver eagle at my feet?"

"Coppers, yes, but an eagle?" Lijena glanced up from the dried apple she munched long enough to give him a dubious frown. "I've never noticed a streak of the braggard in you before."

Chal chuckled, his gaze returning to the street outside. "Nay, 'tis impossible for an Elyshah to lie. A woman dressed in gray robes and black shawl, walked by, smiled sweetly, and dropped an eagle."

"And you're certain it was only your music she was interested in?"

"This woman was much too matronly to harbor more than a delight in the artistry of my music," Chal answered with a chuckle. "Judge for yourself. Unless my eyes lie, I believe the same woman enters the house across the street."

"Across the street? The house is deserted." Lijena's head snapped around in time to watch a woman in gray and black disappear through the doorway to the Pusdorn House. "Grisella!"

"Huh?"

"I know that woman. She's an old friend of my family." Lijena grabbed another sausage. "Wait here. I want to talk with her. Perhaps she can provide us with a clearer picture of all that has happened here in Bistonia."

Not giving Chal the opportunity to reply, she turned and ran from the bedroom. She took the stairs down three at a time to reach the front door, unlocked it, and opened it a crack.

Outside the street was empty except for a lone beggar who stood at the corner, waited a few minutes, then heaved a sigh before plodding on to find better pickings than those along this poorly travelled avenue. When the derelict had vanished, Lijena moved from the house, climbed the fence, and crossed the street.

A rap on the door to the Pusdorn home brought no answer. She tried again and received the same results. Quelling the urge to call out, Lijena tried the door. The brass handle moved without resistance; the door swung inward.

The entrance hall appeared as deserted as her own home. Crossing the threshold, Lijena called out in a low voice, "Grisella?"

No answer came. The only sounds were the creaking protest of settling ancient beams and walls and that of the floor beneath her soles as she advanced. Now and then wind whistled through broken glass and around boards nailed over the windows in a disturbing, mournful wail.

Something was wrong here. Lijena unsheathed her blade. She *had* seen a woman enter the house. And earlier she had thought she had glimpsed a movement here.

Cautiously Lijena opened a door leading into the kitchen. Small hints of recent habitation were visible here and there. Bits of breadcrust had fallen to the floor, not yet carried off by insects or rodents. The counters showed no indication of use, yet they were free of the dust that cloaked everything in her own house. It appeared as though someone had gone to great lengths to make this house seem unoccupied—while people came and went.

She stepped into the kitchen and paused. Her head cocked

from side to side. Voices, muffled and distant, rose from beneath her feet.

Lijena dropped to hands and knees to press an ear against the floor. Clearer now, she discerned at least four separate voices rising from a basement below. Anger hung in the tones as though those concealed beneath her argued bitterly. Fragments of words rose and on several occasions she heard the name "Jun" spat in contempt.

Pushing to her feet, Lijena crept to a door behind which lay the basement stairs. She opened the door a crack and paused. A trap had been laid for the unwary. A string was fastened around a jar filled with what appeared to be water. Opening the door more than a finger joint would tip the container.

Lijena frowned. The contents would spill down the stairs. What sort of trap was this? None at all, she realized, but an alarm. The spilled water would alert those below. *Which means they have ways of escape*.

Lijena slid her sword through the crack and severed the string. She carefully checked for other hidden alarms, then opened the door and quietly slipped through. While she waited for her eyes to adjust to the dim light, she listened intently. The voices were louder now, nor did she notice a hint that they had detected her.

One step at a time, Lijena descended the stairs with the Sword of Kwerin Bloodhawk extended before her in the dark. The soft yellow glow of a burning tallow candle came from somewhere to her left.

". . . right away!" cried a man. "We dare not stay our hands longer."

"We aren't ready for such a move." This from a woman. Grisella, Lijena was certain.

When a second man spoke, a voice Lijena also recognized, she boldly stepped to the basement floor, turned sharply, and confronted four people, three men and one woman, sitting at a small table. "Greetings, Magister Pusdorn. And to you, Grisella."

In the light of a single candle at the center of the table, she saw them all reach for daggers. Grisella and her husband Reslo Pusdorn halted, recognition melting their surprise. Pusdorn's eyes darted to his left and to a small tube overhead. Lijena smiled. If the tube had started dripping, it would have revealed that an incautious intruder had tipped over the jar of water at the kitchen door.

"I am not careless, Magister," she told the man.

Pusdorn and her father had been partners in petty business dealings over the years, but Chesmu Farleigh had never liked nor respected the way Pusdorn interpreted the law or meted out justice.

Of his wife Grisella her father had a higher opinion—as did Lijena. Grisella Pusdorn was unaffected by her own social position. Matronly she was, and her heart flowed out to those less fortunate than herself. Lijena doubted many knew that Grisella worked long hours at an orphanage or that she contributed considerable sums of money to this and other charities. Least likely to know the latter was Magister Pusdorn, who never parted with a bist or eagle without protracted wailings and teeth-gnashings.

"Who is this?" demanded a small man with a thin moustache and a ferret's look and movement about him.

"Lijena Farleigh." The magister's eyes shifted between the swordswoman and the ferret of a man. "Count luBonfil."

"A loose tongue is unwise, Pusdorn." The count's fingers tightened on his dagger, his knuckles turning white.

"Rest easy, Count." Lijena sheathed the sword, but warily remained beyond the man's strike range. "I've known the Magister and his good wife all my life."

"You vouch for her?" luBonfil's gaze shot to Pusdorn.

"Of course we do." This from the gray-haired Grisella. "Her father was a loyal supporter of Prince Felrad."

The count's thin, dark eyebrows rose and a smile more unpleasant than friendly crossed his lips. "*That* Farleigh? She is Chesmu's daughter?" Count luBonfil dropped his weapon to the table.

Lijena kept her cautious distance from the man until Grisella bade her come closer.

"How did you get in?" demanded the fourth at the table.

This man had the look of the gutters about him, and struck Lijena as familiar. For a few seconds she struggled to identify him, then did.

"You're the beggar walking the streets in the neighborhood. I saw you earlier."

"This is Old Pen. He provides us eyes and ears in the city when we cannot go forth," Reslo Pusdorn said.

"How'd ya get past the alarm?" Old Pen asked in a cracked, gravelly voice.

"Go see." Lijena tilted her head toward the stairway. "Perhaps your eyes and ears can be put to better use at the head of the stairs."

Old Pen grumbled and left to discover how she had evaded the water alarm. Lijena guessed he'd installed the device and now distrusted her for the ease with which she had circumvented it.

"Prince Felrad sends his regrets on the death of your father," Count luBonfil said in an unctuous voice.

"The prince knows?"

"He will," the count went on smoothly. "I, as his emissary, am empowered to offer royal sympathies on the death of such a supporter as Chesmu."

Lijena liked the count less with each word he spoke.

"Your father realized that Prince Felrad's wondrous victories reflected not only on Bistonia but all Raemllyn. He also . . ."

"Count," Grisella interrupted again. "This child has lost as much as any of us to Zarek Yannis."

"And to Jun." The name slipped from Lijena's tongue seething in hate.

"So?" said luBonfil, eyebrows arching again. "You come to us desiring to stand in your father's stead? A noble course to take!"

"What do you mean?"

"He means, dear," said Grisella, "that we are plotting to kill Jun and his pet mage."

"Mage?" Lijena asked in mock ignorance, wishing to milk these three for any information they might know about Aerisan.

"You must be recently arrived not to fear the name Aerisan. Jun ordered the construction of the tower that shadows our city—a shrine to Black Qar—but all know it's Aerisan who directed the foul deed. He deals with slavers for sacrificial victims." Grisella closed her pale green eyes and swallowed hard. She aged a dozen years in that instant. "You remember little Teela? The slavers sold her to Aerisan."

Lijena said nothing. Teela was—had been—the Pusdorns' daughter. Tadzi had spoken the truth; children *were* sacrificed to Qar! This Aerisan matched Jun horror for horror.

"What plans do you make?" Lijena inquired after a long pause. "If it serves my own purpose, I will offer what aid I can." She turned and stared at Count luBonfil. "Does Prince Felrad support us?"

"Only in spirit. The Prince fights for his very existence."

luBonfil lowered his voice to a conspiratorial whisper. "Few know, but since you are Chesmu's daughter and these fine freedom fighters vouch for you, I will reveal this. Prince Felrad's fought many battles and won few."

"I saw the aftermath of such a battle in my travels to the north." Visions of that spell-scorched battlefield wedged in Lijena's mind. "There could have been no victors at that site."

"Yannis' demons turned the battle. Prince Felrad's forces fought well against human troops, but when the Faceless Ones attacked, it turned into bloody slaughter. The prince is in retreat to regroup and try once again."

"And?" Lijena pressed. The count let his statement dangle in a way that begged for further explanation.

"Prince Felrad fortifies the city of Rakell. It is costly, both in men and material. Yannis nips constantly at his heels."

"You've been sent to Bistonia to raise money for this venture," stated Lijena. "And you found the city firmly in Yannis' grip, cutting off all aid."

"Lerel lent support," said Magister Pusdorn, "against a possible victory by the prince. Zarek Yannis discovered this and sent his master mage."

"So this Aerisan used Jun to assassinate Lerel," mused Lijena, grasping the intricacies of Yannis' scheme.

"So it appears—on the surface. Aerisan is the true power in Bistonia," luBonfil answered.

"Aerisan works for Zarek Yannis' best interests against Prince Felrad," Pusdorn said with a contradicting shake of his head.

"Not necessarily, dear," Grisella said. "We think Aerisan may have other masters."

"The shrine? Black Qar?" Lijena couldn't keep the horror from her voice. To serve Zarek Yannis was a travesty, but to serve the God of Death was an obscenity against all things human.

Grisella nodded. Magister Pusdorn said, "We plot to slay Jun. Another sword will be welcomed."

"Without overt aid from Prince Felrad, we would be only a handful against the power of Bistonia's ruler. And Zarek Yannis' mage." Lijena hesitated to declare her true intentions. Joining a cabal might increase her chances of killing Jun, but it also increased the risk. Her father had never fully trusted Magister Pusdorn, and his wife had not shown courage in matters beyond hiding her activities and expenses from her husband. Of Pen she knew nothing.

And Count luBonfil hardly inspired her to shout hurrahs to the new order.

"Prince Felrad cannot directly aid you. He is needed in the north, at Rakell. With that base secured, he can sally forth to do battle and stand a better chance for victory. If those loyal to the true heir know that Rakell is the new capital, Prince Felrad stands to gain more recruits, better supplies, much needed money," luBonfil added.

"Bistonia needs free of this mage at once," Lijena countered. "If Prince Felrad doesn't consider Bistonia worthy of support, why should we care to give him our blood in battle against the Faceless Ones?"

"Would you rather have the usurper or the true heir?" asked Count luBonfil. "I read the answer in your face. Prince Felrad's father, Bedrich the Fair, earned his appellation. Never did any complain of capricious decision or cruelty. Bedrich ruled fairly and well. Only Yannis' foul magicks at Kressia defeated him."

"The Faceless Ones defeated him. It is said mere mortals cannot hope to stand against them." Lijena searched the faces of the conspirators.

"Prince Felrad can, given the chance. They are demons, yes, but they are not invincible. Many were killed when last Felrad's army clashed with the usurper's forces," luBonfil said, defense in his tone.

"How many?"

Count luBonfil's eyes darted from left to right, avoiding hers. He finally swallowed and admitted, "One."

A humorless laugh came harshly from Lijena's throat. She had slain three of the demons that distant day in the forest of Agda.

She sobered at the thought. The sword she carried might spell the difference between victory and utter defeat for Prince Felrad. But she had other uses for it. The Sword of Kwerin worked best against magic. Aerisan brought the peril of Qar to her home. Could Lijena meekly turn over her precious sword to Felrad and let Bistonia's citizens, her friends and neighbors, suffer under Qar's reign of death and terror?

"Prince Felrad has many victories when he does not oppose the demon riders. He is not some cur running with tail tucked between his legs. Prince Felrad fights. He wins." luBonfil took a deep breath. "He wins, but not enough. Without Bistonia's aid, Rakell's strength may never come to pass."

"Without this island fortress he may never triumph over Zarek Yannis," finished Lijena.

"They go hand in glove." Count luBonfil leaned back and crossed his arms, staring at Lijena.

"I will join your band," she said.

Lijena spun at the creak of wood behind her. Her sword had cleared half its sheath when she saw that Pen merely returned. He spat on the floor and squatted down a few feet away.

"She reached through the door and cut the damned string with her sword, she did," the beggar said. "Fixed it so nobody's going to do that to us again. No chance, no chance." He spat again and glared at Lijena.

"We," said Grisella, "have a chance, dear. We are not dreamers going against a tyrant without resources of our own."

"I was Prince Felrad's tactician," said luBonfil. "Second only to Berenicis."

Lijena tensed at the mention of Berenicis' name. One day she would repay the deposed ruler of Jyotis for all she had suffered at his hands.

Apparently mistaking her moment of dark reflection as awe of his credentials, luBonfil went on. "Magister Pusdorn has placed monetary resources at our disposal. Old Pen provides us intelligence concerning Aerisan and Jun's movements. But, as mentioned before, we have use for swords pledged to Felrad."

"I've said I'd join you," Lijena replied. "I ask only one condition."

"That is?" asked Pusdorn, suddenly suspicious of her.

"It will be my sword that slays Jun."

Pusdorn relaxed, then smiled broadly. "Agreed."

The magister glanced at his companions. "Let us pledge our unity in overthrowing Jun and Zarek Yannis' power in Bistonia!"

He drew his dagger and placed it atop the table. Grisella's followed, then luBonfil's. Old Pen shambled over. A wicked looking stiletto crossed the others' blades. Lijena stood, unsheathed her sword and laid it on top.

"Death to Jun!" The whisper hissed through her clenched teeth. The other conspirators echoed the sentiment.

As they withdrew their blades Lijena noted Count luBonfil's gaze linger on her sword. For a moment, she grew cold. Did the man recognize the blade for what it truly was? When he said nothing, Lijena pushed it from her mind with silent relief. There were plans to be laid, assassinations to be plotted, revenge to be exacted!

chapter 15

"THIS BEGGAR?" ASKED Chal, suspiciously eyeing the man in tattered rags who waited outside. To Lijena's trained ears his words came with only a hint of the awkwardness that betrayed his tongue was not completely recovered from the razor bite of a soldier's blade. "Can he be trusted?"

Lijena pursed her lips while she considered the question and the reasons behind it. For a week she and Chal had followed Pen through Bistonia's streets tracing the route that the procession would use on the morrow. Only now did he give voice to the doubts she had sensed in a murky swirl about the Elyshah since the attack plan had been formulated.

It is the closeness of the deed that stirs in his gentle breast, Lijena decided when she answered, "Old Pen's trustworthy enough. He won't betray us. Any of us. He served as a captain to Bedrich the Fair before the usurper rose to the Velvet Throne. Nor do I doubt his mettle."

The worry-haunted furrows lining Chal's face remained. "What of the other two—your father's friends? You trust them with your life?"

"Yes, especially Grisella Pusdorn. She has a center of steel that her husband has never appreciated. The magister has buried himself overlong in the petty crimes of Bistonia and ignored his wife's finer points." The rucksack Lijena donned slipped from her left shoulder. "Help me with this. The strap is too loose."

"Can a man accustomed to convicting criminals strike out against his ruler, even if that ruler is evil?" Chal asked while he tightened the strap, then gave the pack a wiggle with a hand; it remained securely in place.

"Magister Pusdorn will not stay his hand when the moment comes," Lijena replied with firm conviction that concealed her own doubts about the magister. Reslo Pusdorn was a man of words; would courage flee when the time for deed arrived? "His swordarm matters little, though. Magister Pusdorn, Grisella, Pen and the others are but a ruse to confuse Jun and those in the carriage with him. *My* hand will *kill* the swine!"

"And these 'others' who we have not met, what know you of them?" Chal handed her a soiled cape of faded blue that she flung about her shoulders to hide the rag-stuffed rucksack.

"As I've said, none of us knows them, nor do they know our identities," Lijena replied. "Thus Count luBonfil protects those who strive to overthrow Jun. If one small group is captured, they can not betray others—even under torture."

"These nameless 'others' and Count luBonfil may seek only to use you."

Lijena shook her head, refusing to consider the possibility. Even if luBonfil sought to elevate another to Bistonia's throne, it didn't matter. Lijena's sole purpose in joining the conspirators was to bring death in the form of tempered steel to both Jun's and Aerisan's black hearts! "You worry needlessly. Are you ready?"

Lijena glanced at her lover and did a double take. The Elyshah's complexion changed subtly. She blinked as he went paper thin; the light from the window diffused through his body.

"Chal, you're pale!"

Chal laughed. "Pale? I suspect I fade away before your eyes! It's the damnable overcast and the hours we've spent hidden away in this dark shell of a house. Too long since I last basked in the renewing rays of the sun."

He paused and lifted ghostly fingers to tenderly brush Lijena's cheek. "Do not fear. It does me no harm to simply vanish from sight. Exposure to the sun will reconfirm my solidity."

Lijena blinked. Knowing that Chal was Elyshah and not human did not help her accept his disappearing flesh.

"If anything, this confirms my faith in you, dear lady. Only a demon can see an Elyshah when he vanishes." Chal leaned forward and lovingly kissed her lips. "Mmmmm, and you, fairest one, are very much a human!"

Lijena's smile faded with the weight of Chal's revelation. "The Faceless Ones?"

"Yes." A note of sorrow touched his voice. "That is why we Elyshah fled in the days of Nnamdi and Kwerin Bloodhawk. Humans failed to see us and thereby let us continue on our way unmolested. The Faceless Ones not only detected us, they slew vast numbers."

"You could have fought back." Lijena watched Chal's form return the moment they walked from the house and into the sun.

"We are children of Yehseen—of life. Answers other than violence occurred to us. If the will is strong enough, it can reshape the world." Chal's eyes shifted between Pen who walked fifty strides ahead of them and Lijena.

"The Faceless Ones drove you away from your homes. You chose to flee rather than fight." She could not disguise the contempt that crept into her words.

Chal shrugged. "You see it as cowardice. We viewed it as serving life, the purpose for which the Great Father Yehseen created us."

"You lost your homeland," Lijena protested.

"We kept our souls, our beliefs, that which follows all us throughout life. What is a plot of land to self-esteem and the knowledge that we triumphed?"

"But you lost!"

Chal smiled gently, almost pityingly. "As you wish."

"Don't patronize me!"

"It is said that Yehseen first created the Elyshah, but he discerned a weakness in my people. He had made the Elyshah too dependent on his light. He then created human beings. However, Qar, his first-born, dipped his fingers into Yehseen's Bowl of Life before the first man and woman sprang forth. Before birth, Death touched the human soul and planted the seed of dissent. Humans fight the eternal war of the divine father and child—Life battles Death," Chal replied. "That touch of Qar blinds you to other solutions than death and killing. We Elyshah see only life."

Lijena forced herself to breath deeply, driving away the anger that had erupted. "I didn't mean to demean your philosophy. It's not mine, that's all."

"No."

At that softly spoken word Lijena despaired. She felt that she had lost and Chal won—but what was the game, what was the penalty for loss?

"Chal, I've not asked you to assist me in this task. If you find what I *have to do* repellent, then you may return to Harn and await me there. I'll write a letter explaining all to my uncle. He'll give you refuge. You'll be safe inside the walls of his estate." Lijena said, her aquamarine eyes probing the face of her love for some indication of his desires.

"I do not seek safety."

"Then what do you want?" Lijena could not contain her exasperation. Nothing she said seemed to be right.

"I want no harm to befall the woman I love. No more, no less than any man," Chal replied, his pupilless eyes staring ahead. "Lijena, I'll accompany you on this mission or to the very gates of Peyneeha. I shall be another pair of eyes to aid you. But, my love, I still will not kill for you."

"Come. Stay. Do as you wish." Lijena's eyes flashed with angry sparks as she turned her attention to the procession route they now walked. "I care not."

"Have you grown so tired of me in this past week?"

"No!" She was hard pressed to keep her voice from rising. Each sentence Chal uttered strengthened the sense of defeat within her breast. Nor could she fathom the reason for that feeling. "Chal, would that I could forsake all this and travel away with you. But I can't! Don't you understand that? I *can't!*"

"A thick-tongued minstrel and a humpback." Chal's comment made no attempt to answer her. He swung his lute from his back and began to strum, although he did not trust his healing tongue enough to sing—except within Lijena's mind. "We should fit well in this dismal city."

Lijena glanced at him, struck by the fact that his words paralleled her thoughts as she perused the market they had entered. Straight forward she asked, "Do you read my mind?"

"Your emotions are clear to me—the embarrassment because of your disguise—the pangs of fear—the looming doubts." Chal reached out and squeezed her hand. "The peaceful winds of the olden days will again blow through your hair. Your path isn't mine, but you have the determination to carry you over the rough road. Never lose that. Even if your feet falter, never lose that. Never."

Lijena's hand tightened about his. Had they only met in a happier time when death did not cast its shadow over them. Lijena's gaze swept upward above the tops of the buildings ahead. The partially overcast sky darkened the hue of the ebony tower that rose above all—the shrine of Black Qar!

Lijena's neck grew icy. Everything natural and wondrous in the world became perverted near that awful temple.

"Qar's temple, one can feel death emanating from it." Chal's words once more reflected her thoughts. "I can sense it—some giant kraken with tentacles spreading across Bistonia."

"The more reason to dispatch Jun with all possible haste."

"Jun is dangerous." Chal nodded. "But true power lies within Zarek Yannis' mage's grasp. Aerisan will only find a new ruler when you slay Jun."

"Aerisan dies, too," Lijena answered. The sorcerer, as well as his puppet ruler, would pay for what they had done to her father.

"So it goes. There is no end to the chain of death. Once the first link slips over the edge of the dock and into the waters of Peyneeha, the next must perchance follow," Chal said as his fingers returned to the lute's gut strings. "How long is the chain?"

"It stretches all the way to the usurper who sits on the Velvet Throne."

"Only Qar rejoices." Chal's eyes shifted to Lijena. "The Death God cares naught who dies as long as souls come to nourish his black body."

"Then so be it! But Jun and Aerisan will precede me to Peyneeha!" Lijena pulled her eyes from the black tower to concentrate on the route Jun's procession would travel.

The advent of spring must be celebrated! Lijena thought bitterly, remembering the Spring Festivals of her childhood. Jun—or Aerisan—had decided this was the time for the new ruler to go among his people. Thus a festival had been decreed to celebrate the passing of winter. To begin the celebration, Jun would ride in procession through Bistonia's streets.

While Jun and his parade wound their way, Lijena and her co-conspirators would strike! By morrow noon, Bistonia would have a real reason for celebration!

"This is the place. Here the market is lined with stalls and shops of merchants peddling their wares. The crowd will be the heaviest here tomorrow," Lijena halted, surveying the scene.

Ahead Pen paused to examine dried fruit hung from one of the stalls.

"The masses will conceal Pusdorn, Grisella, and Pen," Chal said. "But what of yourself?"

"The road comes closer to the buildings here near the turn in the street. I will position myself on a balcony overlooking the procession," Lijena explained. "When Jun's carriage passes below, the others will attack to distract the mongrel's attention. I will leap over the railing and drop into his lap. One quick slash and Jun's head is gone from his shoulders!"

"Too simple," Chal warned. "Guards can stop those on the

ground. Arrows can bring down birds in flight. Rule of Bistonia cannot sit easily with Jun. How many others have attempted assassination?"

"Who cares? They have failed. We won't." Lijena studied the buildings facing the market street and found the one best suited to her needs.

Three stories it rose; balconies pushed out from more than half its windows. Neither potted plants stood nor laundry hung from several of the upper balconies, indicating vacancies in the rooms behind those walls. It could be easy enough to gain access to one of the empty apartments. If not, she could always use the roof to launch her attack.

"And your escape route?" asked Chal.

"If we must flee the city, guard captains can always be bribed at the gates," Lijena said. In truth she had not considered escape. Few in the city would mourn Jun's death nor would they seek to punish his assassin.

"You misjudge what it means to hold power. Those who bear the brunt of it despise the ruler. Those who don't aspire to the power in the ruler's hands," Chal said, his own gaze lifting to the balconies overhead. "Do not think, because you despise Jun, all others do. Especially in the troops he depends on for protection. They will be well-screened—and loyal."

Lijena snorted in contempt.

"Fear binds as surely as self-interest." Chal tilted his head toward Qar's dark temple. "To defeat Jun, you must erase the bonds of fear."

"A strong wrist and a sharp sword is all that is needed to defeat Jun!"

Lijena spoke too loudly. Heads turned in her direction and two city guardsmen stopped and stared. One of them put a hand on his sheathed dagger and approached the blue-cloaked hunchback and red-headed minstrel.

"What's that you said?" The soldier shoved out his chin belligerently, held his shoulders squared back, and took a challenging stance.

All of which told Lijena she had committed the ultimate sin for a conspirator: she had attracted attention.

Before she could mutter a reply, Chal spoke up. "That's not the next line. What a churlish way of covering your lack of memory, Janerel."

Chal turned and faced the guardsman as his companion walked beside him. A look of befuddlement clouded the Elyshah's face as he stared at the soldier. "You're not Janerel! How dare you interrupt our rehearsal?"

"What's carrot-top going on about?" asked the second guard. "What rehearsal?"

"Why, we are practicing for Lord Jun's gala party. We are the Harnish Players." Chal performed a low bow with a wide sweep of his arms. "Our magnificent troupe has come from distant Harn to amuse and beguile, entertain and give a moment's relaxation to the worried masses of our fair sister-city of Bistonia."

"There's only two of you," said the first guard.

"What?" Chal jerked around, staring about the market. "I should have known better to employ a low-bred Garodanian! How could I have been so blind! Janerel has gone off again. On a drunk, no doubt."

"I warned you when he came whining and begging, but you wouldn't listen to me!" Lijena fell into the role, following Chal's lead. "Now, I'll have to play two parts, and for no increase in the pittance you pay me, I'll wager."

"Quiet, you ungrateful Iluskan gutter-snipe! If it weren't for me you'd still be earning your living on your back!" Chal's thin chest expanded with mock indignation. "You bicker about something as insignificant as money when my production is faced with ruin!"

"Move along, you, and don't be clogging the streets with your silly plays," the first guard growled in obvious disgust.

Lijena bobbed her head, gathered Chal's arm in her own, and dragged him away still sputtering about the ruin of his glorious work of art. Only when they reached a sausage stand at the street's corner did she pause and glance over a shoulder. "They did not follow."

Chal heaved a deep sigh. "Deception is tiring."

"It seems I have more than your beautiful blue eyes to aid me in my task! Still healing or not, your tongue is silver, my love!" Her arms flew around the Elyshah, hugging him tightly with joy.

Just as abruptly, she stepped back and eyed her lover. "I thought you said Elyshah were incapable of lying? Not that I regret your falsehood, you understand. That guard took me entirely by surprise."

"Lie? Falsehood?" Chal looked at her as though shocked by the accusation. "Are we not come from Harn to this city? And are we not actors in a play that could change the course of Bistonia's future? All of which is not important. The guards were. They make my point—not all in Jun's employ see him as a tyrant."

"You will not stay my hand." Lijena's words were as firm as a holy vow. "I *will* see Jun's blood on my blade."

She turned to begin the walk back to the Street of Five Rings. There was much she needed to do this day to prepare her for the morrow. Though she loved Chal dearly, would gladly spend the rest of her life at his side, he would not dissuade her from her chosen course. The die had been cast. Only Jajhana, Goddess of Chance and Fortune, could change the outcome.

chapter 16

AT THE FOURTH hour of morning, Lijena Farleigh awoke, quietly eased from Chal's warmth, and slipped from beneath their sleeping furs. In the glow of Raemllyn's two moons that filtered through the window, she dressed in homespun brown breeches and tan blouse. Both had been purchased yesterday at Chal's insistence to aid her in blending with the masses should it be necessary today.

Such was the Elyshah's caution. A gentle smile touched Lijena's lips as she lifted the broad leather belt from which hung the Sword of Kwerin Bloodhawk and strapped it about her slender waist. Her caution was her silence.

Fastening sheathed dirk to the belt, she gathered her boots under an arm and crept from the room and down the stairs before donning stockings and boots. Blowing a silent kiss back to her lover, she stepped into the night. By the time Chal awoke, sunlight would bathe his gentle face, and it would be too late for him to join her. It was better this way. The bloody work she did this day was not of his making, nor did she desire his involvement. Assassination was not the way of the Elyshah.

"A lovely spring morning for a stroll." A man stepped from the shadows as she passed the stables at the rear of the house. "Though a tad early to be truly enjoyed."

"Chal?" Lijena froze, her right hand poised above her sword's hilt. "How?"

He ignored her question, stepped to her side, and kissed her chin. "I grew cold and found you gone."

"Damn your Elyshah ability to flit from one place to another! There is still time to reconsider the path you walk." Lijena did not return his playful affection. "The vendetta is mine. There is no reason for you to be involved."

"If I wish to one day bounce our grandchildren on my knee, I must make certain their grandmother doesn't get her lovely throat slit," the Elyshah replied with the wave of an arm, indicating that Lijena was to lead the way.

Cursing Chal's ancestry, Lijena stalked into the night, damning the Elyshah's hypersensitive senses. There would be no time for protecting spring blossoms this day.

Lijena sat on the bare floor, arms hugged about legs and chin balanced on knees. Her gaze moved around the room's emptiness. Ancient cracks marred both walls and ceiling. The floor was worn and weary.

How many had lived and died here? The idle thought drifted through her mind. Although, she refused to ask herself the question that trailed on the first—*will this be the last room my eyes will ever behold?* Were such shoddy trappings forever the province of conspirators and assassins?

Reaching the third floor and finding the vacant room had presented no problem. In the darkness, Chal and she had found a flight of stairs behind a potter's shop over which the rooms had been constructed. The third door latch she tried had opened and admitted them to the room.

Lijena glanced at Chal who lay curled in a ball beside her with one arm tucked under his head. The Elyshah had fallen to sleep minutes after they had begun the long wait.

For her sleep remained elusive. Countless times she rehearsed the part she would play this day. Leap from the balcony with sword in hand—land in Jun's carriage—rake her blade across the alley mongrel's throat—then a final slash for Aerisan, if the mage was bold enough to ride beside his puppet.

The sound of distant trumpets drew Lijena's attention to the balcony. *The royal fanfare . . . the swine leaves the protection of his palace walls!"*

"The procession begins," Chal spoke while he pushed from the floor. "The crowd gathers outside to watch the spectacle."

"Aye." Lijena rose and stretched almost leisurely in the hope of hiding her mounting tension. "Instead they'll gain their freedom."

"A deed that will be glorified in song." Chal's pupilless blue eyes met hers for a moment then moved about the vacant room. "Humans forever delight in such bloody sagas."

Ignoring the touch of sarcasm in the Elyshah's tone, Lijena walked to the balcony and leaned on the railing. The sharp bend in the street obscured her view of the palace. Until Jun's coach rounded the corner, she would have to judge his approach by the clatter of chains, the neighing of horses, and the cries that rippled through the crowd.

Lijena rested a hand on the pommel of Bloodhawk's sword to assure herself that the magic-forged blade remained with her. The sword's touch was cool. If Jun surrounded himself with magicks, the spells were too distant for the blade to detect.

Her gaze dipped to the market street below. Those gathered to each side of the procession's route looked as though they assembled to watch a funeral march rather than celebrate the return of spring. Gone were the bright colors, the arrays of flowers, the laughter, and music that once marked this festival. The crowd below huddled together, hugging gray and black winter cloaks close to their bodies.

Magister Pusdorn! Lijena caught sight of the man across the street, standing at the forefront of the crowd. She leaned over the balcony enough to see his wife Grisella on the opposite side of the street.

"There's Pen." Chal nodded to the rag-cloaked beggar who stood on the corner as a lookout for the conspirators.

"All is as it should be," Lijena said. "At least twelve mingle in the crowd to divert the guards when Jun's carriage approaches."

Chal peered over the rail to the street thirty feet below. "It's a long fall for one so small."

Lijena's smile was without humor. "I'll have the Emperor of Thieves' belly to cushion my landing."

Her hand tightened about the Sword of Kwerin Bloodhawk. A warmth that glowed from the heart of the steel flowed onto palm and fingers. Lijena's heart raced; her temples pounded like a hammer on an anvil.

"Jun comes." She eased sword from sheath, the morning sun glinting along the polished length of steel.

The clip of shod hooves on cobblestone pulled her gaze to the sharp bend in the street. Around the corner rode ten mounted guards five abreast. Each held a lance with a blue and silver banner furled beneath a wickedly pointed head. Behind the lancers marched a full hundred of the city's guards each armed with sword and shield.

"The carriage . . ."

The clatter of the open coach's wheels drowned out her words as it rolled into sight. No cheers rose from the crowd, though neither Jun nor the blue-robed mage who rode at his side seemed to notice.

Both are here! Jajhana the Goddess of Fortune smiles on me this day! Lijena estimated fifty strides and a thirty foot drop separated her from the two below. With Kwerin's sword in her right hand, she grasped the rail with left ready to leap atop it and hurl herself into the carriage.

Forty strides. She drew a deep breath to quell her stomach's nervous churning. No mistakes now. One chance and one chance only lay before her. She had to kill Jun and the wizard before the guards reacted.

Twenty.

A cry rose from the street. "Death to the tyrant. Kill Jun! Kill the tyrant!"

Lijena swung atop the balcony's rail and crouched like a panther ready to spring on unexpecting prey.

"No!" Lijena's mind railed.

A man with a short bow raised and an arrow notched pushed through the crowd. Stepping before the carriage, he released the shaft. The ill-aimed missle buried itself in the side of the carriage, feet from either Jun or Aerisan.

Then all moved as if drenched in treacle.

Magister Pusdorn leaped from the crowd with a heavy club lofted above his head. He swung and missed!

Aerisan came alive. Standing in the carriage with the folds of his blue robes aflow about him, he raised his arms. His fingers wove their magical paths; his voice called out, resounding like the grinding of massive boulders in the bowels of the earth.

The air about the sorcerer boiled. Five columns of dark, swirling air were born from nothingness. Aerisan's wrists flicked, and the miniature cyclones swept outward.

The first of the raging funnels struck Reslo Pusdorn at the center of his chest. With eyes wide in mute terror, Lijena watched in horror as the cloud sank into the magister's body, disappearing into his flesh. Pusdorn screamed; that wail of anguish died abruptly when his body exploded in a bloody shower of shredded flesh and bone.

The archer with the bad aim died next. The tornado that engulfed his fear-paralyzed form merely swept him into nothingness.

Grisella Pusdorn turned and tried to run. Too late! A third swirling cloud danced over her matronly body, tearing flesh from bone, leaving only a blood-stained skeleton in its wake.

As Lijena poised on the railing, the dark, swirling clouds

raked into the crowd, mindless of whether man, woman or child stood in their paths. Conspirator and innocent alike died.

A hand clamped about the broad belt encircling her waist—and tugged. Balance lost, Lijena tumbled back, sprawling atop Chal. Together they hit the floor in a tangle of legs and arms.

From below came the crack of whip and the panicked scramble of hooves on cobblestone.

"Jun escapes!" Lijena pushed to her elbows. With the Sword of Kwerin Bloodhawk still clenched in her hand, she had but one thought—revenge. "Chal, I'll have your . . ."

The words froze in her throat. Above her, she saw the cause of the Elyshah's action. One of Aerisan's churning cyclones shot over the railing and hovered above the balcony. The raging maelstrom of air expanded, swirling out to swoop down and envelope the pair who stared into the face of descending death.

Like a white-hot coal, the sword burned in Lijena's hand. She grasped it tightly as the funnel's mouth opened and dropped. Her screams drowned in the unholy howl as the deadly walls of air closed upon her.

chapter 17

DARKNESS—THE TOTAL absence of light—enveloped Lijena Farleigh. In a raging fury it boiled and seethed like some living creature. This she sensed, felt, rather than saw. Her eyes perceived only blackness—a blackness that was all consuming, a devourer in which even the rays of the sun were absorbed!

A gale like a thousand hurricanes sweeping off the Sea of Bua tore at her clothing, her hands, her legs, her hair, her face. Worse, the whirling vortex sucked at her very soul as though the demon winds sought to rip it from her still living body!

"Chal!" she screamed in pain and panic. "Chal!"

The roar of the airborne maelstrom shredded her cries before her lips gave them birth.

Yet, there in her mind the Elyshah answered. "Your hand. Give me your hand."

Lijena's left arm groped out. Fingers touched and clasped in desperation.

"We live." Chal's emotion-words flowed calm and soothing, edging aside Lijena's horror. "Why has it not devoured us like the others?"

The sword! Lijena's mind slid the pieces together. The Sword of Kwerin Bloodhawk protected them!

Right hand still clamped about fiery hilt, she wrenched the blade upward and sliced blindly into the blackness. Blue-white bolts like jagged legs of lightning rent the darkness. About her she felt the whirling black recoil. The wind screamed, yowling as though it were some animal the ensorcelled blade cut to the bone. Again and again the miniature bolts struck.

The morning returned! As abruptly as Aerisan's hellish whirlwind had sprung to life, it dissipated.

Ears ringing and chests aheave, Lijena and Chal stared at one another, afraid to believe that they still lived.

Above the horrified screams of the crowd on the street below resounded the clank of armor, the bark of command, and the heavy trod of booted feet. *Soldiers!* Lijena realized as she shoved to her feet and staggered forward to brace herself against the balcony's rail.

Amid the mass confusion that reigned on the street, Lijena's eyes saw and her spinning brain registered two things—Jun, carriage, and mage, were nowhere to be seen—and the city guard swarmed everywhere. The latter moved through the crowd using spear hafts and sword hilts like clubs to clear an avenue toward the building in which Lijena and Chal hid.

"We've got to make a run for it, Chal." She spun around and strode to the Elyshah, helping him to his feet. "The soldiers know we're here. They'll be up the stairs in seconds!"

The narrow hallway outside the vacant room offered two means of egress. At one end were the stairs, which led right into the arms of the city guards. At the opposite end of the hall stood a ladder that dropped through a square-cut trapdoor in the ceiling.

Lijena chose the ladder. Pointing to their means of escape, she shouted. "Up!"

Chal didn't question; he darted down the hall and scrambled nimbly up rough-hewn wooden rungs while she stood guard with sword in hand. The instant the Elyshah disappeared through the ceiling, she climbed after him, drawing the ladder up behind her and slamming the trapdoor shut.

"That should slow them down a few minutes." Lijena peered about the dim attic they had entered. Chal wasn't at her side.

The golden-red haired minstrel crawled atop a beam to a wooden air vent at the far end of the dusty attic. He glanced outside, then swung around to kick the vent open. "It's ten feet to the next roof. A mere step to one who intended to hurl herself from a third story balcony!"

Before Lijena could reply, Chal shoved through the open hole. On hands and knees, she crawled after the Elyshah and jumped out the vent to once more stand at his side seconds later. In a crouch, concealing themselves from eyes below behind the building's coping, they hastened across the roof and onto the next, and the next, and the next to elude Jun's guards who searched an empty apartment streets behind them.

"It would have worked!" Lijena took a swig from the wine jug then passed it to Chal. She leaned her head against the wall and closed her eyes. "Why didn't they follow the plan?"

"Mayhaps they did?" Chal lifted a questioning eyebrow as he sat cross legged on the floor of the Farleigh house beside the frosty-tressed blonde.

"But they didn't! No one made mention of an archer. . . ." Lijena's words trailed off when the Elyshah's meaning penetrated. "Surely you can't be right. They knew I was trustworthy!"

"You had only come to their numbers recently." Chal shrugged. "They might have schemed to sacrifice you while another . . . or others took Jun and Aerisan."

"But . . ." a protesting creak of wood below silenced her. She glanced at Chal and lifted a finger to her lips.

He shook his head and reached for his lute. As he strummed a chord, he whispered. "Silence will alert our visitor that we are aware of his presence."

Lijena nodded when Chal began to sing a light, rolling tune, then pushed to her feet and freed her blade. Cautiously, she crept from the bedroom and edged to the stairs. One glance below revealed the source of the sounds—Pen!

Although still dressed in tattered rags, the man no longer appeared to be the age-bent beggar Lijena had come to know. He walked boldly like a seasoned warrior with straight shoulders thrown back and eyes alert. In his hand gleamed a razor-edged broadsword.

Ducking back before the man noticed her, she retreated down the hall and stepped into a room directly opposite the bedroom Chal and she shared. She closed the door after her, leaving a narrow crack through which to peer. And she waited.

Pen came with sword raised and ready. The moment the man stepped into the open bedroom's doorway, Lijena threw wide the door hiding her, stepped forward and pressed the tip of her blade between his shoulder blades.

"The sword, knave—or your life!" She nudged him a bit to illustrate the ease with which she could run him through.

"I came only to talk," Pen sputtered.

"Drop the sword, then we talk," Lijena answered with another pointed nudge.

The blade fell from Pen's hand. Using her sword to guide the former soldier, Lijena pressed him against a wall. "Now tell me why you come creeping into my house like some assassin."

"I came to tell you that Count luBonfil had advised that it would be wise for all who are loyal to Prince Felrad to flee the city," Pen answered, swallowing when Lijena's sword tip menacingly touched his throat.

"He lies, my love." This from Chal who laid aside the lute and rose to stare into the beggar's face. "He came to kill you—and me, I dare say."

Lijena increased the pressure of the tip of the blade. A drop of blood oozed from Pen's neck. "Why kill me?"

Pen merely licked dry lips, but Chal answered. "The Count ordered it. You were recognized this morning. Jun and Aerisan now search the city for you. luBonfil is afraid you will reveal his identity if you are captured."

"Demon!" Pen hissed, venom in his tone. "How could you know . . ." He swallowed his words as though he realized that he had said too much.

"So the whoreson luBonfil wants my head!" Lijena grinned grimly, twisting the sword a fraction of an inch. "It's I who should be seeking blood! Why did the Count send the archer after Jun this morning? He was to die at my hand. It was the plan we all agreed to."

"Your plan!" Pen spat. "No one trusted you. Figured you'd show your heels and run at the first sign of trouble. You did, too! Eight died today, and you still live! We should have slit your throat the night you crept into the basement! It would have been cleaner."

Lijena resisted the urge to thrust her sword arm forward. Pen was but a pawn—deadly, but still a pawn maneuvered by another hand.

"It seems we've over stayed our welcome in this city," Chal said. "Count luBonfil sends killers skulking about, and Jun is equally desirous of your pretty head."

"The count is no more than a bothersome gnat. But I think it's time I paid Jun a visit," Lijena answered. "I made the mistake of casting my lot with bunglers once. I won't do it again."

Pen laughed dryly. "Then my sword won't be needed. You're as good as dead this very moment! Go visit Jun! The rat has run back to his sewers while Aerisan commands the search for you. Yes, go find Jun. One of his thieves will carve a new mouth on that pretty neck of yours the moment you step into the sewers!"

"So be it!" Lijena fought back the cold fear that squeezed about her heart at the beggar's revelation. She had been in the underground maze beneath Bistonia but once. That visit had been more than she wanted. "If Jun's fled to the sewers, then that's where I go."

Lijena glanced at Chal. "Gather torches while I lock this pig in the cellar. We'll need all the light that we can carry where we're bound."

Chal's pupilless eyes rose to hers and hung there for a heavy moment before he nodded.

"A strange spot to enter." Chal watched Lijena open a corroded grate to a sewer pipe that fed into the River Stane. "Couldn't we have entered off the Street of Five Rings?"

"This is the way I escaped Velden's men. I think I can find my way back to the audience chamber." She stepped into the pipe and held out an arm. "Hand me the torch."

The Elyshah passed her their one burning torch, then with three spare torches tucked securely under an arm, followed her into Bistonia's sewers.

Fifty feet in Lijena reached a familiar junction. Straight ahead lay a yawning mouth of darkness, but on the left was the ledge atop which she had slept the night she had killed Velden. Taking the left branch, she climbed the five feet to the filth-covered ledge and proceeded down a wider passage.

"By the gods!" Lijena jerked back as something dropped from above to land sputtering on the torch.

Chal touched another of the oil-soaked, rag-wrapped torches to the flickering flames an instant before they died. In the new light the "something" that had fallen proved to be nothing more than moss and slime that had lost its hold on the ceiling.

With a curse, Lijena tossed away the doused torch, took the new one from Chal and pressed on. "We can ill-afford such a loss. Unless you have some Elyshah magic that might light our way."

"Aerisan is the only magician I know of in Bistonia." Chal moved beside her and shrugged. The light from the torch passed through his fading body. "Poet and minstrel I might be, but I am no mage. The Elyshah have abilities not granted to humans, but humans possess skills we Elyshah can never share."

"Such as?"

"We can never cast a spell. In all our history no Elyshah has been a sorcerer." He laughed without humor. "Would that I had been born the first. I would feel a greater comfort at this moment, knowing I could weave magicks to shield us. Especially when that sound grows nearer."

"Sound?" Lijena's head cocked to each side, but she heard only the gurgle of flowing sewage.

A fact that did not prevent her from unsheathing the Sword of Kwerin Bloodhawk. The hilt warmed in her palm, and tiny sparks of green witchfire danced along the blade's cutting edges.

"Can you not hear it?" Doubt furrowed Chal's translucent face. "A slithering that whispers beneath the sound of the water. It comes from . . ." his head jerked to one side then the other ". . . I can not tell. The echo here confuses me."

Repressing the desire to turn and run, Lijena sloughed forward through the ankle-deep muck. Obscene sucking noises accompanied her every footstep, but she heard no slithering. Nor could she see anything beyond the torch's glow.

"There are magicks near." She nodded toward the blue-green light that now bathed the sword.

Where eyes and ears failed, Lijena's nose alerted her. Swelling over the overwhelming stench of sewage, came the gagging effluvium of carrion left to rot in the sun for days. Then she heard it—not a slithering, but a hurried splashing.

The blackness before her took form. A hideous dog's head with eyes of burning rubies and mouth gaping wide to expose yellowed fangs appeared at eye level in the air before her. Those monstrous jaws snapped closed a fraction of an inch from her left hand.

Lijena reacted without thought. In a tight arc, she swung her sword upward into the blackness, aiming for the spot where head joined the creature's indiscernible body.

The glowing blade found a meaty though invisible berth. Blue-white sparks showered through the air. Again that grotesque maw gaped wide, but not to attack. The creature howled its deathcries, though no sound issued from its twisted mouth. Pain flamed in its burning orbs—for a heartbeat. Then it vanished.

Dead or retreating into the sewers, Lijena knew not. But it was gone. The Bloodhawk's sword no longer glowed and the heat was gone from its hilt.

"Qar's black hound!" Chal's voice was a low whisper. For the first time since she had rescued him from Yannis' soldiers, Lijena felt apprehension flowing from the Elyshah. "Is it possible Aerisan commands such powers?"

"Qar's hound?" Lijena glanced at Chal; his visage grew dimmer. "Are you certain? Such creatures guard Hell!"

"I hope that I am wrong," Chal answered as they moved

deeper into the sewers. "I have never seen the beasts, only heard of them."

Blackness held prisoner in blackness swirled ahead. And from out of that darkness came slithering.

"You hear it now?" Chal asked.

"Aye, but it is directly ahead," she answered with a tilt of her head to a feeder tunnel that opened on the right. "We go that way."

Together they leaped into the tunnel. Two more turns and a league into the sewer's maze, Lijena halted. Kwerin Bloodhawk's sword once more danced with green sparks.

"Do we wait here for these new magicks to come to us, or march to face them?" Chal leaned wearily against a wall, barely visible now.

"Forward," Lijena replied and started sloshing through the muck once more.

"Lijena, wait!"

"What is it? You hear something?" She strained and heard only the drip-drip-drip of condensation within the sewers.

"The walls. Touch them!"

She reached out, expecting slime-covered stone to meet her fingertips. The wall pulsed with vibrant life. Lijena took an involuntary step back. All around them the walls and ceiling quivered from this light touch.

"The sewer's alive," she said in a choked voice.

"Nay, we stand in the throat of a living creature vomited forth from Peyneeha itself!" Chal cautiously moved away from the wall. "Back. On feet of feathers move backward before we awaken the Qailuhn!"

"Qailuhn?" Ice flowed through Lijena's veins at the sound of that dreaded name. It couldn't be—only the black sorcerer Nnamdi had ever commanded Qar's worm. It defied all logic, yet her senses told her that she now stood in the legendary creature's belly.

Fearing the pounding of her heart would awaken the monster, Lijena lifted her right foot and took a tentative step. Nothing. She moved her left foot.

The world rumbled! The walls, the floor, the ceiling about her contracted!

"It swallows us," Chal cried out. "The Qailuhn swallows us!"

Finding balance in a wide stance, Lijena tossed Chal the torch and hefted the Sword of Kwerin Bloodhawk in both hands. With all the strength she could muster, she swung.

The magic-glowing blade sliced into the rippling flesh overhead. Black ichor sprayed from a deep gash; the Qailuhn convulsed. Again Lijena swung, and again. A dark, dripping wound the width of a man opened in the giant worm's gut.

"Up and out!" she cried, slashing the blade into the nightmarish creature one last time. She then followed the Elyshah atop the quaking gargantua.

"There's a tunnel leading to the right." Chal held the torch high as he ran along the worm's shuddering length, pointing to another feeder tunnel.

Together they jumped from the back of Qar's serpentine servant and darted into the tunnel. And together they ran. Behind them came the grating rumble of unholy flesh writhing against granite.

"It cannot find us," Lijena panted as she stumbled to a shaky halt. "Rest a moment. The sword no longer glows, and I must gather my breath."

She drew but one lungful of air, when her head snapped around. The slithering sound had returned, this time behind them and near!

"Lijena, the air comes alive!" Chal pointed to a fly-sized speck above their heads, that swirled outward, growing in to a miniature tornado.

Grabbing the Elyshah's hand, Lijena tugged him after her. "There was a tunnel leading to the left . . ."

She skidded to a halt, nearly spilling herself and Chal into the muck. The source of the persistent slithering sound rose ahead of them. Two yellow eyes, each as large as a child's head, poked from the water and inched upward on honed stalks. A leathery tentacle equal to the thickness of an adult *pletha* snake whipped out of the muck and wrapped about Lijena's right thigh.

"Run, Chal! Run!" She cried as she wrenched her sword high and brought the edge down on the tentacle. The blade bounced off, leaving neither cut nor scratch.

She had no time to ponder the lack of injury. The howling maelstrom of wind dropped about her, its walls rushing inward. She screamed a curse into the face of death as the crushing force closed about her.

chapter 18

THE BLACKNESS TEEMED with nameless obscenities, loathsome *things*. Lijena fought the smothering presence, straining to breathe, to draw life-giving air into screaming lungs. Nothing! Muck clogged nostrils and mouth.

Panicked, she clawed at the darkness trying to swim free of the lodestone that dragged her downward. From out of the churning black an invisible fist slammed between her shoulder blades. Her body resounded from the force of the impact. Vibrations quaked up her spine to set her head abuzz, chiming and shrilling until it exploded in a shattering shower of sound and light.

"She still lives. Good. It will make torturing her more satisfying."

"You would have tortured a corpse?" a second voice, one higher pitched, but commanding, asked incredulously.

"Of course. Alive or dead, she deserves it. Velden should have let me finish the whore when last she ventured into these fine estates."

Both laughed. Lijena recoiled from the brutal cruelty contained in the two voices. From the black *things* swarmed over her. A thousand tiny talons raked, dragging her downward. Another unseen fist hammered her back. She coughed, spitting out the vile tasting flotsam that blocked mouth and nose.

"Not so hard, fools! I don't want her damaged—yet." A man's voice ranted. "Hold her against the wall and let her get her breath back."

Lijena's eyes fluttered open. A hazy blur of variegated grays gradually focused, and she stared into the face of—

"Jun!" Lijena cried in alarm.

Twisting and tugging against the hands locked about her arms, she struggled to get her feet under her, to find her missing sword, to kill the smirking emperor of Bistonia's thieves. Her boots found no purchase on slime-blanketed stone. She flailed about like a fish out of water and tumbled to her knees in stinking muck.

A chorus of laughter accompanied her fall.

"I see you know how to pay proper obeisance to the ruler of Bistonia." A man in dark blue robes strode before Lijena, roughly grasped a handful of blond hair, and wrenched her head back.

Lijena glared into the face of the mage Aerisan. A grin devoid of the slightest trace of human emotion belied the youthful smoothness of the wizard's features. While Aerisan's body might be young, his soul was older than the world itself.

"I can see why you might want to amuse yourself a few days with a wench as comely as this." Aerisan released his grip, turned, and strode back toward Jun.

Lijena caught her breath and blinked in disbelief. The sewer muck retreated from the hem of Aerisan's robes, sizzling and boiling. The cloth slippers on his feet trod not in refuse and offal, but atop unsoiled, dry stone.

"Yannis' lackey!" Lijena hissed in contempt. Her gaze coldly shifted from the wizard. Leisurely, to hide her anxiety, she glanced around, searching for Chal. Had he run as she had commanded? Or was the gentle Elyshah now dead? She shoved the thought away, refusing to even consider that possibility. If Chal lived, then she had not totally failed.

"She recognizes me? How interesting." The mage turned to eye her. "How is it you know me?"

"All the usurper's lackeys carry a stench about them!" she spat.

With arm lofted to deliver a blow, Aerisan took two strides toward her before stopping abruptly and checking his anger. A sneer that imitated a smile curled his lips. "You know *all* King Yannis' minions? I doubt this. Do you know this fine gentleman?"

The fingers on Aerisan's right hand danced, tracing patterns of power in the air. Beside him nothingness gave birth to a swirling cloud of blackness. A flick of the mage's wrist and the cloud solidified into a shifting amorphous mass. Tentacles with recurved claws dotting their undersides grew and stretched toward Lijcna's facc.

Coldness beyond the simple measure of ice and snow, a coldness that lacked any sensation suffused every cell of her body. One brush of those tentacles—the merest touch—and she knew that she would dissolve into that empty cold forever! This was no spell-sparked illusion, but one of the many guises of Death. This was Black Qar, the Great Destroyer!

A scream that encompassed all that was terror and horror rose in her throat. Sweat popped on her brow as she fought to contain that cry. If Death now came to claim her, so be it. But her captors would not know the pleasure of seeing her fear!

"Stop it!" Jun shouted. "Stop it! I command it! She is mine!"

The mass quavered. Like mist in the sun, the blackness evaporated and left behind the wet, stinking reality of the sewer.

Aerisan turned and stared at the Emperor of Thieves for an instant, before his eyes moved back to Lijena. "Would you like to see more? It can easily be arranged."

"Black Qar . . . you command . . . the Death God!" Lijena forced words over the lump of fear still clogging her throat.

The mage's eyes widened and color left his cheeks. "You know? How?"

Abruptly the sorcerer spun around to face Jun. "This one *cannot* be allowed to live. She must be delivered to the temple immediately!"

"She's mine for a week, as we agreed." Jun motioned with an arm.

Thieves, at least fifty, who stood concealed in the sewer's dimness stepped forward to stand between Lijena and the young wizard. Four of them yanked her to her feet and dragged her from the muck into an immense chamber bathed in the gentle light of phosphorescent moss that hung from the ceiling. *Jun's throne room.* She recognized it from the time she had once stood before Velden in this very subterranean room.

"A word of caution, Lord Jun. This wench is more than she appears." Aerisan protested as he and the thieves' leader entered the chamber. "How is it she penetrated so deeply into the sewers? Ask yourself that? My magicks were thwarted. Is she the offspring of sorcerers?"

"Merchants," answered Jun. "Why such concern over her reaching this room? We took her neatly enough."

"Chains! Good thinking, Beff!" Jun grinned at a man who entered the room on the right. "Bind the bitch before she turns into a panther and rips out Aerisan's throat!" Jun chuckled as he sank atop his throne.

Harsh hands grabbed Lijena and thrust her against a wall. Clammy tapestry rubbed against her back and cold iron bracelets clicked shut around her wrists and ankles.

"Mock not my caution, Lord Jun! You are blinded by her beauty. But this one is more than she appears. I ask you again, how did she get so far into the sewers?"

Lijena detected a hint of hesitation in the mage's voice. Was there something here she didn't see? What would give pause to a man who summoned Black Qar to do his bidding? Was it the small army of thieves Jun assembled? Were they too many for even Aerisan's awesome power?

"What difference does it make, Aerisan? Are you worried that your powers are failing?" Jun waved the man away.

"I am *not* worried." Aerisan lied. Today strained his abilities to their limit. He walked to Lijena and stood staring into her unblinking eyes. " She met a vestige of Black Qar's body and lived. That is impossible."

"What do you mean?" Jun asked, uneasily shifting on his throne. "What spells did you cast to protect me?"

"No ward spells," said Aerisan. "Any mage could circumvent them. I prayed to my patron for assistance. She met and defeated aspects of the Great One that I set loose within the sewers. Tiny parts of Qar, to be certain. No segment was Black Qar's entirety, but no mortal could pass without falling into the Death God's embrace. I want to know how you passed the aspects of Qar."

"Which one?" Lijena asked. The shock on the mage's face revealed what she suspected—Aerisan was vulnerable! She aimed verbal daggers at the chinks in his armor. "The small whining puppy I slew with my sword? Or the shriveled worm I hacked in twain?"

"Qar's hound," muttered Aerisan. Then, "Qar's gut! You entered a god's intestine and lived? Impossible. You lie, bitch, you lie!" Aerisan struck her.

Salty blood welled inside Lijena's cut lip. She spat but missed Aerisan.

"You unleashed Qar in *my* sewers?" cried Jun. "How dare you? My thieves come and go. You told me that the ward spells would let them pass and keep out any assassin."

Aerisan shrugged, as if it mattered nothing to him whether Jun lost all his thieving subjects or not. "She got past the aspects of Qar in the tunnels. How? How?" The mage stared at the chained woman, a slow smile crossing his full lips. "Of course."

Aerisan turned in a swirl of blue robes and pointed at a guard to one side of the audience chamber. "You. Fetch her weapon. She must have carried a sword. Get it. And there'll be a sheath with it. Bring me both sword and scabbard. Now!"

"Lord?" The guard glanced at Jun for his approval. The Emperor of Thieves nodded. The thief walked back to the sewers.

Lijena contained the smile that tried to move across her lips. In spite of the magicks—the god!—he controlled, Aerisan did not rule this underground kingdom. Here Jun still reigned, and Jun was a mere man quite capable of dying at the end of a sword or dirk.

"What is he searching for?" asked Jun.

Aerisan did not answer. He turned and stared at Lijena, his cold smile becoming more pronounced. When the thief returned with Lijena's lost sword and scabbard Aerisan jerked them from the man's grasp. He wiped away the thick muck clinging to both.

"The Sword of Kwerin! And its sheath!" Triumph fired his hazel eyes.

"Those are myths." Jun leaned forward in his throne, hands on the broad arms. "Kwerin Bloodhawk had no mystical way of defeating the Faceless Ones."

"This!" cried Aerisan, holding the filthy blade up at arm's length. "This is the blade of antiquity."

Lijena laughed. *"That's* magical? 'Tis no more than an ordinary blade of steel purchased in Harn."

"You used it against Qar's hound—and the other aspects of the Black God. It served you well—for a while. Then its power was no more." Aerisan shoved the blade back into its sheath. "The blade glowed when you first drew it. How it must have danced with power! Yet, each time it passed through a part of Black Qar's body, it shone less and less. Finally it died."

"Why?" Lijena blurted before she realized what that single word revealed.

Aerisan laughed. "The Sword of Kwerin Bloodhawk is but mortal magic. Even the greatest spell of mortals pales next to a god. Black Qar is all . . . and all that is mortal eventually dies. The Great Destroyer *always* triumphs."

Aerisan whipped forth the blade. It gleamed a pale green in the wan light of Jun's audience chamber. "Without the sheath, the blade is nothing. The sheath regenerates its magicks. With this, Zarek Yannis would be invulnerable!"

Lijena looked past the sorcerer to Jun. The Emperor of Thieves frowned. He leaned back and motioned to his men.

"Lord Aerisan," Jun called. "This sword. Does it take a sorcerer to wield it?"

Aerisan sneered at the seated thief. "No, it doesn't. You already know that, fool. She used it against aspects of Qar himself."

"And your plans for this mystical blade?"

"None of your concern, Lord Jun." Aerisan's words dripped scorn for the master thief.

"Oh, but it is, Aerisan."

The menace that came into Jun's words brought the mage around. Aerisan eyed the Emperor of Thieves contemptuously. "Does the rat develop fangs? No, that's not possible. He needs me. Don't you, Lord Jun? Who else holds the hordes of assassins at bay?"

"I've considered that, mage. The attempts on my life came the moment I took Bistonia's throne—too early to be organized, yet there was an air about them. I've dabbled in such killings myself. Explain how no one in all Bistonia knew who tried to kill me. Explain that, Aerisan."

"The merchants loathe you, Jun. Those in the city guard and palace service who gained promotion at Lerel's hand saw only death at yours," Aerisan replied, his eyes narrowing.

"Easily said, and untrue." Jun's face clouded with anger. "The most obvious explanation of the murder attempts is that someone closer at hand was behind them. Someone like . . . you, Aerisan."

"You play the fool," Aerisan shook his head, although Lijena noted the hesitation return to his voice. "If I'd wanted you dead, Black Qar would have already gnawed your bones."

"True. You didn't want me dead. You wanted me frightened and in your debt. I actually thought only you could protect me after the incident in the garden. But they were not serious assassination attempts that failed, they were merely attempts at assassination," Jun continued.

"You babble."

"You saw no need to remove a valuable pawn. You worked to keep me frightened." Jun paused and stared at the young mage. "You did not tell me you were ringing me with bits of your god. You said only that ward spells had been cast."

"What difference is it to you? Your precious hide is still intact. I've kept my part of our bargain."

"This fascination with Black Qar, the temple you forced me

to construct, the dabblings with different aspects of the Death God, all this leads me to think you have plans for Bistonia that aren't shared by Zarek Yannis—or myself."

"*You* worry about our High King's best interests?" Aerisan's eyebrows lifted in disbelief.

"The Bloodhawk's sword is a potent weapon against the usurper." Jun frowned, lost in thought. Then he said, "With this magical sword fully powered, you can defeat Yannis' Faceless Ones. Would this defeat convince Black Qar that another might be a better choice for the Velvet Throne in Kavindra?"

"Yes, a man such as yourself!" Aerisan answered, holding the sword of Kwerin reverently to his breast.

While in words he mentioned Jun to replace Zarek Yannis, Lijena saw the wizard's hazel eyes. Aerisan no longer thought of himself as a mage, but as High King of Upper and Lower Raemllyn!

This she saw as surely as her eyes caught the gleam of light on naked blades slipped from hidden sheaths. Seven of Jun's men inched toward Aerisan to enclose him in a loose circle.

Lijena's heart raced and her temples pounded. Jun's intent was clear; he wanted the mage dead and the sword in his hands. *Good! A mere man is easier to deal with than a sorcerer.*

"What?" The movement had not gone unnoticed. Aerisan wrenched the sword from its sheath. "You betray me?"

The mage swung the Sword of the Bloodhawk in a wide arc. The blade bit to the bone in one thief's upper arm. The man yelped and jerked away, a crimson fountain spraying forth. However, Aerisan's mistake was the same Lijena had made the night she faced Zarek Yannis' three soldiers. The sword's magicks only turned away magicks. Against the physical it was a simple blade of fine steel.

"Kill him!" Jun bellowed.

A blow from a broadsword-wielding thief with a white scar above his left eye sent the Sword of Kwerin Bloodhawk flying from Aerisan's grip and careening across the floor of the throne room. The mage's hands lifted; fingers wove the air.

Too late! Four thieves fell on him, daggers flashing. Aerisan screamed and then collapsed beneath the weight of his assailants. The thieves rose, but the wizard remained on the floor, his body deadly still.

"Bring me the sword and the sheath," ordered Jun. He took the weapon and its scabbard gingerly, as if the magicks it held might turn against him. He shook his head. "It is difficult to see how this works against demons, but it must. I saw that lying, backstabbing mage's face."

Jun's gaze lifted from the spell-bound blade and stared over the faces of his men. "With this we insure our future in Bistonia! If Aerisan thought to turn it against the High King, think how Yannis will reward me for delivering it into his hands!"

"No more will my loyal subjects be your puppets, mage!" Jun rose and walked to Aerisan's crumpled form. His right foot slashed, viciously kicking the wizard's side. "No more! No more will the Emperor of Bistonia and his men jump at your smallest command. The ruler of the sewers will show all that he is fit to rule all Bistonia, below *and* on the streets."

Jun slammed the sword back into its scabbard and turned.

Lijena gasped. Aerisan rose from the floor like a bloody apparition. His hands shot out, seized the sword, and wrenched it from a horrified Jun. In the blinking of an eye the sorcerer staggered toward the door leading into the sewers.

Jun's terror fled. "Don't let him escape. Kill the whoreson!"

Simultaneously the master thief pulled out a jewel encrusted dagger from his belt and sent it cartwheeling through the air after the mage. Aerisan gasped as the blade bit deep in his left shoulder. The Sword of Kwerin clattered to the chamber floor, but Aerisan slipped through the door and disappeared.

The rush of thieves blocked Lijena's view. She heard the scurry of booted feet outside the chamber. None knew the sewers under Bistonia better than Jun's legion of thieves, but they sought no ordinary man. They hunted a mage who had ample time to send his accursed demons after them.

Jun hefted the fallen sword, then hung it from his belt.

"Your aspirations exceed your grasp." Lijena spat her disdain when the Emperor of Thieves once more turned to her. "Velden contented himself with ruling the thieves of Bistonia. You might do well to follow his lead."

"That was Velden's failing. He limited his ambition. He never thought beyond petty filching."

"Aerisan was not the only one trying to kill you." Lijena goaded him. While only two guards and Jun remained in the throne room, she had to make a move. She had to create an opening through which to spring.

"I know. His swift response in the market told me much. But I think most of your group—it was your cabal?—died within the vortex of his magicks. I will miss that. I enjoyed having him remove my enemies in such dramatic ways."

Jun paraded before her like a motley peacock. His soiled uniform sported as many unearned medals as when she'd known him as captain of Velden's guard. But now authority accompanied his every movement. He had learned to command—that made him doubly dangerous!

"Aerisan made one fatal mistake. He never should have allowed me to return to the wellspring of my power. My thieves had fallen into sorry disarray. None rose to replace me once I sat on Bistonia's throne. But once I returned, ha!" Jun snapped his fingers.

Lijena listened with but one ear. Her attention focused on the guards to either side of her. She needed something to divert their gaze long enough for her to leap atop the Emperor of Thieves and free him of sword or knife.

"Emperor!" shouted a tall, scrawny man who staggered into the chamber. He stood swaying from side to side. Pools of dripping slime gathered at his feet.

"Did you kill him, Scrounge?" Jun turned to face the man "Did you?"

"Emperor, we lost him. He did something. A spell." Fear trembled in the man's words. "It confused us. When we got back on his track, a windstorm kicked up."

"Wind? In a sewer?"

"Magic it was, Emperor, magic. Had to be. He got away. We think he got aground near the palace. We got men out on the streets huntin' him down this very instant."

Anger clouded Jun's features. "He won't elude me. I'll feed him to the sewer rats!"

"You'll get'em, Emperor. You will." Scrounge's answer lacked even mock confidence.

"Yes! Yes, I will have the bastard! In time." Jun pivoted, glaring at Lijena. "But for the moment, at least I have this bitch! Take her to a cell. Take her to *the* cell. The same one we held her in before. But don't torture her—yet. I will attend to that myself."

Jun walked to Lijena and traced a broken, dirty fingernail along the line of her jaw. "Perhaps before that, I will again have my pleasure with you."

Memories of that cell, of the things Jun had forced her to do to sate his lusts flooded Lijena's mind. In desperation, she lunged at the Emperor of Thieves. The effort was wasted. The guards' hands held her like steel bands.

"Take her away," Jun waved to the two men.

Jun's echoing laughter drowned Lijena's curses as the guards dragged her from the throne chamber.

chapter 19

IRON MANACLES CUT vicious, bloody, raw bands into the flesh of Lijena Farleigh's wrists. Alone in the darkness, she hung suspended, chained to the ceiling of a cramped cell whose features she knew as surely as they had been bathed in light.

It was here Velden had kept her prisoner under the watchful eye of his captain Jun. Then glowing moss had matted the ceiling, and a straw cot had been shoved against one wall. Now there was her, the blackness, and the damnable chains holding her strung in the air like some side of beef awaiting the butcher's blade. Only the tips of her booted feet brushed the floor beneath her.

To relieve the pain tearing at her wrists for a brief moment, she strained to balance on extended toes. It was a mistake! She gained just enough purchase on the slime-coated floor to set her body swinging to and fro like an awkward pendulum. Renewed waves of nerve-jangling agony washed through her, setting her brain reeling dizzily.

She prayed to Raemllyn's gods, pleading with them to bless her with the merciful oblivion of unconsciousness. The whispered prayers rose to deaf ears. Her mind and senses remained alert to the slightest throb of fiery pain coursing through muscle and nerve.

And there was pain! It began at the wrists to lance down her hyperextended arms to shoulders that separated at the joints with excruciating slowness. Nor did it stop there. Downward it flared through chest and ribs to her hips where it plunged like a white-hot brand into knotted thighs and calves.

She bit her lower lip to stifle the cry that tried to push from her throat until the warm saline taste of blood filled her mouth. Here she might dangle until the flesh rotted from her bones, but neither Jun nor his army of thieves would ever hear one moan pass over her tongue. She would not give her captors that satisfaction.

Or did she lie to herself?

Velden had broken her spirit in less than a week inside this cell. Could she last longer against Jun? Worse than death would be to find herself transformed into the weak, whimpering, fear-wrought woman she had been then. She would end her own life before she allowed the Emperor of Thieves to destroy her thusly.

She shuddered and winced as burning embers of pain flamed in her shoulders. From where did these doubts spring? She had boldly ventured into Jun's subterranean kingdom with a single-minded purpose—to drive cold steel through the swine's black heart. Now she considered the means by which she might quickly send herself into Black Qar's cold embrace.

Afraid that the slightest movement on her part might start her body swinging again, Lijena cautiously rolled her eyes from side to side. Whether Jun realized it or not, the blackness enveloping her was far more horrifying than the agony of his manacles. No light penetrated the cell's darkness; it equalled the jet that engulfed her when the creature in the sewer had caressed her flesh with leathery tentacles.

Things! The terror of the nightmare-spawned creatures that had dwelled in the blackness swelled and broke over her like a tidal wave. Did Aerisan's magicks linger? Were things lurking in the darkness around her—waiting?

No! She caught herself before she defiantly shook her head. Zarek Yannis' mage no longer served Bistonia's lord of thieves! This blackness was simply an absence of light. What did she, who had faced and killed two aspects of the Great Destroyer, have to fear of the dark?

Killed? She swallowed as a chill inched up her spine with naked realization of what she and Chal had faced. *Nay, not killed, but merely defeated. Death cannot be killed. How can life be sliced from what is already dead?*

Tears welled in her eyes. *Chal? What have I done to you?* Had her desire for revenge destroyed the gentle Elyshah? Or did he now walk the streets above thinking her dead, killed by the monstrous creature they had met in the sewers? *Father Yehseen, let him live . . . let him bask and drink in the strength of your light.*

The rattle of metal on metal clinked through the darkness.

In the next instant harsh brightness flooded the cell. Lijena blinked. Two guards stood silhouetted in the doorway to the small room.

"Ain't no way for her to get down from there," one of the men said to the other.

"Don't matter. Jun's orders is to check on her once an hour to make certain she's still here," the other replied.

"And we ain't to touch her?" the first asked. "Even to have a little fun?"

"Jun'll have your hands, man!" the second warned as he closed the cell door once again.

The muffled sound of their voices continued for a few seconds, then Lijena once more hung alone in the darkness. Her ears alert now, she heard scurry-scurry of tiny clawed feet to the left. *Sewer rats!*

For a grateful moment the sound faded. When it returned, it came from the right and left. As though testing the safety of the darkness, the scratch of claws inched toward her, then retreated with needless caution. If the rodents sought to dine on her flesh, how could she stop them?

The scurry of small paws moved toward her again. Lijena shuddered. Something—something *big!*—brushed the side of her boots.

A rat, just a rat. She tried to quell trembling repulsion. It didn't help. Her mind's eye saw what she had felt—a rat as big as an alley cat!

The click-a-click-squish of clawed feet on stone and slime whispered through the darkness. On all sides it came, creeping toward her.

Sweat prickled on Lijena's brow and trickled into her eyes. The cell swarmed with the filthy creatures. They sensed her helplessness and came pouring from the sewers through cracks and holes to feast.

"Yehseen, give me strength!" she prayed aloud.

Tiny claws tentatively reached up and raked at her boots. She heard them sniffing, trying to identify the scent of this unexpected bounty. She felt sharp, oversized incisors nibble at her boot heels.

Unable to contain her disgust, she kicked out!

The toe of her right boot slammed into a meaty, solid side. A rat screeched as it sailed through the air and thudded into the cell wall.

Its protests and the hasty retreat of its companions was lost in the cry that wrenched from Lijena's throat. That simple motion woke lancing agony within every joint of her body.

The metallic clack of a lock being slid from its niche cut into the darkness. The cell's door swung open to reveal a lone guard in the eye-burning light that cascaded into the room. The man stalked forward and stared at the prisoner dangling from the ceiling.

"What'cha sniveling 'bout?" His gaze rose to examine the manacles and chains.

"I would expect it's the odor that rises from your body, my good man." A disembodied voice floated within the cell.

Chal! Lijena's heart leaped.

"Huh?" The guard spun about. "What is this?"

"The lady gags on the stink you carry with you, my ill-mannered lout." Chal's voice sounded on the opposite side of the cell. "How many months have passed since last you made the acquaintance of soap and water?"

"By Nyuria's arse!" The guard pivoted again, freeing a sword from the sheath at his waist. His eyes went wide and round, then narrowed while he probed empty air with the blade.

"I think the lady has suffered your presence long enough, don't you?" The Elyshah spoke from the left now. "Why don't we release her? Your stench is far greater than any punishment Jun intended."

The guard jerked around and stabbed his sword into nothingness. "Magicks! That's what it is! The whoreson Aerisan is returned to taunt us."

"Nay. It's merely the voice of your conscience, my thick-headed, unwashed friend. Time has come to right all the wrong you have wrought. I think we should begin with these!" Chal's words floated until they stopped directly behind the guard.

A brass ring hung with two keys tucked under the guard's belt abruptly jumped free and floated in the air.

The guard swirled. His sword hissed as he hacked at the unseen hand that tauntingly dangled the keyring before him.

Lijena saw her chance and acted. Grasping the chains attached to the manacles with pain-numbed hands, she pulled herself up and lashed outward with both feet.

"Ahuuhgg!" The guard groaned when Lijena's heels slammed into the back of his head. Off balance, he stumbled forward. With a hollow thud the man's head collided with the wall in front of him. He moaned again as he toppled to the floor unconscious.

"Chal?" Lijena's eyes darted about the cell.

"Here, my love," Chal whispered tenderly into an ear.

"I thought you were dead!"

"Merely faded from sight, awaiting the opportunity to free you." Chal chuckled. "Neither Black Qar nor these thieves even suspected I was at your side."

An invisible arm eased about her waist, lifting her. She moaned as the pressure of biting iron eased from her raw wrists. The keyring floated in the air, unlocking her right hand and then left. She collapsed gratefully into the Elyshah's unseen arms

"At my side?" Lijena stood on quivering legs. "But I didn't *feel* you?"

"I couldn't allow you to. Mages are often sensitive to Elyshah." Chal's hands encircled her arms and lifted them. "Your wrists need salve and bandages."

Lijena jerked her hands away. "Later, I've still unfinished business here." She stepped to the unconscious guard and liberated his sword and dirk.

"Jun?" Sorrow enrobed Chal's single word.

"And the Sword of Kwerin Bloodhawk. The low-bred mongrel intends to deliver the blade into Zarek Yannis' hands." Lijena slipped to the open cell door and stared down the hall outside. No thief was to be seen or heard. "Come, we can get to the throne room from this corridor."

"Would it not be wise to seek help from those on the streets above?" Chal asked.

Lijena ignored the question and darted into the tunnel. By the time she found the way back to the surface, Jun would be on his way to Kavindra with the sword. She couldn't allow that. More than revenge guided her steps now.

"You need rest and balms," Chal said beside her. "And I need the sun."

She halted; she hadn't considered Chal. "Are you endangered by . . . by your present state?"

"I've been only one day from Father Yehseen's light," Chal replied. "Like a human, I can go a week without nourishment."

"Then we proceed." She started down the dim corridor again, sword held ready for attack.

There was no attack. Nor did she catch sight of man or woman. How strangely deserted the maze of tunnels was. When last she walked these halls thieves and slaves trod everywhere.

Reaching a junction of two tunnels, she paused again to

whisper, "The throne room lies to the right. See how many guards stand outside."

She heard a shuffling of invisible feet, then Chal's voice. "None. I see a curtained entrance, but no guard."

"No guard?" Lijena stepped into the corridor and stared in befuddlement. "Where are Jun's men?"

Chal offered no answer as they crept to the throne room's draped entrance. Voices came from the other side of the curtain. Cautiously Lijena edged the heavy cloth back enough to peer inside.

"Deserted me?" Jun shoved from his throne and stared at the thief Scrounge.

"Aye, Emperor." Fear trembled in Scrounge's reedy voice. "'Twas the sorcerer Aerisan. His voice roared within the sewers demanding allegiance to him. 'Serve me or greet your death,' he called. Wilit and twenty others charged him. In the next instant they were ripped asunder by one of the wizard's damnable whirlwinds! When the cyclone died, Aerisan was no where to be seen, but his voice remained, promising life and wealth for those who left the sewers and joined him on Bistonia's streets."

"Damn!" Jun collapsed back to his throne, his eyes lifting to the five men who stood before him. "How many remain loyal to me?"

"These and maybe thirty more," Scrounge replied.

"The son of a pox-ridden bitch! Aerisan thinks he's snatched my kingdom from under my feet. Let him gloat and believe he's won." Jun rose again. "Take those who still serve the Emperor of Thieves and go into the streets above, Scrounge. Let it be known to all citizens above that I place a ten thousand bist reward on the mage's head."

"Emperor?" Scrounge eyed the master of thieves. "You haven't such a princely sum."

"But I will—and more. And I shall share it with all who now stand with me." Jun held up the sheathed Sword of Kwerin Bloodhawk. "I ride to Kavindra. When I return, it will be with Zarek Yannis' armies. Bistonia will be ours, Scrounge, and Aerisan shall finally meet the god he worships!"

A broad grin split Scrounge's face. "Aye, my liege. Me and the others will go to the streets. Aerisan's head will be waiting for you when you return."

"Go then," Jun waved the men from the chamber, then stared at the sword and sheath in his hand. A humorless chuckle pushed from his throat. "To think a Farleigh placed such power in my hands!"

Lijena shoved the curtain aside and stepped into the throne chamber. "And a Farleigh has come to reclaim the sword, swine!"

"You! How?" Jun uttered two words of amazement, then questioned no further. He wrenched sword from scabbard and lunged.

Lijena danced aside, letting the thief's sword tip thrust into emptiness. Her own arm shot up. With her full body weight behind the naked steel, she thrust. There was a brief instant of resistance as tip met flesh and bone, then the sword drove home. Inward it sank, skewering the heart of Bistonia's Emperor of Thieves.

A death shudder quaked through the robed man. The Sword of Kwerin Bloodhawk fell from his shaking fingers as his gaze lifted to Lijena. Total incomprehension filled his dark eyes. His lips worked in silent denial. His body jerked spasmodically, wrenching the hilt of the stolen sword from Lijena's grasp as he crumpled to the ground.

Then it was over.

In the blinking of an eye, before she realized what she had done. She had killed Jun—erasing a name from that list etched into her brain. Hollowness consumed her.

"There should be more," she muttered unable to understand the emptiness. This was a moment of triumph, the victory she had ached to savor for months upon months. And she felt nothing. Jun was but a corpse whose bladder and bowels emptied as his black soul fled his body. "There should be more."

"More?" Chal's disembodied voice floated in the air. "There is no more. Only life and death."

"Life and death," she repeated, chilled by the bitter simplicity of those words. Only life and death.

"Let it rest, my love." Chal's hand squeezed her shoulder. "There is no more. Gather the sword and sheath, and let us return to the world above."

Numbly, Lijena scooped the Sword of Kwerin Bloodhawk from the floor and fastened it to her belt. She felt Chal beside her and groped with an arm until she found his hand. "You're right. It's time we returned to the land of light and living. We've been here far too long. This place stinks of death."

With the Elyshah's hand still clenched tightly in her own, Lijena left Jun sprawled on the floor before his throne and entered the maze of Bistonia's sewers. Two hours later, she halted at a junction of three feeder pipes.

"Is anything wrong?" Chal questioned.

"Nothing, if you don't mind spending the rest of our lives down here," she replied. "Chal, I'm lost!"

chapter 20

LIJENA AWOKE ALERT for sound. Only the gurgle of the sewer's sluggish flow met her ears. Denying herself a sigh of relief, she edged the Sword of Kwerin Bloodhawk from its sheath. No sparks or glow came from the ancient blade.

She pursed her lips, uncertain if she should be pleased with the sword's lack of life. Although the blade's inactivity assured her no spells threaded the area, she wished for the sword's fiery light to illuminate the ground about her.

Chal stirred beside her when she edged the blade back into its scabbard. He moaned softly, then the gentle rhythmic breathing of sleep returned.

Lijena closed her eyes and whispered a silent prayer that they would soon find a way from the subterranean maze. Without the rising and setting of the sun, she had no way to accurately gauge the passing of time, but she estimated they had been lost at least two days, maybe three. The long absence from the light was beginning to take its toll on Chal. His invisible body grew colder with each passing hour, and the emotion-words they shared were mere whispers in her mind.

Not that I'm any better, she admitted. Neither food nor water had filled her belly since they first ventured into the sewers. The lack of nourishment was gradually leeching away strength and reason.

Wearily leaning her head back against the slimy stone of the sewer's wall, she considered allowing Chal to rest while she ventured deeper into the tunnels. She immediately discarded the thought. They had to remain together; an invisible Elyshah would be impossible to find again.

We waste time. We should be walking. She opened her eyes and searched the darkness overhead. Except for a single dim star, there was nothing. *What did I expect? The moons' bright, silvery light?*

Reaching out, she nudged Chal's shoulder. The minstrel groaned a protest, shifted, and spoke. "I dreamed we were back in Tadzi's marvelous palace. Your uncle had spread a magnificent feast before us."

"Aye, and each time you glanced at Susonna there were loving stars in her sultry eyes." Lijena grunted, recalling her uncle's serving wench and the adoration for Chal that had been so obvious in the woman's lusty gaze.

Chal chuckled. "My love, the only stars I care to see again are those above, reflected in your eyes."

Stars! Lijena's mind spun. "Stars, Chal! The star! Look above, to the left!"

"Huh?" The Elyshah sat up. "Have you lost . . . By Great Father Yehseen, *a light!*"

Together they scrambled to their feet and with necks craned back moved directly beneath the pale gray spot. Neither spoke for several long minutes, but simply stared upward.

"Can it be a true star?"

Lijena felt Chal move beside her, then he answered his own question. "Nay, but there are iron rungs inset in the wall. A ladder, my love, we've found a ladder that leads upward!"

Without reply, Lijena groped in the darkness and found the rungs. Slime-coated they were, but neither time nor the sewer's ever-present moisture had corroded their strength. She climbed toward the dim star with Chal just behind her.

"An old grating covered with moss and weeds," she announced when she reached the light's source. She pushed at the criss-crossed pattern of iron overhead with a hand; it refused to budge. "Let me get my shoulders under it."

Lijena wedged beneath the grating so that the top of her back pressed firmly against the iron, and she strained upward. Rusted metal creaked in stubborn protest, then broke free; the grate pushed into the air.

Bright sunlight flooded the darkness, momentarily blinding Lijena. She blinked and squinted until her blurred vision focused on an empty street she did not recognize. "Hurry, Chal. There's no one about."

She shoved back the grating and scrambled onto the street. Signs of relief softly came from the still invisible Elyshah as he climbed into the open air.

"How long until you regain your form?" she asked while she replaced the grating.

"An hour, a day?" Chal replied. "I know not. I've never been so long from the sun."

"We'll find some food, then return . . ."

The words hung in the air. Five mounted lancers wearing the uniforms of city guardsmen turned a corner to the right. Their long, steel-tipped spears dropped instantly, and they urged their horses forward. Lijena wrenched her sword free to face the five soldiers in a wide-legged stance.

The riders encircled her, their wicked lances ready for the kill.

"Do we run her through or take her to the Count, Gareit?" one of the riders questioned a companion.

"If it was my choice, I say be done with the wench. I've no liking for dealing with thieves," Gareit answered, his voice like gravel. "But she may be with Scrounge's crew. Only one way to be certain."

Gareit leaned forward and prodded Lijena with the point of his lance. "Start walkin', wench."

Uncertain what was happening, Lijena did as the lance commanded and started walking toward the heart of the city. Beside her, she felt nothing—Chal was gone!

"Aye, she's the one that done it." Scrounge eyed Lijena. "Don't know how, but she escaped the cell and done Jun in. Sword right through his heart."

"It doesn't change anything," This from Pen, whose head turned to Count luBonfil. "Kill her, then take the sword and sheath. If it's what Scrounge claims, it'll serve any man's hand as well. I'll carry it, if ye want!"

"Be not hasty, my friend. If this sword is the legendary blade—and I say *if*—little is known of its powers. She might be the only one who can control its forces." Count luBonfil's voice flowed like oil while he leaned back in his chair and steepled fingers over his chest. "Besides, she did rid us of Jun, and we have need of all the allies we can muster in this time of peril."

Time of peril? Lijena blinked. What did the Count mean? And why had she been brought to this old cobbler's shop? Why did the city guard obey the Count's command? And where did Jun's captain of the guard fit into the picture?

"What say you, Scrounge?" luBonfil glanced at the scrawny thief.

"I've no feud with her," Scrounge answered. "Did me a

favor, she did. Saved me from having to remove Jun one day myself. As Bistonia's new Emperor of Thieves, I'd rather she sided with me than against me. This one's single-handedly killed the last two who ruled in the sewers. If she'll fight against Aerisan, then I welcome her."

"Bah!" Pen spat. "What care you of thieves, luBonfil?"

"Scrounge has been an invaluable source of information, friend Pen. Without his eyes, we'd have been blind to Jun's and Aerisan's activities." luBonfil shook his head. "Even now his men spy for us in battle."

"Battle?" Lijena could no longer hold her peace. "What battle?"

Prince Felrad's emissary looked up. "I forget you've been lost below for these past three days. All of Bistonia is at war. Aerisan has claimed the throne and commands Jun's army of thieves."

"And a full half of the city guards have thrown in with the magician," Scrounge added. "Worse than thieves they are."

"Bistonia's citizens could endure no more," luBonfil said while he straightened in his chair. "They have taken up arms and risen in revolt."

Lijena's mind rushed. *Revolt!* The reason for this strange bond between noble and thief was clear now.

". . . Aerisan and his forces hold the central portion of the city," the Count continued. "Our men contain them, but barely. Aerisan has more than sword and spear in his command."

"Black Qar," Lijena said with a nod. "He can summon the Death God—or at least aspects of the Great Destroyer."

"So Scrounge has informed me," luBonfil replied. "And you supposedly defeated these aspects in the sewers. Or at least, the sword did. Is the blade truly the Sword of Kwerin Bloodhawk?"

Lijena hesitated. Did she dare confirm the blade's identity to these men? "Aerisan claimed so. The steel does have power when magicks are engaged."

"Mmmmm," the Count mused aloud. "Would you wield the blade against Aerisan?"

"He killed my father," Lijena said. "I would give my life to see the mage dead."

"That well may be the price you pay, if Aerisan does summon Qar to do his bidding . . ."

"You ain't seriously thinking of letting her keep the sword are you?" Pen pushed from his chair. "Kill the bitch and be done with it. Take the sword yourself and drive it into Aerisan's heart!"

"Would that I could," luBonfil said. "But both you and I now command Bistonia's forces. Neither of us can risk our lives heedlessly. She, however, is expendable. And she has some understanding of the blade's powers. If she will serve us, then we must accept that service."

Lijena detected more than a general's weight of command in the Count's voice, but said nothing. "I will serve."

"Then you shall be given the chance," luBonfil said. "Is there anything, other than the blade, you require?

"Food, water to cleanse myself, fresh clothing, and a few hours sleep," Lijena replied.

"Food, water, and clothing are yours." The Count waved a guardsman to fetch the items. "However, sleep will have to wait until after you've faced Aerisan."

"Agreed," Lijena nodded. "Is there a place I can bathe and discard these filthy clothes?"

"Of course. There are rooms upstairs." luBonfil pointed to a wooden stairway on the right. "I'll have the sergeant bring up the food and clothing."

A rap came at the door as Lijena strapped the Sword of Kwerin Bloodhawk about her waist.

"Aye," she called out. "Enter."

The door swung inward, and Scrounge stepped over the threshold. "The guards have a man below who claims to be a friend."

"A friend?" Lijena questioned. "His name?"

"Chal son of Chalt. A minstrel and poet by profession, he says." Scrounge shrugged. "Do you want to see him?"

"Yes!" Lijena's heart raced. "Send him up."

The thief left, and seconds later a fully visible Chal, hemmed between Scrounge and a city guard, was escorted into the small room. The guard left when Scrounge nodded, but the thief remained. Lijena contained the desire to rush forward and throw her arms about the Elyshah's neck and smother his face in kisses.

"I saw the soldiers take you earlier and thought you might have need of me," Chal said aloud, while his emotion-words flowed, *I barely managed to prevent myself from being trampled to death by the guards' horses. I followed to see where they took you, and then I hid until I regained solidity.*

"Chal, I thought . . ." Lijena's thoughts stumbled. The Elyshah had no reason to be here. She and not he must face Aerisan and the dark deity he served. ". . . I thought I told you I never wanted to see you again!"

"Lijena?" Chal stared at her. *What are you doing?*

What is best, my love. Today I must walk alone. When I return, our paths will be as one, forever. But today, I must face the wizard alone. Lijena turned to the thief. "Scrounge, this man is a harmless rogue who seeks to woo me. I haven't time to be bothered with him. Throw him out, please."

Lijena? What do you intend?

Lijena closed her mind to Chal's tumultuous emotions.

"Certain you wouldn't rather be done with him for good?" Scrounge touched the dirk on his belt.

"No," Lijena answered. "He's amusing enough at times. However, this isn't one of those times."

Scrounge signalled to a guard, who dragged Chal away kicking and cursing. The thief chuckled. "Never had much need for the likes of him. Although minstrels often draw crowds, which is nice for pickpockets."

Lijena closed her eyes to hide the tears that welled there. Chal's vehement protests eventually faded. One day he would understand her actions—if she lived to share another day with the Elyshah.

Drawing a deep breath, she looked at the thief. "Scrounge, I need your help."

The lanky thief's eyes widened, but he listened quietly as she outlined a plan for her assault on Aerisan's keep.

Scrounge halted and held his torch high, illuminating a shaft that opened in the ceiling of the sewer. Lijena's gaze traced along a ladder into the darkness.

"This is as close as I can get you to the accursed tower," the thief said. "Remember, this opens in front of the Temple of Yehseen. It's a full block to the tower, and you ain't got nothing but the night to hide you."

"I know," Lijena said. "I'll wait here an hour to give you time to return to luBonfil and tell him to signal the attack."

"Aye," Scrounge said then hesitantly added, "If I was in your boots, I wouldn't place much weight in the Count's promises. You might have to make it to the tower without an attack to divert Aerisan's men."

Lijena nodded, surprised by the thief's warning. The same

thought had crossed her mind more than once. After all, luBonfil had openly admitted she was expendable. "I'll heed your words. I would suggest you do the same."

Scrounge chuckled. "Aye, I've my eye on the Count and ol' Pen. They think to use Scrounge then slit his throat when he's served his purpose. But a man doesn't become Emperor of Thieves without a brain. Now that I've got the throne, I intend to keep it, I do."

He paused and looked at Lijena as though he wanted to say more, but only shook his head. "I gotta be going now. May Jajhana smile and grant you good fortune."

"And you, friend Scrounge," Lijena said, watching the man retreat into the sewer's darkness before she turned and grasped the first rung of the ladder.

Metal grated on stone overhead.

Lijena's right hand grasped the hilt of her sword and freed it from its sheath. Above the sewer grating slid open. Stars in the heavens beamed down, then were partially hidden by a man's head. "It's clear. Hurry, before one of Aerisan's men happens along!"

"Chal?" Lijena couldn't believe her ears. "How?" But she knew the answer to her question. She had forgotten about the Elyshah's ability to will his body from one place to another in the blink of an eye.

"Hows are of little concern now," the Elyshah answered. "Enough to say that I had no desire to let you commit suicide alone. Now, please hurry. Aerisan's men are all over the place, and the way won't stay clear for long."

Offering no complaints, Lijena resheathed her blade and climbed to the street. Together Chal and she replaced the grating, then darted to the pillared entrance of the Temple of Yehseen and huddled in the shadows. Lijena's gaze shifted to the end of the street where the black Temple of Qar loomed a thousand feet in the air. No window opened on that dreaded structure. The only entrance was a single doorway at its base.

"Chal," she whispered, "there is no need for you here. I must do this alone."

"And there was no need of me in the sewers, fairest one," the Elyshah answered. "Methinks the Lady Farleigh would still be dangling from her lovely wrists were it not for a certain minstrel-poet."

"Chal, please listen to me." Lijena made no attempt to hide her frustration.

"I always *listen* to you," Chal answered while he scanned the night around them. "Which isn't to say I always do as you wish. Lijena, I've said this before, our philosophies differ. Mine dwells within this temple we stand before, and yours lies somewhere between Yehseen's holy house and that obscene spire at the end of the Avenue of Temples. Differing views of the universe does not make me a spring flower to be protected and sheltered. I am a *man*. If the woman I love faces danger, I will be at her side."

"And I love a fool who hasn't the sense to arm himself with a blade." Lijena shivered, apprehensive of what awaited them in the tower.

"Do we wait for the others to attack Aerisan's forces?" Chal asked.

Lijena shook her head. "I fear that if we did, Black Qar would have time to swallow the whole city. Count luBonfil *will* order his men against the mage's army, but only after he ascertains my . . . our success."

"A cautious general, the Count." Chal sucked at his teeth in disgust. "Shall we pay this Aerisan a visit?"

"On feet as quiet as the breeze," Lijena answered, slipping from the shadows and darting to the side of a temple erected to Ediena, the Goddess of Love and Pleasure.

Whispering a prayer beseeching the deity to watch over the Elyshah, Lijena waved Chal after her. Thusly they worked from temple to temple, shadow to shadow, until their goal lay but two hundred strides across a plaza set in flat, gray slate.

"Where are the guards?" Chal whispered, his pupilless eyes searching the night. "When I arrived men moved everywhere."

Lijena offered no answer. Her attention focused on the looming pillar of blackness ahead of them. Five hundred strides in diameter at the base, the tower's design was meant to oppress and dwarf those who viewed it. It did.

Lijena blinked time and again as her gaze lifted. The surface of the black stone lacked definition. She detected no trace of joint or mortar. It was as though the temple had been carved from one solid mountain of jet marble. Yet, she knew Jun's workers had used a myriad great marble blocks in its construction. Mortal hands might have built the lofty spire, but forces greater than Man now bound it.

"There's not even a guard by the entrance," Chal said.

Lijena glanced at the single doorway set atop thirteen black steps. Surely Aerisan wasn't foolhardy enough to believe the tower impenetrable. Or was it that he had no need of *human* guards?

"Listen!" Chal's head cocked to the side, then he turned. "War cries?"

Lijena followed his gaze to the west. The din of battle rose clearly. Above the tops of the surrounding buildings and temples she saw the streaking flight of flaming arrows. A shifting glow of reddish-orange reflected from low-hanging clouds. Bistonia's rebels fired Aerisan's barricades.

"It seems we've misjudged Count luBonfil. He attacks!" Lijena's head jerked back to Qar's temple. "Now is the time for us to do the same, while the wizard's attention is with his forces!"

Steel hissed as the blond swordswoman freed her blade. Sparks of green witchfire danced along the cutting edge.

"Aerisan weaves his spells!" she said. "We must strike before he can summon Qar to aid his army!"

A blur of motion to the right leaped from thc shadows straight for Chal. Lijena reacted without thought. "Chal, duck!"

The Elyshah dropped flat to the ground. Lijena's sword flew out in a sweeping arc. The clash of steel meeting steel rang through the night, echoing down the vacant Avenue of Temples. Bone-jarring vibrations ran through the Sword of Kwerin Bloodhawk and up Lijena's arm to set her shoulder throbbing.

Gritting teeth to bite back the pain, she danced around Chal's prone form and faced a scruffy, bearded thief with a large golden ring piercing his left ear lobe. Without word or curse, the man raked his blade upward in a slash meant to lay open the young woman's stomach.

Lijena answered with a circular parry that redirected the sword's tip up and out. Her defensive motion ended with an offensive slash. The honed edge of her blade traced across the attacker's throat, opening vein and artery. Blood, black in the moonlight, sprayed in a horrible fountain as the man fell.

And in Lijena's hand the Sword of the Bloodhawk sizzled from guard to tip.

"Magicks!"

"Black Qar drinks your victim's soul." Chal pushed to his feet, his gaze shifted between dead thief and blade. "I *feel* the Death God's presence. Each death increases Aerisan's power."

The Elyshah turned and stared at the distant glow of battle that raged behind them. "Father Yehseen! Can't you sense the obscenity? There's more than mere spells at work this night.

Aerisan transforms himself! The wizard seeks to become one of Black Qar's many aspects!"

"What?" For the first time since their meeting, Lijena felt fear—raw, unashamed fear—radiating from the Elyshah.

"Death feeds on death!" Chal stared at the woman he loved and saw incomprehension on her face. "You, the Count, Pen, Scrounge all play right into the magician's hands. He uses you. War in Bistonia's streets is what he sought from the beginning. Rebel or thief—it doesn't matter! Each man who falls strengthens the mage! By the morrow's dawn Aerisan will be one with his god. He will be Qar come to walk earth in human form. Not even Zarek Yannis with his army of Faceless Ones will be able to stand before him!"

"Then it's long overtime we sent Aerisan's soul to Peyneeha!" Lijena pivoted and strode toward the thirteen stairs that led to the dark tower's solitary entrance.

"Death cannot defeat death. Man can only kill man, never a god!" Chal pleaded as he ran to her side. "Can't you see that? Yehseen is the answer. Yehseen who is *life* and life renewed has always been the answer, the only answer!"

"I see only the fiery glow of this sword! Magicks to combat magicks!"

The Sword of Kwerin Bloodhawk blazed white hot as she ran to the open temple door and paused at the threshold. She halted, scanning the interior of the tower's lowest level. Walls and floor of polished obsidian cast back reflections of a lone woman and a weaponless Elyshah. The chamber was barren except for another thirteen stairs at the opposite side of the circular room. These stairs spiralled up through the floor, leading to a featureless ebony door with a shining golden knob at its center.

Lijena stepped inside. If she held any doubts as to which of Raemllyn's gods dwelled within, they evaporated in that single step. This was the house of Death. Its stench filled her nostrils. A sense of eternal nothingness enveloped her. An empty cold beyond human concept caressed her cheeks.

She took another step. Fear coursed through her veins. No man would she face, but Death itself—and her own death! Her heart tripled its pounding; her temples throbbed, reverberating like the sound of colliding boulders.

And there was fear!

Terror gnawed within her breast, threatening to transform her into a weeping senseless child.

"Trust in Father Yehseen." Chal's fingertips brushed the back of her left hand as he stepped past her.

A warm relief suffused Lijena, and the fear dissipated. While the smell of death still clung to her, thoughts cleared and reason returned.

"Aerisan uses our own fear of death against us. Place your trust in life. Only that can save us." Chal halted and looked back at Bistonia's fair daughter. "The wall . . . the floor . . . are like mirrors that cast our souls' reflections back upon us!"

He held out a hand, waiting until Lijena grasped it. Then together they walked toward the curving stairs. An elusive smile danced on Chal's lips.

Again Lijena surveyed the chamber's interior. No altar, no braziers, no icons to the Death God decorated the walls. Nor were there mystical symbols carved into the stone. She saw only blackness, a mirrored darkness that drew light from some unknown source and threw their reflections back upon them from all angles.

Where are the guards? She frowned and tightened her grasp on the blazing sword's hilt. Was Aerisan so confident of his might that he placed neither natural or supernatural sentinels within this unholy structure?

"The floor!" Chal gasped.

No reflected image was this! Like a fog, a gray mist seeped in curled fingers from the seamless obsidian floor. Lijena shivered. A cloak of numbing coldness draped about her shoulders. "Poison!"

"Qar's breath!" Chal warned. "Breathe not! We must get above it!"

Chal tugged at her, but Lijena stood paralyzed. A thick tendril of the purest black formed in the air above the Elyshah's head. It coiled downward as though to loop about Chal's throat.

She had seen such *things* but once before—in Bistonia's sewers. This was not death, but a small aspect of the Great Destroyer—yet as deadly as Qar's full embrace. Lijena hefted the Sword of Kwerin Bloodhawk and struck.

Blue-white sparks exploded in an actinic glare when the blade touched the dark tendril and severed it. A shriek of agony echoed throughout the temple, dying a muffled death as the thick tentacle dissipated.

Cheeks turning red as he held his breath, Chal renewed his tugging. Still Lijena did not move. Another of Qar's aspects materialized in the mist—a pair of monstrous pincers clacking together noisily, their serrated edges seeking her throat.

She ducked and made a sweeping cut. The blade flared as it struck armored chitin. Excited, high-pitched squeals rent the tower's interior, melting into the agitated click of those great claws while the aspect retreated. In the space of a heartbeat the pincers launched themselves at the swordswoman.

Lijena backstepped.

More than disembodied claws sought her. From the mist lunged a demon-spawned creature that had never dwelled in Raemllyn's realms!

It stood on four legs—fore of some great cat and haunches those of a horse. Like a centaur, its torso was that of a human—a female with dried, sagging paps. And human arms ended in the snapping claws that raked at her face. However, it was an insect's head that sat atop human shoulders.

In those two blue-black, bulbous, multifaceted eyes, Lijena saw a thousand fractured images of herself fall as the leather soles of her boots lost purchase on the glass-slick floor. Biting down tightly and clamping her lips together to contain her breath, she tumbled to her back.

Above the sprawled blonde, Qar's hideous aspect of mismatched creatures reared.

Gripping the hilt of the Sword of Kwerin Bloodhawk in both hands, Lijena thrust upward. The white-hot tip of the spell-bound blade drove inward, burying half the length of steel in human stomach. Flames like the erupted heart of an exploding star burst from the seams of magicks torn asunder.

And were swallowed in a tide of blackness that cascaded downward in a swirling torrent.

Claws, tiny claws, like the paws of a horde of swarming rats, tore at Lijena's clothing, legs, hands, face. Back and forth in frenzied panic, she sliced the blade she clutched. Still the unseen claws ripped at her flesh.

Hands—the tender touch of Elyshah hands—penetrated the madness. Calm, a peacefulness that held the warm caress of a summer morning, bathed her. Those hands locked under her armpits and tugged. The swarming blackness gave way to misted light and Chal's worried face hovering above her.

"The stairs! On your feet and run for the stairs." His voice came strained and weak. He spoke without breathing. "Hurry!"

Closing her eyes to an inky cloud that formed at the ceiling, Lijena shoved to her feet and ran after the Elyshah. Two at a time they took the stairs, until they stood above the gray mist that floated like a murky lake over the chamber's floor.

Unable to hold his breath longer, Chal sucked in lungfuls of air. He stood, waiting expectantly, then when nothing happened, nodded. "The air is as fresh as one can expect in such a place."

Lijena's breath burst from her lungs, and she gulped down cold air. "I killed it, Chal. I *killed* it. Yet, it still came!"

"There is no way to bring death to Death. The sword's magic merely hindered Qar's aspect. You rent its form, no more," the Elyshah said. "Look to your blade."

No fire, spark, or glow flowed from the steel. The magic locked within that ancient blade was no more, drained by the encounter with the Dark One.

Lijena's gaze lifted to Chal. "It's still tempered steel capable of killing a man!"

Clutching the lifeless sword in her right hand, she ascended the last three steps to a black onyx-rimmed doorway above. She reached out and twisted the golden knob at its center.

"That is, if Aerisan remains a mortal man," Chal said when the door opened.

chapter 21

LIJENA DREW A steadying breath to quell the pounding of her runaway heart and prepared to shove the portal wide and stride through.

Chal touched her shoulder. "Caution."

She nodded and used the tip of her blade to edge the door inward. Light flooded into the chamber of mirror-polished obsidian. Lijena blinked in an attempt to adjust to the eye-blinding glare. Thousands upon thousands of candles burned in the room beyond the door.

In the next instant nausea violently churned her stomach. The inescapable stench of burning human flesh assailed her nostrils. Like an invisible hand the stink thrust out from the tower's second level. Lijena staggered back, head spinning dizzily.

Chal's arms circled her waist in support. His voice was taut as he struggled to overcome the gagging odor. "The candles . . . human tallow . . . Aerisan . . . makes full . . . full use of . . . his victims."

Lijena shuddered. The image of human bodies—men, women, and children sacrificed to Death—rendered for their fat brought bitter bile up from her quivering stomach. What other unholy obscenities did Aerisan perform in the name of his Dark God?

"Can you continue?" Chal edged around her on the stairs and studied her face.

She nodded and stood straight. Her own gaze probed the Elyshah's features, detecting a determination she had never seen before. It was as though he intended to continue on his own were she not capable of crossing the threshold into the next of the tower's levels.

"I'll be all right," she reassured him, wishing desperately

for the chance to draw a fresh, clean breath of pure air. "Aerisan is mine."

Chal offered no comment when she used an arm to nudge him to one side and once more stepped to the open door. Eyes accustomed to the harsh glare of candles, she surveyed the interior of the room and realized to what extent the mage used his victims' bodies. Each of the burning candles sat atop a human skull or rested in the palm of a skeletal hand inset in black marble walls as though they had grown from the rock.

"The bastard must die for this," she said through clenched teeth while she lifted her sword and probed the doorway for concealed deathtraps. "No man capable of such horrors has the right to breathe another breath."

"Steel can kill a man, but it's Black Qar we face," Chal warned when he followed her over the threshold. "Only the strength of Yehseen may divert the Black One."

Lijena didn't hear the Elyshah's words. Her attention centered on the chamber they entered. Although chamber did not correctly describe the heart of the tower in which she stood. A narrow stone stairway spiralled up the curving wall and disappeared into a ceiling that loomed hundreds of feet overhead. Other than the multitude of flaming candles and their grisly holders that covered the wall from floor to distant ceiling, the wall was as bare of mystical ornamentation as the entry chamber to the temple.

"Aerisan awaits us there." Chal's neck craned back to stare into the tower's heights. "There at the pinnacle of this accursed house we shall find him. Come, we tarry here over long. The wizard spins spells that destroy the rebel forces."

Cautiously moving to the staircase, Lijena began to climb. Neither mist nor darkness-born demon rose to confront her ascent. Step after step she moved around the candle-lit walls and up the spiralling path of stone.

And with each step felt a portion of her strength leech away. By the hundredth, she could no longer hold the Sword of Kwerin Bloodhawk before her. Muscles cramped and aching, her right arm hung limply at her side, the blade's tip dragging the stone.

"Sheath the sword," Chal said, calling for a moment's rest. "There is no need for it here. The steps are bound by spells designed to leave us as weak as babes in arms. Aerisan has little need of demons. No man can mount to the top of the tower."

"Neither of us is a man." Lijena did as he suggested, glad to let her hip carry the burden her hand and arm could no longer bear. She glanced at the Elyshah. The strain on his face mirrored the bone-weariness that consumed her.

"That is true." A weak smile slid across Chal's lips. "Lead on."

She did, trudging upward. Another hundred steps, and then another and another, she forced leadened feet to shuffle from one step to the next. Time and again, she or Chal signalled a halt to allow a moment of rest—a rest that did not bring renewed strength, only prolonged the agony of the towering climb to yet another ebon door with a gold knob at its center.

"He senses us not," Chal whispered as they stood facing the final obstacle separating them from the mage of Death. "His attention remains with his army of thieves and treacherous city guards. There is no better time to confront his power."

Lijena's right hand dropped to the hilt of her sword. Heat filled her palm! A humorous smile lifted her lips. The sheath once more renewed the blade's energies. Hope beating new life in her breast, she eased the Bloodhawk's sword from its scabbard. It felt feather light in her grasp—as though the blade sensed its wielder's weakness and compensated for her lack of strength.

"It glows again!" Chal blinked. "Not white light, but the green of witchfires."

Lijena shrugged away the dimness of the sword's mystic aura. "That it lives is enough." She reached out and twisted the knob, then thrust the door open.

No creature of void or substance attacked. Aerisan sat on a low stool in front of a basalt altar with his back to the doorway. He neither turned nor stirred. In a low, muffled, unwavering voice, the magician chanted. Three black candles burned atop the altar, their smoke twisting into grotesque figures as it rose and mingled.

Lijena saw faces in the oily cloud of smoke, faces leering at her.

Not smoke! Realization penetrated. The dark cloud was alive! Like a shroud, it enveloped the seated mage. His blue robes transformed to jet.

"He takes on Qar's mantle! He becomes one with his god!" Terror cracked Chal's voice.

"He goes to Peyneeha!" Intent on delivering the mage's

death before the metamorphosis was complete, Lijena pushed into the room.

And ducked!

Two blades of crystalline fire sizzled through the air above her head!

Faceless Ones! Two of the black-robed hell-riders leaped from each side of the doorway and faced her as she swirled about, the green-glowing Sword of Kwerin Bloodhawk poised to meet attack.

An attack that came from the Faceless on her left. Skeletal talons about sword hilt, the blazing-orbed demon hefted its blade like a club and swung.

Lijena easily met the blow. Lightning flashed and thunder reverberated through the tower when the two magic-tempered swords clashed. The angry hiss of a venomous cobra spit from the Faceless One's unseen lips.

In the next instant, Lijena danced to the side, barely avoiding the flaming blade swung by the creature to her right. Her first attacker wasn't as spry. The second Faceless' blade sliced into its companion's chest.

Ignoring the scream of hellish fury that echoed within the chamber and sizzling black steam that fumed from the cloak of the first demon, the blond daughter of Bistonia struck. Lunging, she drove the honed tip of the Bloodhawk's sword into the exposed side of the second cowled creature. Like steel sinking into curd, the blade plunged all the way to the hilt before she wrenched it free.

Together, their visible forms evaporating in a swirling steam, the Faceless Ones collapsed to the floor. In the blink of an eye only two dark robes remained to give testimony that the unearthly creatures had ever existed.

Lijena pondered not where the two hell-spawn had vanished. Her gaze hung on the Sword of Kwerin Bloodhawk. Neither glow nor sparking witchfire danced along the blade's double edge. For the second time since entering the temple, Aerisan's unholy guards had leeched away the sword's powers!

Magicks or not, it did not matter. She staggered around. Silent prayers to Jajhana, Goddess of Luck and Chance, moved over her lips. Five quick strides would bring her within striking distance. One well-swung blow and Aerisan's head would leap from his shoulders, ending the threat he—and his god—posed.

"Stop!" Mountains ground against one another in that command.

Lijena froze, sword lofted over her left shoulder ready for the killing blow. Her brain screamed out; neither arms nor legs responded. She stood like a stone statue in the grip of an icy fist.

"The sword is truly all it is said to be." Aerisan stood and slowly turned. "Although ere the new day dawns, I will have no need of such trinkets."

The dark mist about the mage grew until it appeared to be a swarm of flies hovering around him. He lifted a finger and pointed. From that fingertip a black, threadlike trendril wove through the air toward Lijena. "I become a god, and you shall be the first to feel my sweet caress."

"God? You're nothing more than a butcher! Not even the Great Destroyer will accept such offal!" Lijena struggled to break the unseen bonds that held her.

"So said your father." Aerisan laughed. "Did you speak to him when you entered? His was the first skull I set in the wall, there at the bottom of the steps."

"Whoreson!" Lijena spat while her eyes watched the dark thread weave closer.

"Nay!" Aerisan's laughter rolled. "Yet, your words plant a seed. Not by a simple garrote shall I kill you. No, in your last moments, you shall know a final lover—Death!"

The black cloak enshrouding the wizard shifted. A formless mass, it flowed to the end of the tendril to gradually transform into a blue-black giant with the head of a great horned bull. The demon's member stood engorged and erect.

"Your lover!" Aerisan's voice rose two octaves. His eyes flamed with insane delight. "Smell his lust! Feel his strength!"

From the corner of an eye, Lijena saw Chal step beside her. With hands on hips, the Elyshah stood in a defiant stance and faced the magician.

"This one is not for Black Qar," the Elyshah boldly challenged. "She belongs to Yehseen—to life!"

Aerisan's cold gaze moved to the minstrel-poet. His eyebrows lifted in surprise. "You walk! How?"

"Those of light are not bound by the dark," Chal answered. Hate radiated from the Elyshah. "Stare upon the face of he who will end your reign of terror. Gaze upon the features of Chal son of Chalt."

Aerisan's face twisted in disbelief. He muttered, "Elyshah?"

"Aye." Chal nodded. "An Elyshah, born of the Great Father himself—Yehseen who holds the scales of balance. Yehseen who can destroy the offspring he sired!"

"Destroy Death itself?" Aerisan's laugh was that of a madman. "Fool! Test the power of Qar against your impotent Yehseen."

The black mantle covering the mage surged from him and flowed to the bull-headed creature standing before Lijena. The monstrous giant dissolved in a churning cloud of black and in its stead rose a black kraken with twelve writhing arms. The creature slithered across the floor. Its leathery arms whipped out, wrapping about Chal.

"Strength, Yehseen! Give her strength to face the *man!*" If there were more, the Elyshah's words drowned when the demon slid forward and engulfed Chal.

"Bastard!" Lijena railed, tears welling in her eyes, her fists tightening about the hilt of her sword. "You . . ."

Chal's words, the movement of her hands, and Aerisan's blue robes penetrated her mind in the same instant! Chal had revealed his true nature and challenged the mage not to kill, but to divert the wizard's attention, to focus Aerisan's power on himself.

A ruse that worked! Qar's mantle was completely gone from the wizard. He stood as a man once again—a man of vulnerable flesh and bone! And his full powers were directed at destroying the Elyshah.

Life returned to her own muscles, Lijena leaped forward, covering the five strides separating her from the magician in the beat of a heart. Aerisan jerked around—to greet the razor-edged blade that descended to carve his head in twain.

No god, but a man whose life blood spewed from his twitching body fell across the dark altar—and died.

Lijena spun about, sword raised to attack the kraken that devoured the man she loved. There was no need.The creature dissipated. Its link to the physical world severed, Qar's aspect dissolved into the nothingness where dwell the gods. The warmth of the spring night outside edged away the tower's interior chill.

Chal lay on the floor. Only his pupilless eyes moved, rolling to her.

"Chal!" Lijena sheathed her blade and dropped to the floor, lifting his head and cradling it in her lap. "Why? Chal, why?"

"There was no other way, my love. Qar could not be permitted to walk this world." His lips did not move, only the emotion-words through which they both had first met flowed through Lijena's soul. "Death must never be served, only accepted with the realization that life gives birth to life. Thus the balance is eternally maintained."

"Shhhh. Don't talk. Save your strength," Lijena urged. "I'll carry you below. Dawn is near. The sun will bring you . . ."

"Not enough." Chal's thoughts were a gentle caress. "How beautiful our life together would have been! The love we . . ."

Nothingness. The tender touch of the Elyshah's emotion-words was gone and in their place an emptiness that could never be filled again.

Her whole being shuddering, Lijena clutched Chal's cold body to her breast. Her tears fell on flesh that faded first from sight, then from touch. Alone as she had never been before in her young life, Lijena collapsed to the floor and wept.

Lijena stepped from the dark tower into the light of a new dawn. A cry of victory rose to shatter the morning's peace.

She blinked and numbly stared at the foot of the stairs. A company of weaponsmen stood below. Faces smeared with dirt and sweat lifted to her. Before she discerned whether they were friend or foe, the warriors raised spear, sword, and bow in salute and cheered.

"We routed them!" Count luBonfil stepped from amid his victorious troop and held an arm extended to Lijena. "The citizens of Bistonia will sing your praise. Because of your blade, the city is free once again! Victory is ours! Victory is yours!"

The man's words paraded through Lijena's brain as a string of meaningless, unrelated syllables. Soul and body drained by the night's ordeal, she wearily descended the stairs. Count luBonfil grasped her right hand and wrenched her arm high in the air. Again the soldiers cheered, which deepened her confusion.

"Aerisan worked his magicks against us," luBonfil said. "Our troops fell back unable to stand before the mage's might. Then his spells were gone. In that instant, all knew what you had achieved! Our forces rallied and routed the curs who sought to conquer Bistonia."

"I achieved nothing." Lijena's head moved from side to side in denial. Tears welled anew in her eyes. *Chal! Oh, Chal, how I need you!"*

"Even now Pen leads troops into the sewers after Aerisan's army of thieves," luBonfil ranted on. "Once and for all Bistonia will be free of the scum who have dwelled beneath her streets."

Lijena's gaze lifted to the sky. Bright and warm the sun floated on a field of cloudless blue. How Chal would have savored such a day. The songs he would have sung!

"Lead us!" A voice called out. Another rang in reply, "We follow where you lead!"

"No," Lijena mumbled as she freed her hand from luBonfil's grip and pushed her way through the throng of warriors. "Death has been served enough this night. The time has come to serve life."

None heard. Her words were drowned in another roaring cheer.

chapter 22

"DO IT? OF course the citizens of Bistonia will give their undivided support." Guidon Brill, one of the city's most respected merchants stood at the end of the table and shouted. "Why wouldn't they?"

"Because Zarek Yannis' armies can sweep up from the south in a matter of weeks." The answer came from a twig-thin noble with a face like a prune. "We must choose a course of caution that will insure . . ."

Lijena's gaze moved over the council chamber and the faces of the thirty men gathered within. Of those who had served with Count luBonfil's rebel forces only Scrounge, the thief, was missing.

Old Pen and his troops had scoured the sewers to rid Bistonia of the army of pickpockets, cutthroats, and purse-snatchers who lived in the city's subterranean empire for a day and night after Aerisan's defeat. Thieves who had served the dark mage were caught and summarily executed. However, neither Scrounge nor those loyal to him had been seen since the scrawny thief had led Lijena through the sewers to the Avenue of Temples.

While many believed Scrounge and his crew had fled the city, fearing for their lives, Lijena had no doubt that a new Emperor of Thieves now sat in the throne room below Bistonia's streets. She sighed. At least she had no feud with the latest in the line of master thieves.

". . . I think you misjudge the people of Bistonia," Guidon Brill ranted on.

Once again Lijena turned him and the others off and wondered as she had at least a thousand times the past six days why she was here. Her attention shifted to a window that opened on the chamber's south wall.

In the distance workers busily labored with hammers and chisels, destroying the obscene tower Jun and Aerisan had built to Black Qar. In another week only memories of the temple and its unholy rites would remain in Bistonia.

A taut knot of aching pain awoke in Lijena's breast. Spring ruled the day outside. A scattering of fleece-white clouds lazily drifted across a sky of blue. The sun's warmth could be felt even within the cold marble walls surrounding her.

Chal! She closed her eyes to hide the tears that misted them. How could emptiness be so painful? How many years would pass before she could look at the sun without it unlocking the bittersweet memories of the gentle Elyshah?

Lijena shifted in her chair to conceal the shudder that quaked through her lithe body. The Sword of Kwerin Bloodhawk pressed against her left thigh, a cold reminder of her original purpose in journeying to Bistonia. She had claimed Jun's life and that of the man who murdered her father. Neither deed gave any satisfaction, only increased emptiness.

Davin Anane, Lord Berenicis the Blackheart, Amrik Tohon, Masur-Kell, Lorennion—those who had taken her, used her body and mind, twisted her life marched before her mind's eye. Where hate had raged without bounds, she now found only hollowness. Were the men standing before her at this very moment, her desire for their blood might fire again. But this was not the case. More meaningless was her quest through Raemllyn's realms, seeking revenge. She had seen the course of those who served Black Qar.

You brought this, Chal. You wove these threads of doubt and change within my breast and mind. Lijena slowly drew a steadying breath.

The Elyshah had once said the gods had bound them together, but never hinted their purpose. Now she knew. Raemllyn's deities had reshaped and forged her in a furnace of pain and suffering, created a woman of strength and determination from a pampered kitten. Chal had been the soothing waters in which the gods tempered their creation. Bathed in the Elyshah's tenderness, she relearned what the gods had driven from her heart—love.

Nor did the gods dull the weapons they had forged. They merely gave it purpose. A purpose Lijena had recognized since her flight through Agda's forest, but had denied. One that she would now fulfill.

"Enough bickering!" Lijena pushed from the table and stood. "There is much to be done, and you waste time haggling like old women."

"But we are decided." This from Guidon Brill. "Were you not listening?"

"They wish for you to sit on Bistonia's throne." Count luBonfil smoothed a finger over his thin moustache and smiled with open amusement. "They await your answer."

"But the House of Maslin ruled Bistonia until Zarek Yannis set Lerel on the throne. Barse Maslin still lives. It's well known he and his family are exiled in Leticia." Lijena shook her head. She had no desire to tarry in Bistonia another hour, let alone rule the city.

"Nay," Guidon Brill answered. "The people will follow you. It was your sword that freed them from two tyrants. You've won the throne by trial of combat."

"Aye!" A chorus of agreement rose from those seated around the table. "The throne is yours!"

"It seems you have little choice." This from luBonfil, his amusement growing. "Such is often the burden of a ruler."

One at a time Lijena's gaze met the faces of the men who urged the throne on her. Their expressions revealed more than their words. Each saw her as one to be easily manipulated, to be swayed to support their interests—Lijena Farleigh, puppet ruler of Bistonia. Only old Pen, now suited in the uniform of a captain of the city guard sat scowling at those about him.

Lijena smiled and nodded. "I accept your judgment."

Count luBonfil's amusement vanished in concerned furrows than ran across his brow. Pen's scowl darkened.

"Pen, stand and face me." Lijena's mind rushed, seeking and finding the avenue she sought. "Do I have your oath of loyalty?"

"Aye," the old warrior muttered. "You stand against the usurper and that is enough. My guardsmen and I will serve and protect you."

"Good," Lijena nodded again, then paused and eyed the four guards stationed at the corners of the room. "Then my first command is to cut out the heart of any in this room who dares speak against me or my decrees."

Pen's eyes widened, then narrowed with suspicion, as did those of the others at the table. Although none protested, Pen grasped the hilt of his blade. Whether to challenge or accept the command, Lijena didn't know, nor did she give him time to prove himself.

"For my second act as Bistonia's new ruler, I hereby appoint Pen my regent. Captain Pen will serve in my stead until Barse

Maslin is returned to Bistonia to take his rightful place as the city's ruler," Lijena announced. "As my last act, I hereby abdicate Bistonia's throne to be effective the moment Maslin's backside touches it."

Pen's scowl transformed into a wide grin. Count luBonfil's amused expression returned. Several mouths opened, but no man uttered a sound.

"Now, Pen, I have matters to attend elsewhere and have no desire to remain in Bistonia past the noon hour. I would appreciate it if you would secure passage on a northbound barge for Count luBonfil and myself," Lijena said, watching doubt return to luBonfil's face.

Lijena looked back at her newly appointed regent. "And one more thing, friend Pen. I think it might be wise if all those gathered here are kept under house arrest in their homes until Barse Maslin is brought back from Leticia. I believe it will make the transition of power flow without snag or hitch."

"Your wish is my command," Pen replied, then waved a guard from the room to bring in additional men to escort those assembled to homes temporarily transformed to jails.

"And our mentioned northward journey?" luBonfil arched an eyebrow.

"I have something to deliver into Prince Felrad's hands," Lijena said simply.

"Bistonia will not soon forget your abdication," Count luBonfil chuckled as polemen moved the barge away from the city's wharves.

"Few will remember what happened today within a year." Lijena perused the four horses penned at the center of the barge and the bundled supplies stacked beside the animals.

She smiled. Old Pen had provided more than barge passage for luBonfil and herself. He left them equipped with mounts, food, blankets, and fresh clothing for the journey northward to Rakell.

"You leave your home without even a backward look?" the count asked.

"Bistonia no longer has the ring of home for me." Only the ghosts for those she held dear walked the city's cobblestone streets—her mother and father, and the man she had loved.

"Our journey is an easy one," luBonfil said. "You should stand before Felrad in three weeks, maybe two, and place the sword in his hands."

Lijena's head snapped around. "You know?"

"I suspected the moment I saw the blade's runes that day in the basement of Magister Pusdorn's home," the Count answered. "I was certain when I saw you walk from Qar's temple. No ordinary steel could have defeated Aerisan's power."

"Yes, no ordinary blade could have stood against Aerisan," Lijena answered, knowing that no sword had defeated the mage, but a poet-minstrel with eyes of pupilless blue.

With a toss of her head that cast long, frosty blond hair into the wind, Lijena gazed northward again. The fingers of her left hand crept to the hilt of the sword sheathed on her hip. Soon she would complete the task for which the gods had forged her.

The End

Book Four: *Death's Acolyte* in the *Swords of Raemllyn* series